The Assembly of the Dead

Also by Saeida Rouass and available from Impress Books:

Eighteen Days of Spring in Winter (eBook)
The Library of Untruths (forthcoming)

The Assembly of
the Dead

Saeida Rouass

First published 2017
by Impress Books Ltd
Innovation Centre, Rennes Drive, University of Exeter Campus,
Exeter EX4 4RN

British Library Cataloguing in Publication Data

A catalogue record for this book is available from the British Library

ISBN 13: 978–1–907605–77–2 (pbk)
ISBN 13: 978–1–907605–78–9 (ebk)

Typeset in Garamond MT
by Swales and Willis Ltd, Exeter, Devon

Printed and bound in England
by imprintdigital.net

For Inez

Between the Ocean's rolling billows
And the Sahara's rolling sands
Lies a land of mystic beauty,
Spell-bound beneath a Wizard's hand.

And who owns thee, mystic country,
Dost thou go from sire to son?
Or art thou a trophy only?
Trophy lost and won?
A setting sun?

Who rules thee, marvellous country,
From Marrakesh to Tangier?
Sultan, Kaid, or Kadhi?
Pasha or Ammer?

Do they mete out even justice
Equally to friend and foe?
It is so.

Not so loud, o mystic country,
None at hand thy call to hear.
But should thou be pressed too hardly,
Call! And someone may appear
Off Tangier.

'Ajax'
Al-Moghreb Al-Aksa (1900)

Prologue

Assiya lent against the wall, lost to her surroundings. Resignation poured out of her eyes and onto the ground. Where once she saw possibility, she now felt nothing but guilt. A guilt so strong it churned her stomach and displayed her sins across her once youthful face for all to see. If she had known it would be so difficult she would have avoided the situation completely, ignored his attention and her own desires. But it was too late for that now. She had made her choice, if it were any choice at all. She could not have love without heaping scorn on others. Her freedom would be built on the captivity of the weak. She thought of her mother, who would most likely be pacing the room, waiting for Assiya's return and wondering if she had trusted her daughter too much. To leave her in that state would be to commit the greatest of sins: the sin of ingratitude.

She looked up from her thoughts to find him watching her intently. The quill had ceased its scratching, hovering suspended over rough parchment, the ink staining his fingers. He did not speak. She had used him, exploited his fascination with her for her own ends. Now that the end had come he would demand his payment. Whatever his demand she would fulfil it, if only to silence him and then return to her life and make do with the small joys it offered.

'Shall we begin?' he asked gently.

She nodded and began her dictation.

My darling,

I write this letter with a broken heart and have spent long nights awake thinking of what to do. I have thought of the promises we made and how you will feel now that I must break them. I know I am giving up on myself as much as you. I see two roads ahead of me, but I must only take one.

I can meet you at the gate and we can leave this city. We can go in any direction we want and wherever we end we will be together. We can make our way on the road ahead and perhaps one day we will find ourselves at the ocean. I have never seen the ocean. People talk about it the way they talk about freedom. I have never been free, except when I am with you. With you I am free of everything. I am not limited by the expectations of others or by my fears. I would like to watch the ocean with you next to me. I would like to dig my feet into the sand and run into the water screaming and laughing.

There is another road, one harder to bear but based on a deeper love than ours. I can give you this letter and walk away, then return to my father and mother and never see you again. I can wait for my father to find me a husband and hope he is decent. I cannot abandon my mother and leave her to her fate. I must take the second road. My mother is the strongest person I know, but if I leave it will break her. It will destroy her purpose, her whole reason for being.

I cannot shame my father. He may not be an easy man – few are – but he carries a heavy load on his back. My leaving will not lighten his load; it will only increase it.

Perhaps one day you will marry and be happy. I wish that for you. I will think of you often and imagine you standing on the shore with your children playing around you and your wife with the taste of salt on her lips. By taking the second road I know what I am giving up: you, and the dreams we made. Though I cannot join you, I ask you to honour those dreams.

Your love,
Assiya

He looked up, suspending his quill in his hand once more. Placing it down, he waited until she composed herself. The corners of his mouth turned in the merest hint of a smile. His eyes eagerly watched her face contort as she tried to control her emotions. Anger, fear, sadness flickered, morphing into one another, then into a vacant stare.

'The world has broken you, Assiya,' he said, ending the silence.

She did not reply.

'It breaks us all,' he mumbled to himself.

'I am not broken.'

'I have written your letters since the beginning of this affair, and read his to you. This one is different; there is no joy, no passion. You are ending it. It appears to me you are broken.'

Assiya shook her head in defiance. The world had not broken her. Her strength was buried deep. It was better to appear weak.

'I am not broken,' she repeated. 'It is an issue of choice. I have the choice.'

He walked towards her and stopped close so he could look deep into her almond eyes that revealed what her words sought to hide.

'This world is not made for girls like you, Assiya, nor you for it. You were made for the next. This world is not yet ready for your choices and if it cannot break your spirit, it will break your body.'

Her eyes fluttered for a moment in panic, overcome by his stale breath. It was true; she did not belong here. She belonged nowhere, but the only thing that made any sense was to find a way to fight.

'Then my spirit will not leave until justice is done,' she replied, meeting his glare.

He observed her for a while, wishing things could be different.

'In that case, you will stay for eternity.'

Without warning she pushed against his chest and ducked under his arm to escape. He grabbed her neck and held her against the wall, a triumphant grin crossing his face. Her eyes bulged and she fought to muster a scream as he leaned into her face and whispered, 'This is not how I wanted it to be.' He smashed her head hard against the wall and let go. She collapsed in a heap.

The triumph he felt only moments ago was quickly replaced with disappointment. He looked down at the body lying at his feet, her shallow breathing just detectable beneath the layers of clothes. She would never have gone voluntarily; her rebelliousness was insurmountable. She would have never willingly joined his assembly.

PART ONE

1

A stranger in Marrakesh

Farook al-Alami stepped out of his funduq and lifted his jellaba and selham above his ankles. He checked his shoes, hoping the shine he had given them that morning would survive the dust of the city. Straightening his back, he looked at the small door he had just crouched through. It was made from dark cedar wood, brought in from the slopes of the Atlas Mountains. Despite the hand-carved patterning of rectangles arranged above each other and filled with ornate swirls and loops, there was nothing distinctive about the door. The whole country was adorned with arched doorways, laboriously carved by carpenters or their young apprentices.

All that made this door distinctive was the fact it was set in a larger wooden frame. This too could be opened, for traders with their merchandise and livestock on market day. It set the building apart from the other residences in the alleyway, and Farook hoped it would help him find his funduq again.

The streets of Marrakesh seemed designed to confuse those new to the city. Long, winding alleyways took sharp, meaningless turns that led into dead-ends or even narrower paths, overshadowed by forward-leaning terracotta walls which rose two floors and ended abruptly in flat rooftops. Perhaps confusion was the aim. The alleyways baffled visitors to the city, and its small doors forced those who passed through them to stoop in an orderly queue. Any mountain or Saharan tribe seeking to invade Marrakesh would find their attack slowed and their troops forced into a queuing etiquette not befitting an army of bandits.

Farook's attempt to locate the funduq the previous evening had left him feeling a little disoriented, and, at times, had seemed more challenging than the treacherous journey he had just completed from Tangier to Marrakesh, regardless of the short interruption in Fez.

The funduq came recommended, or prescribed, rather, by a close friend from Tangier. Farook had not seen his friend for many years and was surprised to find a message, delivered via courier, awaiting him in Fez. The proprietor of the respected funduq was eagerly awaiting his arrival in Marrakesh and ready to take care of all his domestic needs. News travelled fast in Morocco, despite the near impossibility of passage between its imperial and coastal cities, and the lack of the long-awaited wireless telegraph.

In the end it worked out well. The funduqs of Marrakesh were in various states of disrepair, some accommodating nothing more than the city's feral cats. Only a desperate traveller would take lodgings in one of them. The howls of hungry cats and incessant bites of ravenous fleas kept even the deepest of sleepers awake long into the night.

This funduq was relatively clean, with the added touch of boiled water for bathing, a writing desk in the room, and coffee, something he had presumed he would not find in the southern city. Despite the difficulty in locating the building and the proprietor's compulsive need to faff and fuss, Farook was relieved to be lodging there, and even more relieved he had not been forced to spend his first night outside the city walls.

He had arrived in Marrakesh the evening before, just in time to enter before the city gates were closed. The gates locked in residents and, more importantly, kept out criminals and vagrants. Farook al-Alami was no criminal, though it was a crime that had brought him to the city. His travels had brought him so far inland the fresh sea air felt like a childhood memory. Even stuck in the middle of the land, he still felt the call of the two oceans no matter how far he wandered.

He awoke early, as he preferred, and though he could not take his usual morning stroll along the coast as he did in Tangier, he would make do with getting lost in the alleyways of this mountain-locked metropolis. Besides, the sooner he introduced himself to the city officials the sooner his work could begin.

The air outside was as still as the alleyway. Nothing stirred, not even the flies. He walked south towards Jemaa el-Fnaa, convinced that regardless of the path he took, he would eventually come out into the square. He had been told in Fez that every alleyway led to Jemaa el-Fnaa and the city always drew you to the square, even if you began your journey heading in the opposite direction. It was like a magnet that pulled the city to its centre, releasing its attraction only after the last snake charmer had placed his fanged cobra in its basket and the last storyteller had told his final fable to a yawning crowd.

Farook followed his long, sturdy nose around corners, into dead-ends and back out to take other paths. Deep in the alleyways, it felt like the day had not fully broken. The buildings left the air crisp and cast shadows ahead. If he stretched out his arms he could touch the walls on either side, not that he wanted to. They were, in parts, so caked in grime it was difficult to see the red earth beneath.

He entered a wider street with shopfronts slightly raised above the cumbersome and dusty path. The smells of the previous evening's market still lingered in the air, the odour of dried mule dung undercut with the souk's merchandise: cinnamon, clove and raw leather.

As foretold by the descriptions of the city he had heard, he found himself eventually in Jemaa el-Fnaa. At this early hour, the square was almost as quiet as the alleyways, but with at least some evidence of life. A group of donkeys had congregated during the night in the eastern corner. Huddled tightly together, they stood sharing a comforting moment before the weight of the city was loaded onto their backs once more, to transport goods as far as its numerous gates and beyond.

Just beyond the donkeys, men offering potions for impotence, powders for infertility, and spells to cast evil spirits from a person's home or body, were beginning to stir under their layers of ragged clothes and blankets, setting up their displays of ornate bottles and magical instruments. Gradually they emerged from their woollen bundles, as though rising from graves on the Day of Resurrection, bleary eyed and uncertain of their whereabouts.

Farook passed these men, avoiding eye contact. He was not a superstitious man. He believed their magic was no different to that of the snake charmers and storytellers also plying their trade in the square on a nightly basis. All relied on fear and imagination to coerce the resigned into parting with a coin or two on the promise of a better life, or, at the very least, a temporary escape from this one. These medicine men, with one foot in the supernatural and the other in the temporal, had seen humanity at its worst, at its most desperate. Farook preferred not to look into their eyes because he disliked peering into the despair they witnessed.

He continued through the square towards the Koutoubia Mosque, its minaret rising up to the cloudless heavens. He had heard so much about this mosque that seeing it with his own eyes felt anti-climactic. It looked exactly how he had imagined it would and not much more. Somehow, its significance as the grandest place of worship at the furthest westerly point of Muslim land seemed lost on its plain sandstone walls and conventional structure.

He swung to the left, leaving the mosque and thoughts of religion behind, and soon entered yet another series of narrow alleyways. This neighbourhood was a vast improvement compared to where he was staying: its walls clean and smooth to the touch, the floor cobbled and swept.

Eventually he came to the house which fitted the description given to him. The arched door was also made of dark cedar wood and at its centre hung a large brass knocker in the shape of a woman's hand. 'The Hand of Fatima.' There to repel the evil eye of passers-by from the threshold.

Farook held the hand, the brass cold in his palm, and knocked twice. He hoped his host would surrender easily and there would be no need for an unnecessary confrontation.

2

By order of the Sultan

There was no answer.

Farook placed his ear to the door, not a sound or sign of life from within. He shifted his weight to his left leg and continued to wait.

He lifted the doorknocker once more and was preparing to release a knock that might wake the entire neighbourhood when he detected the pattering of leather slippers on tile heading towards him from within the house. Directly at eye level a window slid open leaving a small rectangular gap in the door. He saw no one on the other side.

'Who is there?' a meek voice asked from beneath the opening.

'Farook al-Alami, from Tangier.'

The window slid shut and once more he heard the pattering of leather slippers move back into the depths of the house. Stepping away from the door, Farook brushed imaginary fluff from his shoulders and shook out his long black cloak so that it fell into natural folds around his crisp white jellaba. He stood with his feet planted firmly into the ground, straightened his tarboush and continued to wait.

The door was pulled open and before him stood an African girl of about eight or nine. She wore a loose cotton dress over her shoulders that stopped at her knees and her hair was braided tightly around her head. She took a slight bow and gestured for Farook to enter. As he stepped into the corridor it bent sharply to the left and he was plunged into semi-darkness.

'Master was not expecting guests at such an early hour,' she explained and, not allowing Farook an opportunity to answer, scurried ahead of him.

Farook followed as the corridor bent right and reflected that perhaps Marrakesh houses and social protocols were as tricky as its streets.

Lost in his thoughts, he found himself suddenly bathed in bright sunlight. Ahead of him stood an inner courtyard which opened to the sky. Around the courtyard was an elevated path and whitewashed pillars holding up the second floor of the house. In the centre of the courtyard was a fountain delicately trickling a stream of water from its ornate brass spout into a round basin. The floors were covered in deep green parquet tiles that crawled across the courtyard and up the surrounding walls, each carefully placed by hand. The upper parts of the walls were covered in decorative plasterwork, the baroque patterning around the entire courtyard both enchanting and overbearing. In the far right-hand corner stood a young orange tree which let off a sweet citrus aroma. The soft heat collecting in the courtyard and the sound of trickling water would be seductive to any visitor. Farook observed the various details and began to estimate the hours of labour it must have taken to complete the house.

A cough brought his attention back from his mental calculations and he looked down to see the little slave girl staring up at him with mischievous wide eyes and a twitching grin. She quickly turned and scurried around the courtyard to a door opposite. Opening it, she bowed once more and indicated for Farook to enter. Removing his shoes and selham, Farook bowed back to the girl, amused at her playfulness and handed over the items. He stepped into the room.

Turning toward the girl he saw her grin had changed into a contrived grimace. She stood holding his shoes slightly away from her body, as though holding a scorpion by the tail. Looking up at Farook, a small giggle escaped her lips once more, which she made no attempt to contain.

'Qadi Abdullah al-Hassani will be with you shortly,' she whispered, retracing her steps.

Farook was alone in the room. The two windows on either side of the doorway opened to the courtyard, breaking the dimness with shafts of sunlight. He stepped further in and took a seat on the floor divan, which wrapped around the side of the walls. Tapping his index finger against his knee, he waited once more.

Looking up, he admired the wood-carved ceiling, beams running down the length of the room with geometric patterns coloured burnt orange. A large Persian rug stretched across the floor and a grand clock stood against the back wall counting time.

A lot could be learnt from observing what a man surrounded himself within the privacy of his home. So many houses in Morocco were festooned with decorative features: carved wooden ceilings, tiled floors and walls weighed down by the ubiquitous plasterwork. The outside of the house in no way hinted at the beauty contained within. If his home was anything to go by, his host seemed no different to other officials in the makhzan. A position in government provided ample opportunity for personal enrichment, which most officials never shied away from exploiting.

Farook heard footsteps and stood ready for his host. An ageing man entered the room, his frame small and thin. He too wore a white jellaba with a crimson tarboush resting on his head and in his right hand he clutched a pearl rosary with a black tassel.

They greeted each other in the usual way, a combination of head bows and gentle handshakes. This was accompanied by a series of enquiries about the well-being of one's health and family, repeated over and over in varying incantations until all enquiries were exhausted. With the greetings complete they took their seats, Farook waiting for Qadi Abdullah al-Hassani to sit first.

'Bring tea,' the judge called towards the door.

'Thank you, but I do not drink the stuff.'

A silence fell between them. The judge sat gently counting his rosary, a slight murmur escaping his mouth to accompany each bead as it passed through his thumb and index finger.

'You are from the north,' he stated.

'That is correct,' confirmed Farook, his accent revealing more than he preferred. 'Tangier.'

'Has a new drink arrived in Tangier which we in the south are not yet aware of?' asked the judge. 'Or perhaps the proximity to Europe means you Shamaliyin have more refined tastes than us southerners.'

'It is a matter of personal choice,' Farook assured him.

'In the south it is considered a great offense for a visitor to refuse the hospitality of his host.'

'I mean no offence and would gladly take some chilled water if available.'

'Bring water,' the judge called, his attention returning to his rosary.

They sat in silence and while doing so Farook inspected his host as best he could. He noticed the man's delicate hands, skin sagging. His nails were clean and cut close to his fingers. And despite his physical frailness, the judge had clearly not lost his thirst for power, even in the most mundane of conversations.

Farook had been warned in Fez that Qadi Abdullah al-Hassani was a formidable official who had survived tribal raids, changes of Sultan and city intrigues through cunning alone. Farook's one advantage was that Marrakesh had not been warned of his arrival.

The slave girl stepped into the room and presented a silver tray to Qadi Abdullah. He took a glass, a mild tremor in his hand causing some water to spill on his jellaba.

Irritated, he clicked his tongue and she quickly presented Farook the tray, keeping her eyes firmly focused on the floor.

'The girl seems to have taken a liking to you,' Qadi Abdullah observed, as she left the room.

Farook took a sip of water.

'She was a gift from the Sultan. I assume he acquired her while on one of his many expeditions.'

'May God increase your gifts,' said Farook.

'Take her, she is accident prone. What use is a slave after whom I must clean up?' the judge scoffed.

'Thank you for the generous offer,' Farook said, trying to hide his surprise at the Qadi's blatant ingratitude. 'But I must decline. I am sure our Lord the Sultan, may his reign be long, would be most disappointed to hear of her inadequacies and would happily replace the girl if you return her to the palace.'

'Ha!' retorted the judge, 'the Sultan has other matters to deal with. I hear these days the court is filled with Christians and their many useless contraptions.'

'I have heard it said,' Farook mentioned, as he took another sip of water.

Again, a silence descended between them. The judge counted his blessings on his rosary beads and Farook thought of the thousands of ways the Sultan had snatched the blessings of others for minor offences.

'What brings you to Marrakesh?' asked Qadi Abdullah. 'I do not have merchant visitors from as far as often as I once did. My son oversees much of our trade.'

Farook wondered if the judge's reputation was well-founded after all. He had made two errors already, both based on assumptions. Only a fool acts on assumptions.

He slid his hand into the pocket of his jellaba, deciding now was the perfect time to play his one advantage and withdrew a neatly folded piece of parchment. He handed it to the judge.

Qadi Abdullah looked down at the letter, secured with an unbroken wax seal. He gulped hard, as if forced to swallow one of his prayer beads. He carefully broke the wax and unfolded the paper. He continued to look at it long after finishing the short letter. Finally, he gave it back to Farook and returned to counting his rosary, the tremor in his hand more pronounced than ever.

'How is the Sultan, may his life be long?' The judge's voice choked.

'The Sultan is well and sends his regards. He only wishes he could visit Marrakesh to ensure the city is not being filled with useless European contraptions, but the running of the nation keeps him busy in Fez,' replied Farook flatly.

Qadi Abdullah stopped counting his rosary, his fingers frozen over a single bead. Perhaps he had run out of blessings to count.

'Our Lord has nothing to fear in that regard. His brother, Prince Moulay Hafid, makes a fine Caliph. Under his esteemed leadership we lowly judges are humbled to be in his service and deliver his command.'

'The Sultan only commands order and justice for all,' Farook explained.

The judge massaged his throat involuntarily, trying not to picture the executioner's sword making a clean cut. For now, at least, his head was still attached.

'Of course,' he mumbled. 'We do our best and I serve only him.'

'And he serves his people,' replied Farook, not missing a beat in the delivery of justice. 'The report is that you were approached repeatedly by the families to investigate and nothing was done,' continued Farook, observing the judge's jugular as it pulsed spasmodically.

'That is n … n … not true. I assured the families we would investigate and we did. On closer inspection it seemed the families in question were of … how shall I say … questionable character. Their intentions were unclear and to me it seemed they wanted nothing more than to extract blood money from the makhzan to compensate for a crime they could not prove had taken place.'

'All of them?' enquired Farook.

Qadi Abdullah made no attempt to answer the question; he sat with drooped shoulders and glazed eyes, realizing that his recurring nightmare had finally become reality.

He looked suddenly older, worry lines cutting deep across his forehead and the tremor in his hand was crawling up his arm until it looked as though it might consume his entire body.

If it were not for the sheer incompetence of the man, Farook might have felt sorry for him. But his lack of action had consequences: families left in the purgatory of unanswered questions; growing resentments towards the makhzan and accusations that the southern imperial capital was quickly becoming lawless. Situations such as this had a way of escalating out of control and the makhzan was bloated with officials who sat apathetically sipping mint tea in their plush homes. The judge had to feel the outcome of his unquenchable thirst for money and power and the situation had to be resolved, if for no other reason than to bring the families answers.

'Appeals were made to the Minister of Complaints, who presented them to the Sultan. The palace saw fit to appoint me to investigate. And here I am.'

'And who are you?' asked the judge, still having not fully emerged from the darkness of his nightmare. Thoughts of how this situation had developed so suddenly would consume his waking hours, bleeding into sleepless nights as he counted each new minute he survived as a blessing on his treasured rosary.

'I told you. I am Farook al-Alami from Tangier. I am here by order of Sultan Abd al-Aziz. Why don't we start at the beginning? Tell me, whom did you appoint to the investigation?'

3

Forgotten women

Farook sat at his writing desk. A gas lantern offered a faint, flickering light. If it were not for the chill in the room causing his fingers to stiffen he could sit there all day and evening. He placed his quill pen in its box and flexed his hands. The proprietor had promised to bring wood for the fireplace, and, for all his talk about fulfilling every domestic need, Farook had not seen him since.

He reviewed his notes, searching for a small detail that might provide a line of investigation. Three women reported missing to the Minister of Complaints since September the previous year. And that was where his notes effectively ended.

It seemed local officials had failed to take the reports seriously and done little to investigate their disappearance. With the exception of appointing an investigator, a Yusuf al-Mhadi, who also seemed impossible to locate, the pleas from the families had gone largely unheard. The Marrakesh authorities concluded the women were of ill-repute. They had run off to Mogador or Tangier, where they could ply their trade along the docks and earn enough to feed their families for six months, compared to nothing in Marrakesh. It was not unheard of.

If it had not been for the persistence of the families in petitioning the Minister of Complaints in Fez, the women would have been forgotten along with the crowds of others occupying shacks along the coastal towns of Morocco, providing a necessary but unsavoury service to the constant stream of merchants passing through the trading ports.

Farook did not believe the women had gone to Mogador, at least not voluntarily. If that were the case the families would have located their daughters themselves rather than risk involving the makhzan. If the Marrakesh authorities were proven correct, the consequences for the families would be catastrophic: a generation of women unable to find husbands due to the shame, and the men would have to walk through their neighbourhoods with heads lowered, as taunts of children and grandmothers rained down from the rooftops.

But, that did not mean they had not left the city. Perhaps they were forced into an activity many believed was their only natural place, whether institutionalized through marriage or commerce.

Such thoughts made him think of his friend in Tangier, who viewed the debate of such controversial topics as a sport and happily kept others awake into the early hours of the morning in heated discussion. His old friend had an opinion on almost anything.

'*Let the facts speak for themselves; do not draw premature conclusions based on conjecture,*' Farook heard his friend's voice warn from an evening long past.

Farook noted down his thoughts in a ledger. He would ask the initial investigator about people trafficking networks in the city and perhaps visit the slave market to keep his ear to the ground, though he doubted it would be much use. The slave traders tended to steer clear of officials.

At least he thought that was the expression, '*ear to the ground*'. He had read it once in an English newspaper and spent days after trying to understand its meaning. It was only when a British resident of Tangier explained the phrase that it finally made sense and he felt confident enough to use it. And in this way – reading the only English newspaper in the country, and asking friends and acquaintances when he did not understand some linguistic riddle in its pages – he developed a command of the complex and unpredictable language that had proven invaluable in a country suddenly forced to listen to the demands of others speaking in strange tongues.

He placed his pen down onto his ledger and immediately regretted it. It seeped black ink onto the paper. Farook quickly patted it dry, leaving a stain resembling a face in profile with what appeared to be a small, up-turned nose.

That blasted Yusuf al-Mhadi was nowhere to be seen. Farook had sent messages through official channels requesting a meeting, but to no avail. Perhaps news of his meeting with the judge had spread across the city. The investigator was either in hiding or had also fled Marrakesh, much like the women whom he had been so quick to accuse of indecency. But he could not hide forever; his whereabouts would eventually also be uncovered.

Farook picked up the newspaper sitting on his desk. He had brought it with him and read every page over and over during the journey. It offered him the comfort of familiarity as he headed deeper and deeper south into a part of the country he had only heard others talk about, usually with a speed that seemed to allude to their desire to leave as quickly as they had arrived.

Reading the date on the top of the page, Saturday 13 January 1906, he felt the dislocating distance of time and space. He scanned the head story.

'Regarding the police, it will be proposed that the force should consist of natives under the command of a Moorish official, who will be responsible but not nominal head; the European officers and non-commissioned officers of whatever nation or nations will be given a mandate to undertake the duty.'

Despite reading the story for perhaps the third time, the news of a national police force still surprised Farook. It surprised him not just because it was the hot topic of discussion during the very opening week of the Algeciras Conference, but also because it was brutally honest in describing European plans to police Moroccan society. As evidenced by his two days in Marrakesh, the country was in desperate need of a police force committed to keeping law and order, but the way in which Europe planned to structure the force made one wonder where its loyalty would really lie. He was reminded of a story he was once told about the hermit crab. In seeking a larger home within which to grow, the hermit crab will enter a shell, eat the whelk and take up residency. Thus, the shell retains the appearance of a whelk, but is in fact controlled by an occupying crab.

Within certain circles there was no pretence as to whom that hermit crab resembled or whose shell was being appropriated. In Tangier, where it was all anyone talked about, he had been told the French liked to call it 'peaceful penetration,' a phallic expression designed to further insult the young Sultan no doubt. And yet here in Marrakesh, the city residents seemed happy to busy themselves with minor distractions and conspiracies. He couldn't help but question why he had been sent to the city to search for women already forgotten, while further north and just across the Straits, the nation was being *peacefully penetrated*.

Farook made for the door, deciding he had no choice but to visit the home of the initial investigator. He opened it rather more aggressively than intended and almost ran straight into the funduq proprietor.

The proprietor quickly straightened up.

'Si al-Alami, excuse me. I was coming to inform you that you have a visitor,' the man explained, his face flushed crimson and hands flapping in unnecessary excitement.

Farook nodded, hoping silence might calm him. It did not.

'Yes, a makhzan official,' the proprietor rushed on, his arms looking like he might at any moment take flight.

'He says you have requested a meeting.'

4

A girl ignored

Soon after, a tap on the door finally brought Farook face-to-face with Yusuf al-Mhadi. He was dressed much the same as other men of his position, leather baboush slippers dyed yellow and a light woollen jellaba resting just above his ankles with a billowing hood falling down the back. A white turban, giving him a height denied by lineage, framed his round face. Beneath his jellaba, his rounded belly protruded, indicating a healthy appetite and obliging wife in the kitchen. But his most discerning feature was his piercing grey eyes that appeared to look down at his up-turned nose as though in constant surprise by its femininity.

Behind him stood a young Berber boy carrying a basket of firewood. Farook shook his head at the boy and flipped him a coin. Almost dropping the basket entirely, the boy caught the coin and bit down onto it. Realizing his insolence, he bowed and scampered away.

'The country is being overrun with fake coinage,' said Yusuf with a sigh.

He shuffled in and stood casually inspecting the room.

'Si Yusuf …'

'Please,' interrupted Yusuf, 'call me Yusuf, I am no Sayyid and my family are in no way descendants of our noble Prophet, may peace be upon him.'

'In that case, I insist you call me Farook.'

'As you wish,' replied Yusuf waving his hand as he sat by the desk and began to flick through the newspaper.

Farook watched the man's bravado and made a mental note to determine if such behaviour permeated every conversation with an official in the city.

'Yusuf, as I was saying …'

He trailed off, aware that Yusuf, shifting uncomfortably, was not paying attention. The European furniture did not appear to suit him very much as he struggled with the rigidity of the chair and the position it forced him into.

Farook was certain the conversation was going to be laborious in the same way he was certain this Yusuf al-Mhadi and Qadi Abdullah al-Hassani had subjected the families of the missing women to time-wasting demands and perhaps even threats, in the hope they would eventually give up and grieve for their lost daughters privately and without fuss, never knowing the young women's actual fate. He looked at the back of Yusuf's neck with its rolls of fat and watched the man's plump hands rifle through the paper, pausing as he inspected headlines he could not fathom. Farook considered taking a more authoritative tone. Perhaps if he utilized his seniority, Yusuf would stop behaving like a petulant boy and more like the authority he was meant to represent.

But, while it might bring him temporary satisfaction, Farook understood better than most that the man before him had mastered the ability to deflect responsibility and bury orders in fabricated bureaucratic systems. Some men responded to authority, while others held the threat of idleness over you just by the way they casually browsed through your personal papers. The key was to remember the desired end in selecting the most appropriate method to manage them and to put aside any urges to grab them by the scruff of their jellaba and …

'We have much work to do and we must begin by recapping what we know of the three women before we can begin our investigation.'

Yusuf paused in his inspection of the newspaper and watched Farook with a new interest, his thin eyebrows raised slightly.

'Work? Investigation? I am not sure what you mean.'

'The women reported missing,' Farook explained in a slow and protracted voice. 'I have been sent to investigate the complaints made by the families. I understand Qadi Abdullah often appoints you to investigate crimes within the city, which is how you came to be looking into their disappearance.'

'Yes, yes, but investigate is a rather refined way of describing what I do, Si Farook.'

'Please call me Far –'

'I round up criminals and put them in the city dungeons. It doesn't take long for them to confess their crimes. The rest we leave to those ordained to deliver God's justice,' Yusuf summarized, a smile forcing his full cheeks up so that they almost swallowed his eyes.

'I understand the local makhzan's preferred methods. I asked you here to request your assistance in fulfilling the order of the Sultan to get to the bottom of these disappearances.'

'Of course,' Yusuf said, standing up in animated respect, discreetly rubbing his behind while doing so. 'I am here to serve only him and I do that through serving you, may his life and yours be long. Name your request and consider it done. Would you like me to have the families put in the dungeons? That can be easily arranged.'

Farook turned to watch the shadows from the kerosene lantern play gently against the wall, shifting from one shape to another, impossible to grasp or name as this or that.

'Perhaps you will entertain me for a moment to recap what I know so far and then I will explain what I believe to be the next best steps,' Farook explained, ignoring Yusuf's suggestion.

Yusuf looked longingly around the room. Finding no alternative, he nodded his consent and sat back in the chair.

'Three women have been reported missing in Marrakesh since September of last year ...'

'Yes, can I –'

'Please, Si Yusuf. Let me finish and then you can do whatever you wish. If you wish to leave this room and have nothing to do with the investigation you are free to do so. I only ask that you entertain me for a moment,' Farook persisted.

'We have three women, approximately aged between 16 and 21. According to Qadi Abdullah these women are completely uncon-nected and do not know each other in any obvious ways. They do not live in the same neighbourhood, frequent the same public baths, or even use the same public ovens, so it is safe to presume that for the moment they are unrelated. However, three women disappearing in as many months is enough to warrant an investigation would you not agree?'

'Yes, but –'

Farook quickly raised his hand.

'My point is there are multiple possibilities as to why these women have disappeared and where they have gone. Ultimately it is my job ... *our* job I should say, to find out the truth. Thus, the best course of action is for us to speak to each family in turn starting with the first woman who disappeared – preferably without the use of dungeons. We must establish the exact dates they went missing, their last known location and their movements on those dates in order to trace them. Would you not agree, Si Yusuf?'

Yusuf al-Mhadi sat with a slightly dazed look across his face. Realizing Farook had stopped talking and was waiting for a response, he gathered himself.

'Your assessment is correct, Si Farook,' his voice once more tak-ing on an animated formality. 'And I would agree that, yes, it seems the best course of action would be to speak to the family members, though I already have and it bore little fruit. However, I would add one small detail to your summary if you would allow me.'

'Go ahead.'

'There were, in fact, how should I say … well, not three, but four women reported missing.'

Yusuf watched Farook for a reaction, but found like the newspaper, the man was unfathomable.

The Minister of Complaints and the judge had both told him there were three. Farook played back the conversations – yes, he was definitely told of only three.

'Four?' he asked. 'Please explain.'

'Yes, four,' continued Yusuf, bolstered by the politeness in Farook's request. 'I tried to explain earlier but you were so adamant that you wanted to continue I felt it rude to interrupt. One family, I think the second or third, withdrew their report before it was all snuck to the Minister of Complaints.'

'Why?' Farook noted Yusuf's choice of words.

'I presume because the girl returned home after whatever fancy took her heart.'

'You presume … Did you speak to her or see her?'

'Of course not, why would I? Si Farook, I consider it an act of generosity that I did not pursue the report any further. If I had, only God knows the shame it would have brought to her and the family.'

'Why did the judge not mention a fourth?'

'Why would he, Si Farook? The situation was resolved within the family and no official complaint was ever made to Fez. Who ever heard of such a thing? If the makhzan insisted on lifting every pebble in this city we would all be swimming up to our necks in the sewage of our collective immorality.'

Farook pondered the situation. The case was more complex than he expected and no doubt his investigation would be done without the support of city officials. He only hoped they would leave him to his work and not interfere or sabotage his efforts. Four missing women, one of whom was not even on record. Who was to say there weren't more?

'Si Yusuf, this is what we are going to do,' Farook said.

Yusuf started in his chair, realizing his attempted coup through withheld information had failed to subdue this man from Tangier.

'Do?'

'Yes, do. Firstly, if you insist on calling me Si Farook, then I will continue to call you Si Yusuf. Why you insist on it I am not sure, as it was you who suggested we do away with politeness altogether!'

Yusuf looked around the room hoping an ally might appear from behind the strange furniture. Unfortunately, none did.

'First, we will speak to the girl, if we manage to find her. If not her, then the family, to establish why they withdrew their complaint. Then we speak to the other family members to identify any similarities or patterns.'

'Patterns?' Yusuf asked, his confusion overwhelming his ability to construct a full sentence.

'Yes, Si Yusuf ... patterns. Then we will retrace her last steps.'

'Retrace?' Yusuf's voice rose to match his sudden panic at the mountain of work that had appeared before him and every minute, every second, the summit was growing higher.

Farook walked over to the door and flung it open.

'Are you in?' he asked.

Yusuf looked at the open door wondering if God had finally caught up with him, demanding repayment for his years of apathy by entangling him with this riddle. For now, he had no choice but to trust the man from Tangier.

5

Italian shoes

Farook sat on a wicker stool and pushed the clay bowl away from him. Despite requesting a sprinkling of cinnamon, the couscous soaked in soured milk was inedible.

Around him sat other men lost in dialogue or in their own thoughts, drinking from similar bowls. Occasionally, they stole glances at Farook's shoes which were poking out beneath his jellaba. The look was that of guilty men, as though daring to meet the eye of a woman. Looking around, he saw most of the men went barefoot; their feet black and crusted over with hard skin. Others wore rudimentary rubber sandals and none wore leather slippers.

The shoes had been a gift imported from Italy and had he known they would be so comfortable when the measurements were taken he would have ordered a whole shipload. He had always found the Moroccan baboush slipper clumsy to walk in. After a period of use they collapsed into shapeless gaping holes that could fit the paw of a mountain lion. They had never suited him, nor ever would. People could stare, whisper under their breath or accuse him of vanity and treachery all they liked, the feel of the imported shoes on his feet meant he would never give them up for anything. Farook pushed his feet out from beneath his jellaba and inspected them. This city would ruin the shiny leather the way it was ruining his appetite.

The sounds and smells of the souk filled the air as Farook casually watched. He was a far cry from the tearooms of London. Sitting with his back to the hole in the wall that operated as an eating establishment, he tried not to think of what might have swum in the soured milk, or crawled across the couscous, before being served to him.

'Balak … Balak!' cried an old man, as he pulled a wooden cart heaped with fresh mint. People stepped to the side to let him pass, with one or two stopping to buy a bundle. The scent of mint cut through the thick air, offering a mild relief from the smell of sour milk and feet. Shoppers carried woven baskets to store their latest purchases: bundles of mint or Verbena; walnuts and almonds; and meat cuttings for those who could afford it. The street was filled with jostling bodies, the sway of jellabas caused the dust to rise up from the ground, only to be trapped by the dried palm reeds draped across the roofs of the opposing buildings. Amongst the crowd he felt the eyes of women peering out behind their malhafs, carefully scrutinizing the produce on offer and perhaps even Farook and his shoes.

Farook saw Yusuf ambling towards him through the souk. The man was a pain, but in the end he was a natural follower, someone who succumbed easily to hierarchy. Eventually, he sat down on a stool next to Farook and gestured for a bowl of couscous.

'Well?' asked Farook, continuing to look at the hive of activity ahead of him.

'Well not much, I am afraid. The father refused to let me see the girl,' replied Yusuf, watching his bowl make its way from the darkness of the hole in the wall to the low wicker table beside him.

'Did he explain why?'

Yusuf flicked a bug out of his bowl and took a long slurp. Around his mouth sat speckles of couscous.

'He is under no obligation to explain why. I cannot harass peace-loving families in their homes and demand they present the unmarried women of the household to me. There would be riots on the streets and I would be the first to be lynched.'

Farook nodded in understanding.

'What now?' asked Yusuf, as he drained his bowl of its last drops. He peered into it as though cheated out of a fortune.

'We wait,' replied Farook.

Yusuf looked down at Farook's untouched bowl. Frowning at the speckles of cinnamon floating in the milk, he gestured for a second portion.

And so it went the next morning and the one after, Farook was forced to watch with a morbid fascination as Yusuf single-handedly doubled the profits of the eatery. They took turns to walk through the neighbourhood, passing the household in the hope someone would emerge and then reconvening at the hole in the wall only to add more sourness to their lack of progress.

Until the third day, when, as Farook sat once more on the same stool for what he hoped was the last morning, a young boy with hair twisted like copper came running towards him. The boy tugged at Farook's sleeve with an urgency that made him wonder if something terrible had happened, or, worse still, Yusuf had used his initiative.

Jumping up, he threw a coin on the table and followed the boy through the market. Eventually they found Yusuf stood over an old man with a grey-flecked beard. The man sat cross-legged on the floor guarding a pitiful pile of vegetables. Yusuf was fixated on a withered carrot, turning it over in his hand as though its blackened dots might unlock the mystery of the missing women.

He spoke through the side of his mouth.

'To the far left hand corner there is a woman. Can you see her?'

Farook turned his head to the corner of the small square, as did the old man.

There were a number of women dotted around. They were all dressed in the same way. Farook recalled a childhood memory of watching his grandmother put on a malhaf, the long piece of woolen cloth that she tied around her waist and then drew around her head and across her face to tuck behind her ear. His grandmother would transform from a voluptuous woman decked in colours and large jewellery to a heap of material with only kohl eyes visible. As a child, he imagined it was an invisibility cloak.

Yusuf stepped closer to Farook and whispered in an even lower voice, 'She came out of the house about five minutes ago and I followed her.'

The old man leaned his head forward; his right ear almost twitched with excitement while his eyes simultaneously took in the novelty of Farook's shoes.

'There are three women in that corner. Which one are you referring to?' asked Farook.

The old man snapped his eyes away from the shoes and looked over to the corner. He squinted in concentration, and, as though impatient to be told which of the three they were discussing, looked up at Yusuf with a raised eyebrow. Yusuf lobbed the carrot at him. It bounced off the old man's nose and landed on his lap.

'The walls have ears,' Yusuf said, taking Farook's arm. 'Why do you think we have one circling the entire city?'

The old man rubbed his nose as he watched them leave, more disheartened not to have discovered which of the women was being watched than the injury he had incurred.

The woman broke away from the group and entered a narrow alleyway. Yusuf and Farook followed from a distance, picking up pace as she efficiently negotiated her way through the crowd of buyers and sellers.

'Who is she?' Farook asked the back of Yusuf's head.

Yusuf shook his head, the tassel of his tarboush swaying left to right.

They entered another section of the market, the smell changed from rotting vegetables and chickens resting in their nest of faeces, to stale sweat and old musk. Piles of clothes sat on the floor along both sides of the alleyway and by each pile sat a woman or young girl guarding them. The clothes looked like rags, their colours bleached by sunlight and age. The housedresses lifted for inspection were shapeless and unappealing. Farook looked around at the sorry sight and wondered how any of the women survived. There was desperation hidden behind their veils, the young girls already showing signs of the fatigue of failed dreams in eyes that may have once flashed bright. He looked ahead and watched the woman as she crouched to inspect a pile of clothes. Her rounded form was just visible beneath her tattered malhaf and a slight stoop in her back told Farook she spent the best part of the day bent forward in housework.

She stood, waving goodbye to the old woman guarding the pile of clothes. Without warning she took a sharp right and disappeared down an alleyway. Farook and Yusuf rushed through the crowd and took the corner, only to be stopped in their tracks as she stood waiting.

Behind her veil, her dark eyes moved between Farook and Yusuf. They settled on Farook.

'Why are you following me?' The assertiveness in her voice stunning Yusuf to silence.

Farook stepped forward.

'We only want to speak to your daughter,' explained Farook. 'We are concerned for her well-being.'

She fell into silence and continued to watch the two men for a while. Her eyes large as though capable of taking the whole world in with them alone. Farook detected the confidence that sat behind her bold stare and an intelligence which even poverty could not quash. As though coming to a decision, she nodded slightly to herself.

'I have not seen my daughter for many months,' she said.

Yusuf stifled a small gasp. Farook had been right to probe further.

'What happened to her?'

She paused for a moment. There was the response she had been told to give if ever asked about her daughter and then there was the empty void of an unlamented loss.

'Go to your usual place tomorrow morning and wait,' she instructed. 'Wait for me there.'

6

A vacuum of information

'How did she know we were watching her?' asked Yusuf.

'I don't know,' replied Farook. 'It doesn't really matter anyway.'

'What do you mean it doesn't matter?' Yusuf retorted in alarm. 'If she knows then the whole city knows!'

'Do not panic Si Yusuf, we are here on official business after all,' Farook reassured him. 'She told us to wait here for her and so we must wait. We are making progress.'

'But how did she know? And it is almost time for the afternoon prayer. If she is coming, what is taking her so long?'

'Si Yusuf, in order for me to truly answer those questions I would require some evidence regarding her thought processes and intentions. Evidence we do not have the resources to collect. We can but wait.'

Finding himself more befuddled than reassured by these strange words, Yusuf peered at Farook from the corner of his eye. Who was this man from Tangier and why did he have to say such strange things? He considered whether ordering a third bowl would be perceived as greedy.

The midday sun was relentless, even through the canopy of reeds above, the oppressive heat curdling Yusuf's patience.

Perhaps she has changed her mind or been prevented from leaving the house, thought Farook. *If that were the case we would have to start again or attempt another form of contact ...*

'Nevertheless,' murmured Yusuf, persisting in his concerns, 'we must be more careful. We should not draw attention to ourselves by working in ways not befitting makhzan officials. I have seen many a man stumble from lofty positions for the merest infraction.'

'I agree,' Farook conceded.

'Perhaps we can start with your shoes, and maybe don't announce that you speak a European tongue,' noted Yusuf.

Farook looked down at his feet. He understood Yusuf's point. If someone wants blood they will find some twisted logic to use a person's choice of footwear to justify the demand. His shoes were offensive to many, along with his fluency in English, his abstinence from mint tea, his work methods, his lack of wives or children. The list went on and was added to daily, every foreign quirk making him a bigger target.

But fear was a pointless emotion satiated only by conformity, and conformity became impossible once one's mind had been opened by information and experience. Yet, what value was information in a country living under the threat of economic collapse, famine and an invasion of locusts? If the harvest was devastated as some had been predicting, what good would it do if the citizens knew the reasons why? Or if they were aware just how wholly dependent the country had become on European trade and loans? It would do nothing but fill empty stomachs with resentment and an appetite for revenge.

Farook could not go back. It was already too late for him to seek comfort from conformity; he had seen too much of other lives and enjoyed, for too long, the pleasures of personal choice. He did not expect Yusuf or anyone else to understand his choices. He had not arrived in the city to win over its population and officials. He had arrived to extinguish an ember that might ignite rebellion. His task was to help restore internal stability, so that when the hounds of Europe finally arrived they would find the wild beasts of Africa united. It was the country's only hope and even then it might already be too late. Who was to say if, once people knew the full extent of the threat, they would not turn on each other?

'Thank you for the advice, Si Yusuf,' said Farook, shaking the morbid thoughts from his mind. 'Our priority is to discover what happened to the missing women, where they are now and whether they are safe. The mother has information she wants to share with us and information is what we are in desperate need of.'

Yusuf could think of faster ways to gain that information and as he listed them in his mind, logging the advantages of each, Farook watched as the boy with copper hair approached their table. Yusuf scowled at him, having found the answer to his earlier question. Coins did not buy loyalty when others were willing to place a heavier one, or a bowl of hot food, in a desperate hand. If it weren't for the fact that she was a woman, Yusuf might have respected the mother's courage, instead he would have liked to teach her a lesson about her place. The boy dropped a rectangular parcel in Farook's lap and waited with his hand outstretched. At this, Yusuf's eyes grew wide as he prepared to throw him a kick or punch.

'Leave him be,' instructed Farook as he tucked the parcel under his arm. 'We should return to the funduq.'

Farook closed the door to his room with one hand, and in the other he carried a tray upon which lay a silver tea pot, a small glass and a clay mug holding thick black coffee.

'I don't know how you drink the stuff, Si Farook. Are you even from this land?'

'Is it not experiences that shape the man, Si Yusuf?' Farook asked, sipping his coffee from his chair.

'No, not at all,' replied Yusuf. 'It is his place in the world that shapes him. The place where he was born.'

'I cannot fight my tastes, nor should I have to.'

'Very true, but perhaps you should at least fight acquiring them,' warned Yusuf.

'Well, the Sultan seems to see some value in my experiences and what I might, in turn, contribute to the country.'

'For now.'

'And you, Si Yusuf,' Farook asked, 'what makes you valuable?'

'Ha! The Sultan does not even know I breathe and I hope to keep it that way for fear he order me to stop.'

Farook chuckled into his coffee.

'If I may be frank, Si Yusuf, I took you for a simple man,' Farook stated, as he picked up the leather bound parcel from the desk, 'and it appears I was mistaken.'

Yusuf al-Mahdi said nothing and took no offence by the comment. He had long ago learnt that ignorance could save a person's life. Despite Farook al-Alami's strangeness, Yusuf felt a growing fondness for the man. He did not carry the pomp and sense of entitlement that other men of his position and connections seemed to have. Even stranger, he seemed to actually care about what had happened to the missing women. He appeared to be one of those rare officials who were genuine in their sense of responsibility rather than engaged in the pantomime of power. Yusuf had met very few in his long years of service and most ended their days in poverty and nihilism, unable to secure the future of even one lot of descendants, it all being for nothing in the end.

As Farook began to unwrap the parcel, Yusuf wondered what would become of the man, and whether he would survive the plotting of enemies someone in his position would inevitably acquire. He placed down his glass and stepped closer to watch. The parchments were folded neatly inside, with three or four stacked up. A faint scent of jasmine rose from the parcel as Farook lifted each parchment and placed it on the desk. He took the first and unfolded it. Immediately, a few dried jasmine buds fell onto his lap. Ignoring them, Farook looked over the Maghrebi script moving from right-to-left and written in brown ink. He observed its rounded curves and extended horizontal lines. Farook's hand began to tremble. Yusuf glanced from the paper to his friend.

'What is it? What does it say?'

7

Clues wrapped in love

My darling Assiya, my love,

How long must I wait until my eyes rest on you again? Our time together in the garden was too short. When you left, a rain cloud gathered above and drained the colour from the fruit groves. How long until you fill my sight with colour once more Assiya, the light of my eyes? I place in this letter buds from the tree we rested under so that the scent may bring you back to our meeting place and back into my arms.

Your destiny,
K

Farook carefully picked each jasmine bud and placed it in the letter. Folding it, he returned it to the leather wrapping. He picked up the second letter and read it aloud.

Assiya, my love,

I saw you in the market today with your mother. I could not help but follow you. Forgive me, my darling. I saw you lift a yellow housedress, barter with the woman and then drop it and walk away. I stopped and bought it for you, Assiya, so that I can think of it against your skin. In the cold nights you can wear it and think of my love keeping you warm. Meet me at our usual place and time so that I may give it to you, my love.

Your heart,
K

Placing it on top of the first letter Farook looked up at Yusuf.

'When did you first speak to the family, Si Yusuf?'

Yusuf thought for a moment, his eyes rolling slightly, as though rolling dates backward in his mind.

'We are in January now. They made their initial complaint in late September and I spoke to them again when they withdrew it, perhaps mid- to late October of last year.'

Farook noted down the time frame in his ledger, wishing he had exact dates. There was no point in asking for them; makhzan officials were notorious for not keeping accurate written records; even the courts did not record all verdicts.

'Did they say anything about why they were withdrawing the complaint?'

'No, they just said their daughter had been located. The father was very keen for the complaint to be withdrawn. He practically begged me. I felt sorry for him and thought by not pursuing it I would be helping the family. Perhaps I was mistaken,' admitted Yusuf, his mood downcast.

'That is quite all right, Si Yusuf. You did what any decent man would do and should be commended for it. At least now we know why they withdrew the complaint. The shame would have destroyed them.'

Farook picked up the final letter and turned it over in his hand. There were no distinguishing features about the parchment, no watermark or wax seal, just a sheet of anaemic paper that could be purchased from any shop along the Street of Scribes. Even the handwriting was unremarkable and entirely conventional. Farook had once read a paper about graphology and though the article concluded there was no scientific evidence to suggest handwriting revealed anything of use about a writer's state of mind, it wouldn't hurt if someone cast a critical eye over the script. That was, of course, wishful thinking on his part. There were no such people in Morocco, except perhaps the men down in the square who would read the past or future into any object you placed before them in exchange for a coin. Though their craft had its own history, unfortunately its purpose was more therapeutic than scientific and of no use to Farook.

He read the contents to Yusuf.

My darling Assiya, my eyes, my heart,

I do not understand. I am a broken man, lost in despair. Please, Assiya, tell me why you must end this? You ran from me after uttering such harsh words and I have wandered around this city aimlessly ever since. I have not slept; it is as though I have been plunged into eternal darkness from which I will not escape until I gaze upon your face. I am Majnun from the stories told in Jemaa el-Fnaa. You are my Laila, and I wander the city like a crazed man in search of your scent, your smile. I will wait for you in our usual place in the fruit grove until this madness leaves you. Do you love another? Is that your reason? I must know why. Please meet me to explain what has come over you.

Your happiness,
K

'Young love,' Yusuf scoffed. 'If I spoke to my wife that way she would check my clothes for fear someone had stitched a love spell into them.

Even when we were first married we never spoke that way – not that we married for love. Who does? I met her on our wedding day after all. But, I suppose it is a different generation. New ideas ... different dreams. I don't understand it myself. What's so wrong with the old ways? Marriage is ...' He trailed off, realizing Farook had not listened to a single word.

'This is good, Si Farook ... in fact, it is great,' Yusuf exclaimed to gain his attention.

Farook turned to Yusuf. 'Please explain how you have come to the conclusion that this, as you say ... is great?'

Yusuf stifled a frown, why did the man have to frame his questions so strangely? Surely a simple 'How so?' would do.

'Well, I just mean that ... Ah ... I suppose we can eliminate her from the list of missing women ... I imagine her and her lover are far away now.'

'But, from the last letter she appears to have broken off the arrangement with her lover.'

'Ah!' was all Yusuf could muster.

Farook laid the three parchments beside each other. He scanned across them, pausing at a word or a line and then checking it against the contents of the other two letters.

'We could speak to the mother again?'

Farook nodded, not taking his eyes off the letters.

'A bit of gentle persuasion and I am sure she will talk. It is amazing what a night of darkness does to a person's recollections.'

'Si Yusuf,' Farook snapped, 'do not suggest such a thing. That woman has been through enough and she has already taken a considerable risk, without which we would not be where we are right now, I might add. We will return to our spot tomorrow morning. I suspect that is exactly what she anticipates, but we will be sensitive to her situation and not jeopardize the trust she has placed in us. Do you understand?'

'But ...'

'There are no "buts", Si Yusuf. Within these letters are multiple clues that we must pull out and piece together. We can already determine a number of facts about Assiya's lover that increase our chances of identifying him considerably. We must focus on that and try to establish when he last saw her or heard from her and what her mood was at the time.'

Yusuf lifted his tarboush off his head and scratched at his temple. Standing up, Farook placed his hand on Yusuf's shoulder and gently guided him to the door.

'You have done well, Si Yusuf, we make a good team. But for now I must bid you good evening. I have a small personal matter I must attend to.'

'Tomorrow?'

'Yes, tomorrow,' confirmed Farook, as he closed the door.

He returned to his desk and from the drawer withdrew his finest letter paper. Sitting down, he began to write.

8

An intervention

'I suppose you are wondering why I requested your company,' said Qadi Abdullah.

Farook looked over at Yusuf, who seemed needlessly absorbed in a detail on the carpet. He would be of no use.

The judge waited patiently, moving his rosary through his fingers at a slow rhythmic pace. He appeared in no rush to begin the meeting. Any fright caused by his initial introduction with Farook had long passed.

'Would you like some tea?' the judge asked, looking at Farook. 'Of course, pardon me, you do not drink the stuff,' he continued, a wry smile flashing across his face as he turned to Yusuf.

'Thank you, your honour. Yes, if it is not too much trouble,' Yusuf said, continuing to observe the carpet as if it might flap at the edges and take flight at any moment. No doubt, he would jump on it if it did.

The slave girl scuttled from her seat outside the doorway without needing further instruction. Farook looked up at the grand clock and watched the seconds tick, each one was painstakingly slow. The entire morning had been lost and, with it, the opportunity to meet Assiya's mother again.

'I have been a judge in this city for over forty years,' began the judge.

Farook estimated the time for the afternoon prayer. It would be another few hours before it was called across the rooftops. Surely, the judge would not keep them that long.

'I have witnessed Sultans take the throne and I have watched them carried on the shoulders of their loyal subjects to their graves, wrapped in nothing but a white shroud. And I have heard the wail of the women of the harem behind the palace walls. There is a reason I am still here in my position, Si Farook and Si Yusuf, and not thrown out on the streets with nothing but the clothes on my back or had my head displayed on a spike at the city gate.'

The reason was known all too well within the makhzan of course. Survival was not built on justice or fairness, nor was it built on competence. Men like Qadi Abdullah were capable of extreme acts of barbarity if called for and though their hands remained clean, their march into old age spoke their guilt.

'Many young men who are just beginning their position as makhzan officials, like yourselves, ask me how I have managed to survive. And I have thought long and hard on that question over the years. The world around us is changing, gentlemen, and survival in these volatile times is not easy. What is fashionable today may not be tomorrow and you would be wise to heed my warnings,' continued the Qadi.

Farook accepted the possibility that the call to prayer might come and go and the judge would continue oblivious, lost in the throes of his sermon.

'You see, I have survived forty years because I have kept the common good. I have given everyone their due: the Sultan and the common man. It is respect that keeps us civilized and separates us from beasts, nothing more.'

'Your reputation as a fair judge is known across Marrakesh, Qadi Abdullah,' interrupted Yusuf, 'and it is a privilege to work under your mentorship and guidance.'

Farook tapped his knee gently. They still had the afternoon. The mother told them to return in the morning, but if they went to their spot as soon as they were done and found the boy with the copper hair he could discreetly deliver a message. Perhaps something could be salvaged from the day.

'My judgments extend beyond Marrakesh and have reached the Sultan's ear, Si Yusuf. To be clear, I am not your mentor nor did I invite you here to offer you professional guidance. Your job is simple: to follow my orders. So there is no need for false flattery.'

Stunned, Yusuf returned to staring at the carpet. His only use seemed to be to listen, listen and keep his eyes just before the feet of his master, heaven forbid he have an idea of his own. The judge turned his attention to Farook. 'If we, as representatives of the makhzan, undermine the common good then how can we expect any better from the man or woman on the street?' the Qadi asked him. Farook gave no response. 'A husband must be able to allow his wife to leave the marital home assured of the fact that she will return with her honour intact,' he continued undeterred. 'Not accosted in the marketplace like a common thief or worse. This is common decency, this is respect.'

'Si Abdullah, may I just explain ...'

'I do not wish to hear your explanations, Si Yusuf. You would be wise to be like your friend here,' said the judge flicking his rosary at Farook, 'and to shut up and listen.'

'The man of the house paid me a visit. To say he was enraged would be an understatement. Reliable witnesses claim you followed his wife around the market. They heard you talking about her, and ...' looking at Farook's bare feet, 'in the end it was not too difficult to identify whom they meant. With some persuasion, the wife eventually admitted to her husband that you both approached her and forced private family matters out of her.'

Farook wondered what the husband's persuasion methods might be. The possibility of the wife emerging from the house again was now a distant one. They could take up their positions on those stalls for the next week sipping on that awful slop and it would make no difference. He doubted she would ever talk to them again.

'This is indecent and improper behaviour for government officials, regardless of station. You are both lucky I managed to contain the man's anger as he wanted to pursue the matter even further and planned to visit the Street of Scribes to draft a letter of complaint to Fez. To bring his wife's reputation into question in public, and his daughter's for that matter, is a disgrace.'

Farook assessed the damage. The letters were with him and within them a host of clues to be extracted. What's more, the judge gave no hint of even knowing of their existence. Was it possible that the mother had outsmarted both her husband and the judge? If so she had probably saved their investigation. The quicker they left the sooner they could return to discovering the identity of the lover.

'I have assured the man that you two will no longer pursue the matter of his daughter or ever approach his wife or any member of his household again. I hope you both do not shame me or the makhzan any further by flouting this assurance. The man tells me his daughter is soon to be married. We should not deny the family the opportunity to restore their honour.'

'I assure you, Qadi Abdullah, we will leave the family in peace and only hope he can forgive our transgression,' Farook confirmed.

'Good, now that is settled, some tea,' the judge said, a postponed smile of hospitality cracking across his face. 'Will you take water, Si Farook?'

'That donkey, that son of a dog, that …' Yusuf muttered under his breath, as he fixed his attire.

The street they had taken was filled with the sounds and smells of food in preparation. There was the sound of women huffing as they kneaded bread for the lunchtime meal and the smell of chicken broths bubbling wafted over the rooftops and into the alleyway. Yusuf grabbed his stomach as it grumbled.

'There is no need for such language, Si Yusuf, and while the judge may have enjoyed the opportunity to give us a dressing down, we have lost nothing. Our line of enquiry has not been seriously compromised by this small setback. We will comply with his request and find other ways,' Farook assured him.

'I am not referring to the Qadi. I am referring to that bastard, son of a whore, who informed on us. If I see that old vegetable seller again, it won't just be his carrots that are withered! It could have only been him.'

'How the husband came to know is of little significance.'

'Why did you not defend yourself, Si Farook? You are more senior than him and now we cannot speak to the mother again.'

'Because there are some battles that once started will follow you into the future with no definitive end in sight. He can have his victory. We have the letters."

He slapped Yusuf on the back, hoping to lift his spirits. 'Come, I hear there is a shop near Bab Doukkala that has the best couscous south of Fez.'

9

A letter from home

Yusuf leaned forward extending his right hand. His wife held a silver ewer with warmed water and a matching washbasin in front of him. He took a small knob of soap from the bowl and moved it around his palm. His wife held the kettle over his hand as he rinsed away the remnants of lunch, the washbasin collecting the cloudy water beneath. Yusuf shook his hand free indicating for her to stop. Placing the kettle and bowl down, she gave him a cotton napkin. Next, she lifted a matching silver bottle and sprinkled her husband's hands with rosewater. He rubbed them together and patted down his face with the residue. She lifted the bowl and ewer from the floor and made to exit the room.

'Take Aliya, leave Soufian,' Yusuf instructed.

His daughter did not leave without a fight. She fussed and kicked as she was taken away from the game she was playing with her brother in the corner of the room. Yusuf watched impassively. Children were both a blessing and a burden. No doubt, this time next year they would have another occupying a space in the house and perhaps another the following year. It was expected after all, the number of offspring was an indication of a man's virility. He just hoped the world he brought his children into would be kind and that the next generation would honour the ways of their fathers and their grandfathers.

Islam had not only liberated the Arabs from the ignorance of idol worship and shown them the right path; it had given women rights, elevated their station, and even afforded them a portion of inheritance. But he saw in his daughter a defiance that unnerved him, as though the rights afforded by God were not enough. A lack of gratitude would only cause bitterness for his daughter as she grew into adulthood. The girl only had to look to her mother as an example of that. She had to learn to appreciate her good fortune instead of expecting more.

'Take her,' Yusuf snapped as he watched his wife struggle with the wriggling child, 'and bring tea.'

His wife grabbed the five-year-old girl by the hand and pulled her out of the room towards the kitchen. Yusuf called his two-year-old son to him. The boy waddled across the room and collapsed into his father's lap. Yusuf absentmindedly stroked the boy's hair.

Even the imam had addressed the very subject that afternoon at the Friday sermon. While Yusuf sat in the middle row, discreetly scanning the crowd in search of Farook, the imam bellowed his convictions from the pulpit. The family was the backbone of every society, he preached. If one wanted to know the health of a society then he need only look to the state of its family units. God had ordained a station for each of his species and given the world a natural order. He had divided his creation into male and female and it was when we forgot the place decided for us by the Almighty that we disrupted his plans. Submission to the Creator meant submission to the natural order he set and fulfilment of our role predestined by birth. The fight against creeping ideas and ego was played out in the living rooms of families and in the madrasas where young boys memorized the Quran, the imam summarized. It was no doubt a reference to the growing encroachment of European ideas of women's emancipation and mass literacy.

Though the imam spoke truth, Yusuf had eventually stopped listening. It was all well and good talking about the sacredness of the family and the need to protect it, but how a man did that without inviting a sandstorm of ramifications – food served cold, lukewarm water for bathing, clothes not repaired in time, the afternoon nap interrupted and, finally, passive submission during nocturnal duties – was anyone's guess. If the imam just explained how a man kept order without causing such a soul-destroying backlash, perhaps his sermon would be of value. As it was, the sermon did nothing but frustrate the congregation, wedged between the will of God and the vengeance of women. God only knows what reprisal his wife was concocting at that very moment for his earlier shortness of tone.

In fact, the journey to the Koutoubia Mosque had been a total waste of time. Yusuf had not seen Farook. Perhaps the man did not even bother with the Friday prayer, a blasphemy that Yusuf did not think even Farook capable of. He seemed to have disappeared. They had not spoken for a few days, since the awful visit to the Qadi. Yusuf wondered what the man might be up to. Yes, they had not known each other very long and his attitude left much to be desired, but Farook made for interesting company and, without him, Yusuf felt lost and at the mercy of people whose intentions were unclear. He was not sure whom he feared more, the Qadi or his wife.

He looked down at his son as the boy wriggled in his lap, his eyes opening and closing slowly as he fell into a listless sleep. Tomorrow he would visit the other families as instructed and report back to Farook in his funduq, Yusuf decided. Farook would no doubt be impressed with his efforts and hard work. He closed his eyes, also feeling ready for a well-deserved nap.

Just as he felt himself drifting, a thunderous crash from the kitchen yanked him out of his dream.

* * *

Farook sat at his writing desk. The funduq was silent. The owner snored softly in the recess of the building, enjoying a lazy afternoon nap after his Friday lunch of steamed couscous with slow cooked chicken and vegetables, sprinkled with caramelized onions and chickpeas. The whole city was in the midst of a collective slumber. The interior windows of the houses closed – wooden shutters blocked out any natural light that might have found its way in. Women, after spending the morning in their kitchens, had fed their families, tidied the aftermath and lain down on thin mats, placing their babies on their breasts to nourish them while they slept. Men, on returning from their prayers, had taken off their jellabas, filled their stomachs and collapsed onto beds prepared in advance by their wives or daughters. Even the stray cats seemed to have taken note of the time of day, their bodies stretched along alleyway walls and curled on rooftops, purring gently in relief. Everything was silent and everyone slept, except Farook and those unable to find relief from the pain of their empty stomachs. Farook could hear the movement of the young house boy as he rattled around in the kitchen below.

He picked up the letter sitting on his desk and placed it against his nose, inhaling deeply. He hoped to pick up the scent of the ocean, but instead his nose was filled with the smell of stale leather and dirt from the long journey. He broke the seal and read it slowly, enjoying the cursive penmanship. The words bent slightly in unison. He never grew weary of the left-to-right direction of the script.

My Dearest Friend,

It is with great joy that I received your letter. I sleep better knowing you have reached Marrakesh in good health and have been deposited at the funduq safely. I hope it meets with your requirements.

As for my health and wellbeing, I can assure you that I am in good spirits. Old Abu Mosa takes good care of me despite his incessant moaning. I am quite convinced that were his master a local he would not dare raise his eyes, let alone his voice. Alas, I tolerate his moods as he makes the best fish tagine this side of the Mediterranean.

You ask of news regarding the Sultan and the Algeciras Conference. Oh, how I wish that it were good! The young Moulay Abd al-Aziz may soon regret heeding the advice of Germany, as those scoundrels seem already intent on double-crossing him and leaving Morocco to the French and Spanish wolves. I know we are often in disagreement regarding European control of Morocco, but it is naïve to presume that the country can take what it wants from all that is great from the continent and disregard the rest. Progress comes with a price and a glance east proves that the benefits are worth the temporary loss of control. I might point to British India as a fine example of this.

My only wish is that the Sultan understands that at this point in the predicament this fine country finds herself in, the question is not so much how to prevent European influence, but how to ensure that influence comes from a well-intentioned nation. The French are not to be trusted, Algeria proves that case well enough. The British, however, look upon their foreign subjects as partners on the same journey to progress. If only the Sultan had taken the hand of the British when it was on offer. But it is already too late for such talk. I hear Hajj Mohammed Ben el Arbi Ettorres and Hajj Mohammed Ben Abdesselam el Mokri are doing a fine job in Algeciras ensuring the Sultan's concerns are widely known and we can only hope they will be heard.

It is as you describe, the main concerns from both sides of the Straits are security and the flow of money, both its direction and quantity. It is too early to know how Morocco will fair once she untangles herself from this unfortunate crisis and of course it depends on the negotiating power of those fine representatives. But, make no mistake, change is inevitable. I believe that Morocco will ultimately benefit from this change. I am the eternal optimist.

Enough of politics – though I love the subject, as you well know from our late night debates which often ended in exhaustion on both our parts rather than agreement.

I am, in fact, quite intrigued by your case. You say four women are missing from the city, and not three as was reported to you in Fez. I am rather impressed with how quickly you have discovered a new line of investigation for their disappearance and you are correct in your assessment. These love letters may very well hold the key. If there is a connection between this girl and the other women I have no doubt you will soon discover it. Do not let the ways of the southern capital dissuade you from your work. Do not worry about what you do not know and focus your mind on understanding what you do know.

Remember, my dear friend, police work is still a relatively new science within Europe and we are continuously developing and modifying investigation techniques. In fact, the Metropolitan Police are still recovering from their failure to capture the culprit behind the Whitechapel murders to this day. And the lessons learnt from the failed investigation have reached our highest offices of power and caused significant reform. I am in no way suggesting that these young women in Marrakesh have fallen into the hands of a similar monster, a Moorish Jack the Ripper if you like. I would not wish that on the families or this fine nation. I mention it simply to draw your attention to the mistakes made by the British detectives in the case, which perhaps is understandable considering the unique nature of the crimes.

Do not underestimate the usefulness of your partner. Yes, I call him that because he is your partner in this investigation. Despite his quirks you cannot do it without him. Consider his mind a reserve of local knowledge for you to mine. He has knowledge that by your very foreignness you cannot have. Yet, do not make the mistake of losing your objectivity. The Metropolitan Police made a similar mistake. They wasted valuable time at the very beginning of their investigation into the Whitechapel murders by looking within the local crime structure for a culprit and lost sight of other possible explanations. The truth is hidden in the facts and you must uncover it from there, not bend the facts to fit a palatable narrative.

Follow your intuition; intuition, after all, makes for a fine detective. The questions you have must direct your work and until you have satisfactory answers do not shy away from asking them. Yet, I must give you a word of warning, my dear companion, because I am concerned for your welfare so far from friends and protectors. Your work is unheard of in this country and men like us – torchbearers of change – open themselves to danger. Do not presume logic will rule, even though it is the highest form of human intelligence. We are living in uncertain times and even the Sultan may not be able to protect you from those that seek to keep this bountiful land in the dark ages. Tread carefully, keep your methods to yourself and celebrate your victory when it is achieved and not before.

I include with this letter a summary of a recent English translation of the ground-breaking work of Hans Gross and hope his work on criminalistics will help you in what lies ahead.

Your friend and confidant,
W.H.

Farook re-read the letter and then turned to the translated document. He sat for a long while staring into the gloom. Words swarmed his mind: psychology, crime scene photography, fingerprinting, profiling.

Of course, he did not have the resources or expertise to use the techniques described, but it did not matter. The ideas alone were enough to make him feel as though he had made some kind of evolutionary jump forward and to confirm what he already knew. The investigation into her disappearance had to go on, despite Qadi Abdullah's threats. There was no case without Assiya.

10

A precious stone

'So, you say your daughter left the house to run some errands two months ago and you haven't seen her since?' asked Yusuf. Ali nodded gently, his eyes distant as he recollected the day.

'You have heard nothing of her since? Nothing at all?' Yusuf frowned. Ali nodded once more. He was a man of few words, finding solace in silence except when it came to his daughter. He could lie in bed next to his wife all night and speak of nothing but Souad. Memories of her as a baby; she slept so silently, already considerate towards her parents. And then the sun would force in a new day, one filled with the hollowness of her absence. Yet, still he did not speak to Yusuf.

'Perhaps you can tell me what happened that day?' Yusuf pushed.

'When we last spoke, Si Yusuf, I had hoped you would tell me that. But I heard nothing and never saw you again. It is only because the Minister of Complaints – may his life be long – listened to our pleas that you are now here.'

Yusuf searched for an excuse, but finding none he took the scolding without protest. There was no explanation that would relieve this father of his suffering. Although he could try to explain the apathy of city authorities, he knew it would only feed the resentment.

The curtain covering the doorway fluttered. Ali stood up from his position on the hard floor and retreated to the next room. Yusuf looked around him; the room was bare of furniture except for the mattress on which he sat.

Ali returned with a dented brass tray on which lay tea-making paraphernalia and a small samovar filled with hot water.

Yusuf watched as he began the hospitality ritual.

Placing the tray on the floor, Ali took a pinch of green tea from a chipped bowl. Lifting the lid of the silver teapot, he poured the dried leaves in. Next he added some hot water and swirled the teapot. He poured the cloudy water out into a glass cup. Then he broke off three lumps of sugar from a conical block sitting on the tray and added them, tore off some sprigs of fresh mint and poured the hot water over the mixture. Stirring the sugar in, he let it sit for a while.

They waited in silence as the tea brewed.

After a few minutes, Ali poured a small amount of the syrupy liquid into one of the glasses and handed it Yusuf. Yusuf took the glass and after mumbling a short prayer, sipped from it, making an appreciative sucking-in sound. Ali nodded and poured himself some tea.

'She is my only daughter,' he whispered, the sweetness of the tea loosening his tongue. 'I have been blessed with four sons and I know it is not proper, but she is my favourite. She was like a precious stone gifted to us out of the generosity of the Lord. I work in the tanneries washing animal hides. I spend most of the day standing in pigeon shit up to my knees. When I come home my wife and sons hide from me in the back room because of the smell. But Souad ... even when she was a little girl would run into my arms and wrap herself around me. As she grew older, I would return home to find she had already warmed water for me to wash. The day I arrived home to find the water cold, I just knew something terrible had happened to her. She would not abandon me or her family, her love for us was too strong.'

'I regret our previous lack of action,' Yusuf offered.

'My daughter has a happy temperament,' Ali continued. 'She always makes us laugh. And if I am honest, she is smarter than my sons. This is why we often send her to run errands and not them. With my sons, they may come back from the market with last week's vegetables or rotten offal. My daughter knows how to drive a hard bargain and I trust her completely. She is of marriageable age, but has no interest in any such thing. She has always said she wants to stay with her mother to help her in the house. We are a poor family.'

A sob from behind the curtain escaped into the room, the family seemed locked in the past, waiting for something to bring them into the present.

'When did she disappear?'

'As I said, two months ago. It was a Tuesday morning.'

'What errands did you send her on?'

'I sent her to buy some offal from the butcher and she said she would take her slippers to the cobbler to be re-stitched. It was I who sent her just before I left for work; my wife would often protest but I refused to listen. She also went to the spice souk to buy henna. Souad planned to decorate her hands and feet that evening but she never returned. She liked to do that even when there was no occasion.' The father stopped abruptly, and frowned into his teacup.

The sobs from behind the curtain came in quick short bursts. Yusuf tried to block them out. 'Do you know if she completed her errands?' he asked.

'I do not, but suspect she didn't. How could I find that out? I could not approach people. Perhaps we were stupid to let a young girl out alone,' Ali lamented.

'What do you mean?' Yusuf asked, making a mental note to concoct an explanation for the lack of action before visiting the other families. 'Do you know of any reason why she might choose to not come home? There is no shame in this,' Yusuf assured, knowing it was shame that had caused this sorry mess in the first place.

'We do not.'

'Is there anything from her possessions or your family's possessions missing? Did she leave the house in an unusual state?' Yusuf pressed.

Displeased with the direction of the conversation, Ali stopped for a moment and looked over at the curtain. He listened to his wife's sobs with the resignation of someone already familiar with the monotony of grief.

'My wife cannot understand why God would gift us such a special child and then take her away without explanation. I tell her it is a test, but perhaps it is our punishment.' His eyes never left the curtain.

Turning back, he spoke with a determinedness that took Yusuf by surprise. 'We do not care about anything else, we can live with the shame and forgive if it is necessary. But I know something has happened to her. I know this is not from choice. You must find her and bring Souad home, for the sake of my wife's health.'

11

Speaking pictures

Later that day, after visiting the other two families Yusuf made his way to the funduq to report back to Farook. He took a longer route than usual, bypassing the crowds of Jemaa el-Fnaa for the quieter residential neighbourhood east of the square. He walked its streets, listening to the sounds of children playing along the narrow alleyways and behind the walls, and found his enthusiasm to see Farook dampened. It seemed he had gathered nothing but the details that made up the despair of others. Until then he had not really thought about the loss to the families or considered the possibility that the women might even be missed. By bringing into question their morality he had inadvertently denied them their humanity. *What were four girls?* he had told himself before Farook's arrival to the city. The city was bursting at the gates with unwanted girls and boys. What was the value of a single life?

But he could not shake off the image of Souad's father bent over making tea, the act seeming so meaningless and when he reached Farook's door he found that same emptiness waiting for him in the pleading eyes of the kitchen boy. He felt the novelty of the last few weeks wear off as he followed the boy through the funduq.

What had his official work entailed before this moment? Filtering through his memory, he could not recollect a single instance of meaningful work. Yes, he produced results. He caught thieves and adulterers and had them thrown in the dungeons. His success at extracting confessions was noted by others and he had enjoyed some minor privileges as a result. Yet it seemed to him, as he made his way to Farook's room, that the value of his efforts could no longer be quantified by the number of drunks locked up in the city prison on any given night or by the amount of praise people showered on him as he entered a room. For a moment, Yusuf considered turning around. He could speak to Qadi Abdullah and request to be assigned to another responsibility. He would not have to work with Farook and risk his position or favour with city officials or think about Souad and her father. But the sound of Souad's mother sobbing pushed him forward. He would give the family peace if only to dislodge the melancholy building in his chest – the sooner the better.

Yusuf had barely knocked before the door flung open and Farook pulled him into the room. He paced in front of Yusuf, who sat there dumbly taken aback. Stuck on the wall were four blank pieces of paper. He had written 'Assiya' on the top of one of the papers and beneath her name was some scrawled writing.

'I have been waiting for you all day, Si Yusuf.'

'I paid a visit to the three families,' began Yusuf, 'I must confess I believe you were right. The women have most likely come to danger, and the families …'

'We have no time for this,' Farook interrupted. 'Have you ever heard of the speaking picture?'

What could he possibly mean by 'speaking picture?' Had the man turned to black magic to solve the case? Those seers would affirm anything for a loaf of bread.

'Don't look so worried, Si Yusuf. The speaking picture is actually not as strange as it sounds and is being used widely as part of police investigation processes.'

Yusuf looked up at the papers stuck on the wall; they were just blank pieces of parchment ripped out of a ledger. They spoke of nothing but their failed investigation to that point.

'The picture does not actually speak and naturally we do not have photographs of the women. Besides, the only person in possession of a camera in the country, that I am aware of, is the Sultan. I hear it is gold-plated and has never been used. Personally, I have never seen it, but perhaps one day we can request use of it. Anyway, while we are not in possession of a camera and therefore cannot use photographs as part of our investigation, it is merely a technicality and adaptation is the key here, Si Yusuf – adaptation.'

Farook paused to take a breath and Yusuf took the opportunity to raise his hand.

'Si Farook,' he said as he rubbed his temple. 'The families are in desperate need of help and answers. Perhaps this is not the time for fancy ideas and naïve ambitions.'

Farook paused for a moment, a frown of confusion crossing his brow.

'This is the perfect time for such things, Si Yusuf,' he explained. 'After all, necessity is the mother of invention.'

Yusuf was not quite sure what that meant, but decided silence would serve him better.

'It is quite a simple concept, Si Yusuf, and is being used to catch criminals by the London Metropolitan Police and as far as the United States of America. Every time a criminal is caught his photograph is taken and a series of unique body measurements are also taken. This information is put on a poster … or speaking picture … and displayed for detectives and police officers to review. There is speculation that even this method is soon to become obsolete with the recent application of dactylography to criminal investigation.'

Yusuf sank into a mild despair, overwhelmed by the feeling that a wide pass would always run between himself and Farook, try as he might to bridge it. He daren't ask what dactylography meant.

'Si Farook,' Yusuf said despondently, 'we are not looking for criminals, we are looking for missing girls and women. Unless of course you are implying they are criminals, which may I remind you I suggested at the very beginning of this in–ves–ti–ga–tion.' Yusuf stumbled through the word, still feeling its foreignness on his tongue.

'Correct,' Farook said. 'We are looking for the victims of crime and with a bit of creativity we can use the speaking picture in reverse to speak to us … without an actual picture … or any actual speaking of course.' He waited for Yusuf to match his enthusiasm and seeing no such thing he took him by the arm and led him to the wall.

Yusuf stood staring at the empty pages, he read the notes under Assiya's name.

'Do you believe they are dead, Si Farook?' he asked.

'I think it is probable. What do you believe?'

'Well … I believe … I think …' Yusuf stuttered, his thoughts only beginning to formulate as he spoke them. 'I am also of that opinion.'

Farook's smile broadened wider than Yusuf had ever seen it and Yusuf noticed for the first time his even, white teeth.

'I am still not clear how these speaking pictures can help us though,' Yusuf admitted.

'Don't worry, everything will become clear. Now, remind me. What are the names of the other missing women?'

'Souad, Maryam and Leila,' Yusuf stated.

12

The right question

We must continue to investigate Assiya's disappearance,' Farook stated.

Evening had descended. The room was filling with shadows. He lit the kerosene lamp to chase them away. He called down to the kitchen boy to bring more light and he soon arrived with two lamps, which he placed in the corners of the room. The boy went over to the fireplace and stoked it into life before leaving quietly. Shadows danced on the walls and across the now complete speaking pictures. Farook rubbed ink off his hand with a cotton cloth and Yusuf stood reviewing the information. The muffled sound of a baby crying crept through the walls and over it a woman's voice, softly humming a lullaby. Beneath them a mule brayed as it made itself comfortable amongst a merchant's produce, guests crawled into their beds ready for the cold night ahead and the long day to come.

Yusuf prepared to leave, gathering his selham and throwing it around his shoulders. He fastened the front and secured his tarboush on his head.

'Qadi Abdullah will not be happy,' said Yusuf, paused before the door.

As he opened it to leave a draught entered the room. The late January cold crawled up the walls and into Farook's bedding. He turned to Farook, still absorbed in front of the speaking pictures.

'Do you think they will be of any help?' Yusuf gestured to the parchments. He hoped for simplicity in the midst of such a heavy burden.

'I have no doubt,' Farook said, turning to him with a reassuring smile. 'Go home, Si Yusuf, to your family and rest. Travel safe and may God protect you.' Yusuf lingered, watching his friend who had already turned back to the pieces of paper now covered in scrawls of black ink, before gently closing the door behind him.

Farook continued to stand in his place, the heat from the fire behind him warming his back. He reviewed what information they had gathered, carefully going over each one.

Souad (age 15)

Missing since: Mid-November 1905 from Riad Zitoun el-Kheddim area.

Left house to run errands, but has not been seen since.

Visited the butcher, but did not complete any of her other errands.

Farook allowed his imagination to run away, piecing together an image of Souad from details her father had mentioned to Yusuf. Short, he decided, with a small frame, dark brown eyes and thin lips permanently turned down. He played out a conversation with the young girl.

'Why did you not complete all of your errands, Souad?' he asked her. 'Did something or someone stop you or was it by choice? What happened between the butcher's and your next errand?'

The air in the room stirred as the fire behind him gently crackled.

The speaking picture gave up its value and Farook knew the key to her whereabouts lay in the answer to those questions. Yusuf had his instructions and soon enough the answers would be revealed.

He turned to Maryam: the only married one of the four.

Maryam (age 24)

Missing since: August 1905 from the Bab Doukkala area.

Married with three young children.

Left house to visit doctor after complaining of stomach pains.

Left the children with husband but did not return home.

Again, he took a moment to imagine what she looked like. He drew her as slightly plump. Her body was older than her years and tired and her hands were dry and calloused.

'What ailed you so, Maryam, that you had to visit a doctor?' he asked the speaking picture.

Life, she seemed to whisper in his ear.

It was unfeasible Maryam would abandon her three children. According to Yusuf's report she was a devoted mother. Her husband spoke of the loss felt by the children and the absence of laughter that once filled their home.

'What did the doctor do to you?'

He turned to Leila to ask his questions.

Leila (age 18)

Missing since: September 1905 from the Riad Zitoun el-Djedid area.

Left house with younger brother in early evening to visit Jemaa el-Fnaa.

Brother lost sight of her while they listened to a storyteller.

She had a mischievous smile, he decided, and enjoyed playing tricks on her younger brother.

'Did you deliberately lose your brother in Jemaa el-Fnaa, Leila? Where did you go from there?'

The sound of mice scurrying across the flat roof above momentarily caught his attention. He listened to the scratching as they crossed the length of the funduq and back again.

'Did you arrange to meet someone or did someone lead you astray?' he asked.

Then he turned to Assiya. He paused for a moment, clearing his head of the images of the other women.

He imagined her to be tall and slender with a graceful walk. Her face was iridescent, with mocking eyes. She was confident – confident enough to fall in love and secretly engage in an affair, and smart enough to leave some signs from which he could work. But she was also naïve and inexperienced. He had so many questions for Assiya, questions that he had already asked but found no way of answering.

Assiya (age 18)
Missing since: Beginning of October 1905 from Bab el-Khemis area.
Left house to visit hammam; has not been seen since.
Has a lover with the initial K.
They would meet regularly in a fruit grove.
The liaison ended against the lover's wishes.

'Did he hurt you when you ended the affair?' he asked her image. The kersosene lamp sitting on the desk hissed and then popped, plunging the room into semi-darkness. He stepped closer to the speaking picture.

'Who was he?' he whispered. 'Where would you meet and when? What caused you to end it? How long did it go on for? How did your parents react when they found out?' The questions poured out of him, but remained unanswered.

The silence mocked him, laughing at him as he stood glaring at the four papers on the walls. Farook calmed his frustration and understood that the answers lay somewhere between what he suspected and what he did not know. By answering each of his questions, one at a time, he would eventually bring the disjointed facts together and that beneath them lay a single thread that would somehow tie all the women together.

A gentle knock on the door drew Farook's attention back to the darkening room. The kitchen boy quietly reentered, bringing in a tray of food, which he placed on the desk. He left the room, returning briefly with a basket of wood and dry twigs to feed the fire once more. Farook went over to the tray on the desk. A round loaf of bread sat on a small plate cut into four triangles and next to it a clay tagine let off a mild heat and steam. Farook lifted the conical lid and inside succulent cubes of beef bubbled in thick gravy, decorated with juicy prunes and a sprinkling of sesame seeds. The aroma of sweet meat filled the air. Farook replaced the tagine lid to keep in the warmth and watched as the boy stoked the fire.

'What is your name, boy?' He asked.

'Mohammed, master,' he replied before quickly turning back to stoke the fire.

'How old are you?' Farook asked, watching him more carefully now.

'I do not know, master.'

Farook guessed him to be about nine or ten, perhaps older, circumstance having stunted his growth.

'The proprietor – is he your father or uncle? Are you related?'

Mohammed stood up to leave the room, holding the empty basket in his hand.

'No, master,' he replied. 'I am not from here. I came here to work.'

Farook nodded, understanding too well the litany of abandoned children willing to do almost anything for the leftovers of others to fill their stomachs. Mohammed was one of the lucky ones; he had work and a roof over his head.

'Do you have siblings?'

'Three sisters, but I haven't seen my family since I found myself here.'

What did that mean? Maybe his parents had abandoned him late one night at the city gates, hoping that a kind soul would take him in. One less stomach to feed that would do nothing but usurp the collective bowl and then die of smallpox before putting something back in. Or maybe the boy had been sold to the proprietor in return for a hard bed, scraps of food and a few coins sent home to the village, his childhood filled with the worries of a grown man.

'Does the proprietor treat you well, Mohammed? Is he a good man?'

Mohammed smiled the smile of a wise man. 'There is good and bad in everyone, master,' he replied.

Nodding in understanding, Farook lifted the lid from the tagine. 'Come eat,' he told the boy. 'My friend brought me some snacks and so I do not have an appetite tonight.'

Mohammed hesitated, looking past Farook to the meat, which continued to let off a sweet steam. Checking Farook's invitation once more, he put the basket down and walked as calmly as he could to the desk. Sitting in the chair, he placed his nose over the food and inhaled deeply. Losing all sense of decorum, he grabbed a piece of bread and began to devour the stew. Farook returned to the pictures, turning his back on the boy.

'Master, what are those?' Mohammed asked pointing to the papers, his fingers dripping with gravy.

'They are called speaking pictures.'

The boy looked up at Farook confused.

'Can you read and write, boy?' Farook asked.

He shook his head in reply. 'That is only for those who have more than they need to fill their stomachs. My father used to say an empty brain is the friend of an empty stomach and a full brain its enemy. I was never sent to madrasa to learn. I am not clever, master,' he replied through a mouth full of food.

Farook stepped closer to the speaking pictures. He focused on Assiya and re-read the information quickly. A question began to form in his mind. He repeated it under his breath, saying each word to ensure its correct place in the sentence. Turning quickly towards his desk and feeling his mind run ahead of him, he stood next to Mohammed searching through the draw. He pulled out the love letters and opened the first on the pile. Mohammed had stopped eating, a cube of meat cooling in his mouth and the prune in his hand waiting to be consumed.

Looking down at the boy, Farook smiled broadly. 'Not all intelligence is acquired through books. You may be smarter than you think,' he said.

13

The butcher

The smell of blood and guts turned Yusuf's stomach. He stood back from the makeshift wooden block and apprehensively watched the butcher slam a cleaver into the leg of lamb. The cleaver hit the leg at the knee joint, cutting into bone, muscle and sinew, and the butcher let out a deep satisfactory grunt each time metal met flesh. Precise blows rained down until the lower part of the leg was completely severed from the upper. The crunch of bones breaking left Yusuf feeling dizzy. Throwing the lower part onto a bed of reeds beside him, the butcher began attacking the upper leg.

He was a fat man, grown accustomed to the sight and handling of flesh. He sat on a stool in front of the wooden block looking up at Yusuf. His large round belly hung between his knees so that it almost touched the floor. His white jellaba was spattered with blood and flesh and around him sat his offerings.

On the floor to his left rested an earthen bowl filled with sheep stomach, thick and colourless like bleached leather. An old man stood bent over it, inspecting the strips with his index finger and sniffing the bowl for freshness. Yusuf felt his stomach turn once more as he raised his hand to his mouth, regretting the hearty lunch of meatballs cooked in a spiced tomato sauce with fried eggs.

On another tree stump sat a lamb's head, stripped of skin with eyes locked in terror. Against his better judgment, Yusuf inspected the head. Observing the muscle lines and bone structure beneath, he felt bile rise within. The mouth was completely stripped away leaving the teeth and gums exposed, above which sat two cavernous holes where the nose once was. The eyes, still in their sockets, seemed to be watching Yusuf as if to say 'it was you, you did this to me.'

Yusuf turned his attention back to the butcher.

'As I explained,' he was saying between grunts, 'she came in, bought half a kilo of intestine and then left.'

Yusuf nodded, the bitter taste at the back of his throat making it impossible to speak.

The old man next to him indicated to the butcher. The butcher stopped what he was doing and plunged his hand into the bowl of stomach. He pulled out a handful and threw it onto scales encrusted in blood and layers of fat. Weighing the stomach, he added a bit more from the bowl and then wrapped and tied it in a palm leaf. The old man handed the butcher a coin. The butcher aggressively wiped his hand on his jellaba, leaving a smeared red print. He dropped the coin into a small jar at his feet and withdrew a small writing implement from behind his ear, which he used to record the sale in a small bloodstained book.

'Did you speak to her?' Yusuf thought to ask.

'Of course I spoke to her. I asked her how much offal she wanted,' snapped the butcher, as he watched Yusuf fidget in his crisp clothes.

'I think you know what I meant, Si Khalid,' he retorted, his patience for the man and the stench thinning.

'I have known that girl since she was a baby. At one point I thought perhaps I would take her hand. My wife can no longer give me children. I asked after her family. The family is wretched, they can barely eat,' the butcher grumbled on. He leant over and took the lamb's head from its block and positioned it in front of him. He withdrew a thin knife from beneath his stomach and began working on the top of the head, the movement of his hands transforming from a brutish wildness to the delicacy needed for crochet.

'You said you thought you would marry her. Why did you change your mind?'

The butcher paused to consider the question, the knife hanging in the air between them. 'Her father refused my offer.' He returned to his work of cutting out the eyes from the lamb's head. 'At first I thought he was mad as well as stupid, but then I realized he had done me a favour. It is unwise to tie your horse at the place of the donkey. Everyone wants to progress, to leave something for his children when his Maker calls him back. Marrying Souad would have only meant more responsibility, more mouths to feed.'

'Did her mother approve?' asked Yusuf.

'How am I to know, Si Yusuf? It was a momentary insanity on my part. Sometimes I become fascinated with an idea and then get over it.'

Yusuf recalled his younger days, before marriage and children. He too had been driven momentarily insane. He had spent a considerable amount of his late childhood convinced he would marry his neighbour's daughter. He could feel her watching him from the opaque windows on his way to madrasa and caught glimpses of her as she sat on the roof with her mother in the evenings. But the day he was told he was promised to a cousin and would go into the makhzan he forgot about her completely. Since then the opposite sex, except his wife, held very little fascination for him.

'Was Souad aware of the proposal?' Yusuf asked. There was something about the man that did not sit right. The brutality of his words seemed to match his skill with the cleaver. Perhaps he did not take rejection well.

'Absolutely not. I never discussed it with her directly. Thankfully I came to my senses before my wife removed my eyes with my very own knife,' he joked, holding out the now severed eyeballs for Yusuf to see.

Yusuf's stomach lurched forward. Despite wanting to ask more questions, he quickly left the shop.

14

The cobbler

The twenty-minute walk from the butcher's had given Yusuf time to clear his nostrils and settle his stomach. He stood in a small shop that was set slightly below street level. The ceiling was low with wooden beams running across it, precariously held up by rotting pillars. The floor was a dusty red earth and Yusuf checked his yellow baboush slippers for dirt. Set near the back of the shop was a wooden workbench that took up most of the space. It was stacked with an assortment of shoes and slippers. They were of different shapes and sizes, some rubber and others leather and spilled onto the shelves inlaid into the back wall. In the corner behind him a gentle smoke filtered up from a small clay pot on the floor, the scent of musk wafting across the room. He moved towards the bowl and carefully encircled it with his selham. He looked over to the closed door in the far left corner of the room. The old woman said she would return shortly, but his patience began to fray much like the sorry excuse for footwear scattered around him.

This was not what he had intended for his life. He thought back to when he first entered the service of the makhzan. With a young beautiful wife at home to take care of his needs and an auspicious career ahead, his days were filled with the promise of success.

But the truth was he had hardly moved from his entry position. The flames of his ambition had been dampened by the mistakes of his naïvety. And it had cost him his future. If he had been shrewder and less nostalgic for a lifestyle he could not even prove existed, he would not be standing in a cellar fearing at any moment that the ceiling might come down and bury him in a pile of ragged second-hand shoes.

He understood now, of course, there were men born into enough privilege so as to make their incompetence irrelevant and there were men who made their competence relevant. People like Farook. He had worked his way up the hierarchy through proving his indispensability. With the lack of privilege and obvious talent, Yusuf was doomed to do all the legwork. However, perhaps Farook was the person to give him the long overdue acknowledgment he deserved.

The old lady entered the shop from the back room. She was round and short, with a slightly crooked spine that left a permanent hunch in her back. She wore a simple house kaftan; age had liberated her from the need for modesty. A light cotton cloth was tied loosely around her head, her hair the last vestige of propriety. Yusuf estimated her to be in her late seventies, but she could be younger.

She took a position behind the counter and began rearranging the shoes into what appeared an identical pile, just placed further along the counter. From beneath a pile of mismatched leather slippers she withdrew a tattered ledger, the only evidence of organization in the surrounding chaos. 'My son will be with you shortly,' she said through the collapsed muscles of her cheeks.

A stout man soon entered, and his presence seemed to fill the small shop space. He was of considerable height so that he had to stoop to fit into the shop and had a broad frame with strong arms. He had a large face with a wide nose and long lips stretching across it.

'Hajj Mohammed Mesfewi,' he said with a voice that seemed not to fit his physique

'Yusuf al-Mhadi,' Yusuf replied .

The old lady moved into the shadows, behind her son.

'I am here about a girl,' Yusuf began, already feeling the tediousness of the questions to follow. 'Her name is Souad and she has been missing from the city since November. Do you know her? She planned to visit your shop but never made it.'

'I can only account for the customers who come into the shop, not those who don't,' said the cobbler.

'But do you know the family?' Yusuf snapped. 'According to the father they are customers.' These craftsmen fancied themselves clever with their wisecracks.

'I would not say "know" exactly,' replied Hajj Mesfewi. 'I heard about the disappearance but unfortunately I do not recollect the girl.'

'And you?' asked Yusuf to behind the cobbler.

'My mother does not sit in the shop,' the cobbler responded.

Yusuf nodded his understanding. First the butcher and now the cobbler. Would he not be allowed to rest until he visited all the craftsmen in the city and was humiliated by their insolence?

'Son, why don't you check the ledger just to be sure and to give this gentlemen some ease,' the old lady suggested. 'It is a tragedy that the young girl has not been seen and if ...' The cobbler cut his mother a stare that silenced her mid-sentence. Drawing the ledger towards him he flicked through the pages while keeping his eyes on Yusuf. Yusuf stepped closer.

Disappointed, he saw the cobbler's records were not as organized as he had hoped. Names, dates and descriptions of shoes scribbled randomly across the pages. Mesfewi snapped the ledger shut.

'There is no record,' he said with finality.

Yusuf stepped back to his original position and looked around the shop, taking in more details. He had not noticed the stack of baskets leaning against the wall or the wooden Berber box poking out from behind the door.

'What exactly is it you do here, Hajj?'

'I fix shoes,' he said confused. 'I am a cobbler.'

'Only shoes?'

'If customers ask me to fix a bag or basket, I take it. Times are hard,' he explained.

'They are indeed. Tell me, do you declare all your earnings to the treasury? Including the ones not entirely legal?'

Both the cobbler and his mother gasped in offence.

'I am a Hajj,' he blurted out. 'I have performed the pilgrimage to the holy city twice.'

That was twice more than Yusuf had.

Yusuf smiled broadly. 'Thank you for your time, Hajj Mohammed,' he said. 'You have been most helpful.'

15

The doctor

Across the city deep in the mellah, encircled by a high wall demarcating the line between Jews and Muslims, Dr Jacques Delacroix sat in his wooden chair writing notes in a patient's file. Draped across his chair lay his dusty grey coat, its weight a constant bane in his daily life but something which, out of principle, he could not do away with. Its matching waistcoat fitted loosely over his white shirt, unlike when he first arrived in the city. His black dress trousers, starched so much they could stand upright on their own, were beginning to crack and gather around his groin. He shifted awkwardly in his chair, rearranging himself into a more comfortable position. On his large oak desk, imported from Paris along with the other furniture in the room and which had been unwrapped in front of the excited eyes of the neighbourhood children and grandmothers, sat his black bowler hat. It was another legacy of his heritage. Dr Delacroix persisted in wearing it, unlike the other French residents of the city. He also insisted on taking it off when indoors, unlike the less civilized Moors who wore their head attire when lying with their multiple wives – or so he was told.

Beneath his white collar he wore a grey cravat. An angry rash was just visible, as it crawled up his neck and towards his long chin. Delacroix pulled at his collar to let in some air, resisting the urge to scratch. The rash was not the only evidence of the doctor's discomfort. His pale lips, hollow cheeks and the dark shadows around his narrow eyes had set the neighbourhood grandmothers gossiping that he may soon need to see a rabbi.

Finishing his notes, the doctor rapped his fingers on his desk impatiently. He had repeatedly explained the protocol to his assistant, but the young man still could the most simple of tasks. 'Wait five minutes patient,' was the most complex yet the doctor already knew he would leave the comfort of his surgery himself to fetch and remind him to call the next patient.

When the young man had first been presented to him – or, with hindsight, thrust upon him – Delacroix had high hopes that he could groom him to one day become the most medically informed and efficient doctor's assistant in the whole of Marrakesh, if not Morocco. He soon realized, however, that the Jews of North Africa, much like their Muslim counterparts, found the concept of timekeeping challenging to say the least. As it turned out, after two years in this God-forsaken city, the tardiness of the locals was something he had learnt to tolerate. This was not because of the flexibility of his character. The Jews, at least, seemed willing to acknowledge it as a cultural flaw, whereas the Moors were likely to appear even later than usual if you exposed any hint of irritation. He had come to tolerate the nation's inability to keep time because, when compared to the host of other strange and uncivilized native customs, lateness was the least offensive. Perhaps once these people learnt to take their hats off and keep their shoes on when they entered a room, they would be ready for training on punctuality. He feared such a time was a long way into the future.

Besides, it was not the nation's tardiness that irritated the doctor at the present moment. It was the fact that the Moors, rather than turning up late, did not turn up at all. He was warned in Europe of Muslims and their distrust for all things modern, particularly Western medicine. At the time he dismissed the warnings, seeing them as both mockery of his grand plans and fuel for his ambitions. Hearing the rumours after his arrival into the city, he had no choice but to revaluate. After spending years dedicating himself to learning medicine, establishing a respectable practice in Paris and giving all that up to move to the frontiers of civilization, he was aghast to hear he had been called a Christian witchdoctor, a Crusader magician and even a peddler of poison planted in the city to feed the natives potions to make them infertile. As if infertility would ever be a plague in these parts.

His surgery was filled with Jewish women from the mellah on any given morning, their exposed faces showed the wretchedness of their daily lives and the screams of their children followed him into his dreams. The Jews, at least, learnt quickly the value of European medicine. The Alliance Israélite Universelle had made significant headway in establishing schools in the Jewish quarters of Arab cities and in the mellah of Marrakesh they were active in encouraging the women to seek him out for medical assistance. But, in a city of 100,000 the Jewish population made up a minority. It was the Moors he wanted, the women in particular. Yet, they continued to stay away.

Despite the explanations Dr Delacroix offered to the other foreign residents over cigars and port, he knew the real reason they refused to cross his threshold. They had a treatment system of their own, which consisted of incantations that sounded like the ravings of a mad man; potions drunk according to the sighting of a particular moon; or cocks slaughtered over the grave of one of the seven saints dotted around the city. Until these uncivilized and primitive practices were stopped, Delacroix feared the Moors would never seek his help in the kind of numbers he hoped for.

Of course, some had turned up, visiting the white witchdoctor and hoping his magic would work where that of others had failed. And when they did, he lectured them profusely on their ways, warning them of the dangers of public baths, the risks of bearing too many children and the importance of a daily walk. He could see in their eyes that they did not listen, their minds already identifying the next quack to visit. Most refused even to remove the malhaf, let alone allow him to complete a physical examination.

Delacroix banged his fist onto his desk in frustration. A tap on the door made him wonder if this perhaps should be how to call the attention of his assistant. The door opened and to Delacroix's surprise a Moor entered. The doctor looked the man up and down as he entered the room and was shocked to see beneath the traditional clothes he wore European shoes. Meeting the man eye to eye, Delacroix had no recollection of having even stood up.

Farook took the seat in front of the doctor's desk and introduced himself.

Delacroix found himself flummoxed as he observed his visitor. In Paris, Moors who had absorbed French culture were often called mimic men, but the Moor in front of him did not seem to be mimicking anyone. He was too comfortable in his clothes and shoes, the combination of which appeared to cause no internal conflict.

'I have come about a woman who visited your surgery in August 1905. Her name was Mariam, a Muslim woman.'

The doctor recalled the previous summer. He remembered her of course.

'I cannot divulge patient information, Monsieur al-Alami,' the doctor heard himself say, irritated that the Moor spoke better English than him. He wondered if he should try his Arabic with the man, perhaps he could give him some hints. He had made significant progress with the script, but the spoken form remained mostly a riddle of throat gurgles and hisses.

'I understand,' Farook sympathized. 'You took an oath.'

Delacroix nodded energetically, feeling understood for the first time since his arrival in the city.

'I am unsure how I can be of help, as much as I would like to be,' said the doctor.

'I do not expect you to divulge her medical condition or the treatment you prescribed, but if there was anything about the visit you feel was interesting or unusual perhaps you could describe it to me,' Farook requested.

The doctor thought back to his first summer in the city, the ungodly heat. He decided not to refer to his patient notes, fearing his assistant would take the rest of the day to find them. He remembered the woman clearly. How could he not?

'Her very presence in my surgery was unusual, Monsieur al-Alami,' he began. 'It is not often I see Moors ... I mean Muslims. They do not trust me unfortunately, despite the great benefit it would do them if they visited my surgery. Perhaps you could put in a good word for me with the city officials. If they were to endorse my medical expertise I imagine ...'

Farook tapped his knee with his index finger.

The doctor stopped. This man must be an apparition. A Moor who got straight to the point, doing away with unnecessary frivolities. He grabbed at his collar, forcing it away from his neck.

'She came with abdominal pains. I must confess I was very surprised by her willingness to be treated. She undressed and lay on that medical bed behind you and I gave her a physical examination. She was the first Muslim woman I have touch- ... physically examined.'

The doctor paused for a moment, recollecting the disappointment he had felt on seeing her face and tired body. Despite the paintings displayed at the Louvre, beneath the malhaf Moorish women were not seductively beautiful, but quite worn and battered. He recalled discreetly watching the woman from his desk as though observing the unveiling of a statue, but rather than excitement at being privy to a sight denied almost every European in the country, he felt nothing but repulsion at the sagging skin and smell of stale sweat. He shuddered in his seat. The doctor continued, furnishing Farook with as much detail as he could in an attempt to prolong the meeting. 'Beneath her outer garment she had some very fine jewellery on. It took her a while to take it off and put it all back on again and if I am honest I am not quite sure why she bothered … considering they … I mean she was covered from head to toe. Perhaps that is the norm, I do not know.' The doctor stopped abruptly. He felt a drop of sweat develop between his shoulder blades and trickle down his spine.

Farook did not speak, extending the doctor's misery. He continued to tap his knee and the doctor sneaked a look at him. He wondered what the man was thinking, what machinations were turning behind those dark eyes and what caused that subtle frown between his thick eyebrows. Perhaps he was offended.

Suddenly breaking into a broad smile, Farook thanked the doctor and stood up to leave.

'Wait,' the doctor called to him as Farook reached the door. Farook turned. 'Perhaps we can meet again, under less formal circumstances,' the doctor requested, hearing the desperation in his voice.

Farook paused with his hand on the door. 'Yes, perhaps.'

* * *

It was only later, once the doctor had arrived home and allowed the houseboy to treat his rash with a paste made from the plants growing in his garden, that he realized how dangerous a man like Farook al-Alami could be to his plans.

16

Latifa

The young girl perfumed her wrists and neck with a block of rose-scented wax. She sniffed at her armpits. Disappointed at the smell of her unwashed body, she decided that next time, if she were able to muster the courage again, she would visit the hammam first. She listened for sounds around the small house, detecting her father's deep breathing and besides him her mother, an occasional restful sigh escaping her tired body.

The post-lunch nap was typically instituted at the first sight of her father's yawn and ended when he opened his eyes, thirsty for water. Between those moments the house was deathly quiet. Whatever the family were doing would stop. Activities were suspended in time until the father returned from his afternoon dreams to bear witness to the domestic harmony. Today was different, her father retreated to the bedroom before the designated hour, struggling to stifle lifeless yawns.

The girl had rushed her morning chores, smacking the clothes on the rock outside the back door with a strength that surprised her mother. She ate little of her lunch, and picked off the fragments of chicken from the bone. Her two brothers had left the house, choosing to roam the alleyways of Marrakesh. They would be back just before the sunset call to prayer, in search of food to revive them before the evening entertainments pulled them out of the house once more.

She removed the bottle of kohl from her underclothes, tucked away earlier in the day and took out the thin wooden stick within. With only her hand to guide her, she drew the stick across the inside of both her eyelids. Her hand trembled slightly, the adrenalin interfered with her certainty.

Carefully, sure not to make a sound, she took her mother's jewels from behind the plates on the shelf. The necklace felt heavy in her hand and as she raised it to her neck she experienced a moment of doubt. Holding the necklace in front of her, its turquoise stones hanging like tear drops, she thought of what might happen if she were caught. She would be ruined; her father's fury would be felt across the whole neighbourhood and her mother's cries carried across the rooftops.

What is the worst that could happen? She thought to herself. *No man will marry me and I will be confined to this house for the rest of my life.* She placed the necklace around her neck and clipped it at the back. It hung down, stopping where her nascent cleavage began. *What does it matter who your captor is? Your father or husband, you must sleep when he sleeps and eat only after he is full.*

But not all men were like that. Some were sensitive and generous. Some fed you with their very hand and listened as you dared to speak your dreams.

She heard her father cough and froze. She had added the exact amount to the tea, had followed the instructions to the word. She waited until his breathing regulated once more and quickly wrapped her malhaf around her. By the time they woke she would be in the back yard, cleaning away the lunch dishes and sweeping the dust from

83

the ground. They would never know. She left the house with a smile hidden beneath her veil.

She walked for fifteen minutes through the city, cutting across the square, and keeping a watchful eye in case one of her brothers saw her. She had already decided her excuse if accosted by them or anyone else. She would tell them she had been sent to the public bakery in time for the evening meal of tea with bread dipped in olive oil.

She passed the prison and shuddered at what lay beyond its walls. Heading southeast, the area grew quiet and her nerves calmed as she passed the walls of the cemetery, where former Jewish residents of the city turned in their graves, and soon after walked along the mellah wall beyond which their descendants scratched a living.

She stopped at a series of gardens behind the mellah. She turned north, tracing her fingers over the top of the wall, feeling the roughness of the rocks on her fingertips. She continued for a few minutes until she felt a mound of jasmine flowers placed there for her hands alone to caress. Looking around she saw the area was empty on her side of the wall and tucked the flowers beneath her malhaf. She lifted her clothes and jumped over. She landed steady on both feet and found herself in a small olive grove. The stunted trees were lined up in rows, the thin leaves offering a natural though fickle canopy. The season for olives had passed, the harvest of that year being meagre anyway. The leaves looked withered, the trees' potential snatched from them before they could open and bear their fruit.

She walked through the grove until she came to a small opening. Ahead, she saw he had laid out a picnic and sat waiting patiently for her company beneath one of the trees.

As she stepped forward, the man heard her rustle and looked up. His face lit up with a broad smile and she felt the last pangs of doubt disappear. Moving closer, she loitered at the edge of the picnic rug laid out, unsure whether to sit or wait for his invitation. He gestured for her to sit down. She sat awkwardly on the edge, taking note of the bottle of wine with two goblets beside him. He handed her a goblet, filled in anticipation of her company and took the second for himself.

'Drink,' he said softly.

She did not expect this. She had never drunk wine before, or even seen it. She hesitated. Her mother would smell it on her breath or she might become intoxicated and give away her secret.

The man took a long sip from his goblet and watched her.

'I am so glad you came,' he said. 'If I am honest, I thought you wouldn't and felt ridiculous sitting here on my own. But, seeing you I do not feel ridiculous at all.' She looked away, shy of the attention.

'Show me your face.'

Slowly, she removed her veil, not meeting his eyes. Her malhaf fell around her, exposing her mother's jewellery and her youthful curves. He smiled mildly as he took in the sight and she hugged her body for comfort.

'Drink,' he insisted. 'The wine will warm your blood.'

She took a large gulp from the goblet. The bitterness hit the back of her throat instantly and the smell of fermented fruit filled her nostrils. She coughed gently into her hand, suppressing a hiccup.

He threw his head back and laughed. She giggled with him and drained the goblet.

Emboldened by her daring she flashed him a challenging look and then coyly turned her head away.

'Do you remember my name?' she asked, testing his previous testaments of love.

'Of course,' he said, bending his head slightly to look into her lowered eyes. 'Your name is Latifa.' The wine rushed to her head.

After a while he took her delicate hands in his. Reaching out, he stroked the stones around her neck, making her jump with fright at the proximity of his hand.

He dropped his hand from her neck. 'Do you remember mine?' he asked.

She nodded assertively, happy to be able to continue the game. 'Your name is … You are …' She frowned. Her head was spinning; she tried to recall his name. It sat just beyond her memory, but she struggled to retrieve it from the fogginess surrounding her. 'I … I know you,' she stuttered as she tried to stand, stumbling back onto the rug. She relented, surrendering herself to the effects of the wine. Feeling the weight of her head on her neck she swayed slightly back and forth.

'Why don't you lie down for while?' she heard him say, his voice called her as if beyond the garden wall. 'Perhaps you drank too quickly.'

She did as he suggested, resting her head on the rug and stretching out her legs. *Just a few minutes*, she thought to herself, *and then I will get up and return home before they find me missing.*

The leaves of the tree rustled above, releasing small jasmine buds so that they fell around and on her chest. She felt herself reach out to catch one. She caught her breath as the man's face came into view above her. Her skin prickled and the air suddenly felt cold. As the world around her faded into darkness, his name finally came to her. She uttered it beneath her breath. It was her final word.

17

A pomegranate seed

This city of red, why did it go on?

In the north, the taste of sea salt in the air gave hope that whatever became of the place, whatever it resorted to, it could be sanitized, born again. If the Mediterranean Ocean refused to send a cleansing wind, the Atlantic would soon oblige. Not Marrakesh, not this city of red. Was it the blood of its residents that coloured the earth, crawling up its mud walls so that from a high point it looked like it was bleeding from its arteries? What gave it life and the will to persevere when it had so much to fear and very little left to fight for? Fear of drought, famine, disease and invading tribes, one terror replacing another or sometimes occurring together. Why did it choose to continue? Trapped by the Atlas mountains to the south and east with flat lands as far as the horizon in all other directions, it had nothing but itself. It had no choice but faith and no spectacle but its own image; its life force came from within. The novice would look at the baked earth and wonder how its people found their sustenance and why they even bothered, never realizing that beneath the burning red lay a river flowing formed by the sweat of its inhabitants.

By day the residents scratched a living. Some left the city walls to forage for edible plants amidst the cacti and locusts, others begged for a coin. Some sold their worldly possessions for a loaf of bread. Most went hungry, except for the lucky few who had provisions to withstand times of hardship and the excess who controlled which way the hardship flowed.

And as night fell and the late January cold seeped into frail bones, the city's residents would seek heat from each other by gathering in Jemaa el-Fnaa. They would huddle together in circles, shoulder to shoulder, turning their backs on the city and all the despair it caused. While waiting for the evening's distraction to begin – whether a storyteller, a dancing monkey, acrobats or a man who could tell the future by looking into the stares of a hungry child – they would momentarily lock eyes in recognition of their continued existence, finding rebirth where the dead assembled.

Farook al-Alami stood back from the circle of men and children. He waited for Yusuf, not wanting to refuse him his moment of denial. Yusuf al-Mahdi hugged himself from the cold and stamped his feet into the red earth. Many of the other men in the circle did the same so that it looked like they were caught in a divine dance. With their hoods raised and feet stamping they appeared to be in a trance, locked together in one movement. In the centre of the circle stood an old man, his hood also pulled over his head. His jellaba was made from wool once dyed black, but now a dusty grey. His face was wrinkled and the inward curl of his lips spoke of the loss of teeth, pulled out one by one as he progressed into old age. In his right hand he held a thin cane, which he raised to the sky and shook at the men encircling him. At his feet stood an iron lamp, within which sat a stunted candle offering a pathetic glow.

The storyteller circled the crowd before beginning his tale, absorbing each man as though harvesting his energy, pulling it from their core to then return it as a ⸻ carpet weaved by the Berbers of the Anti-Atlas.

Farook watched wi⸻ ⸻nterest, his thoughts on the missing women and how the⸻ ⸻aved together. He was certain they did, convinced among⸻ ⸻nants of the life they lived lay a single detail, a comm⸻ ⸻hat would unravel the whole thing before his eyes.

The storyteller stopped at Yusuf and looked at him. He read his face as though reading a book, a look of curiosity shining in his eyes. As though having acquired all that he needed, the storyteller returned assertively to the centre. A prickle of anticipation made its way around the men as the feet stomping subsided and the circle tightened. Farook extended his neck to look over the crowd of turbans at the storyteller.

'Once upon a time,' the storyteller began in a booming voice, 'There were two sisters, Mimouna and Aicha, who could not have been more different. Mimouna was ugly and mean, while her sister was pretty and kind. Aicha would try to help her older sister, but Mimouna was jealous of the beautiful young girl and would treat her badly.

One day the two girls were amusing themselves in the garden. Mimouna was eating a very ripe, perfumed pomegranate. Aicha thought it looked delicious and asked if she could take a piece of it.'

"Certainly not," replied the older sister. "I'm not sharing this with you."

As the greedy Mimouna munched on the fruit, a seed fell to the earth and Aicha leant down to eat it. Mimouna was furious and, because she had forbidden her sister to taste the fruit, she lashed out, striking her sister violently. Aicha fell, smacked her skull on a rock and died instantly.

Mimouna was terrified that someone might have seen her do this, but fortunately for her, no one was watching. That night under cover of darkness, Mimouna dragged her sister's corpse to a forest outside the walls of Marrakesh, dug a shallow grave and buried her there.

One day, a wandering minstrel happened to be passing through Marrakesh. He loved to play the drum, but the leather that had been stretched over the instrument had been torn. As he walked outside the city he saw a shady forest, where he thought he would sit down and rest from the fierce heat of the sun. But, as he entered the woods he stumbled over something. Turning around, he expected to see a tree stump or root, but imagine his horror when he saw a foot sticking out of the earth. When he cleared the dirt, he uncovered the corpse of the delicate Aicha.'

The old man paused in his tale, waiting for the story to seep into the imagination of his listeners. The circle of men stood transfixed by the conjured sight of a corpse still beautiful in its decay. Some of the children had sat down, cross-legged with their heads resting in the palm of their hands. Farook stepped closer to hear the story better.

Pointing his cane at Yusuf, the storyteller continued.

'He was a simple man and did not know what to do. He thought he should bury her properly, but as he turned her over and gazed at the fresh pale skin on her back, he had an idea.

"Maybe I can use her skin to repair my drum," he thought.

So, he cut out a section of her skin from her back with his knife, washed it in a stream and stretched it over his drum. Then he dug a deeper hole in the earth and buried the fair Aicha in the ground.

The musician was delighted that his drum worked again, and he sat there in the forest playing a tune that enchanted the birds. But, as he beat the drum with his fingers, the most extraordinary thing happened; it began to speak.

"I died from a pomegranate," the drum said. "I died from a pomegranate."

He thought maybe this marvellous, magical instrument would draw the crowds in Marrakesh, so he set off again for the Medina. As he entered the city he passed a house.

"I died from a pomegranate," the talking drum continued to say. "I died from a pomegranate."

The musician could hear cries from the house. He knocked on the door to see what was going on, and when it opened, he was welcomed by an old couple, who looked very sad.

"Please come in," they said. "Have you, by any chance, come upon our youngest daughter? We've not seen her for several days."

"I died from a pomegranate," the drum said, as the musician sat down. "I died from a pomegranate."

"Why, this is the most extraordinary musical instrument I've ever seen," said the old man. "Why does it say those words?"

"I was walking in a forest and I came upon a body that was buried," the musician replied and recounted the story.

"I did it," wailed Mimouna, as she burst into the room in floods of tears. "I killed my sister. I would not share a pomegranate with her, so I killed her."

For many months the magician played his drum in this square, and soon everyone knew about the tale of the beautiful Aicha, who was killed because she ate the seed of a pomegranate, and her sister Mimouna, who was betrayed by a talking drum."

The spell broke and with it the circle of men. Some wandered off while others stood a moment, blinking as though waking from a heavy dream. The children continued to sit on the ground mesmerized by the tale. Yusuf lingered for a moment, placing a coin in the storyteller's hand. Farook stood pondering the case of 'The pomegranate and the talking drum'.

'He knows nothing,' said Yusuf as he joined Farook, nodding his head at the storyteller now busy counting his meagre collection of coins. 'Has no recollection of seeing Leila and her brother.'

Farook nodded, Yusuf confirming what he already suspected. They began to walk around the square, passing other crowds gathered with their backs to the city.

'Assiya left the letters. They are our talking drum,' said Farook.

Yusuf took a while to make the connection. 'Assiya's lover!' he blurted out. 'By his behaviour we already know him to be an indecent man.'

'Not true,' Farook countered. 'From his letters we know him to be a man in love. That does not necessarily make him indecent.'

Yusuf would one day like to learn what Farook defined as indecent. Whoever he was, the lover had broken a moral code.

'If he sent her love letters, it is safe to assume she also wrote some to him.'

'Ha! A young girl able to write,' laughed Yusuf. 'It's less believable than a talking drum.'

'My thoughts exactly. Her family is evidently poor,' Farook confirmed. 'She must have had an accomplice in her love. Someone to write for her from dictation and read her lover's response. It would have to be someone she trusted.'

'It would be a mistake to approach the family again, Si Farook,' warned Yusuf. 'We should focus our energy on the other girls.'

'We look for the lover and Assiya's accomplice,' Farook concluded, ignoring Yusuf.

'How?' asked Yusuf, already weary of the answer Farook would give. 'Do you know how many fruit groves there are within the city walls? Then there are the gardens outside. We do not even know what day and time they would meet. It could take weeks to find him …' Yusuf rattled on, angering at the amount of work he was creating for himself. Perhaps he should just shut up.

But he could not resist the urge to continue. 'As for her accomplice. Let's assume it's a man, if it's a woman we have no way of knowing who without approaching the family. There are dozens of registered scribes in this city, dozens. To locate the scribe she used could take weeks if not months, and that is assuming she used a registered scribe. It is too much for us to do, it's impossible …' Yusuf trailed off.

'Tomorrow, visit the Street of Scribes. Collect as many samples of writing as you can. We will compare them to the letters first to see if any match. It is unlikely we will find a match; she was probably not that stupid. But we must eliminate registered scribes first. Use your position and do not reveal the reason behind requiring the sample. Meet me in two days at my funduq. Come early, we have much to do.'

Yusuf stayed silent, preferring the task of visiting the Street of Scribes than trudging through every garden in the city.

They stopped at a barber stool. The barber aggressively pulled at a young boy's head and brought a rusty blade to the top of his forehead. The boy winced.

'I did not like the butcher. He seemed cold and indifferent about the missing girl, even though he has known the family her entire life and even considered marrying her,' said Yusuf.

Farook frowned. 'And the cobbler?' he asked, watching the barber at his work. A thin line of blood appeared across the top of the boy's forehead. The barber wiped it away with a dirty rag.

'He has completed the holy pilgrimage twice, but I did not like him either. He seemed … insincere.'

They stepped away from the barber and walked in the direction of Farook's funduq.

'You said you visited the French doctor. I have heard of his work. They say he prevented a bout of dysentery escaping the mellah walls.'

'I am sure he would be happy to hear such a rumour. Leave him to me,' Farook said. 'You continue investigating the butcher and the cobbler. I will handle the doctor.'

Continuing around the square, they stopped at the narrow street leading to Farook's funduq and shook hands. Yusuf watched Farook walk down the alleyway. His bones ached, but his head hurt more. When would the hard work end? When would he be the one to tell others what to do without need for explanation? When would his commitment to maintaining the rule of law in this anarchic city finally be acknowledged?

18

The Street of Scribes

The Street of Scribes was filled with people and yet deathly quiet. The only sounds were the scratching of quill on parchment and the muffled instructions of clients. The letter-writers sat on low stalls with makeshift wooden desks raised just above the ground or in tiny shops that had enough room for two patrons at a time. It was the only market area in Marrakesh where traders did not scream their wares. There was no need since the increasing demand for the written word surpassed the city's capacity to produce it. What's more, the scribes needed silence to concentrate; a dot in the wrong place and they would have to start all over again. So patrons and those just passing to grab a moment of quiet amidst the commotion respected them and their working needs.

The scribes sat deep in concentration looking down at their writing equipment. In their line of work there was no need to meet customers in the eye to make a sale; hearing was the most important sense to harness. Their ears were pricked for their client's instructions, zoning in on the sound of their voice and shutting out the mutterings of others. Occasionally, quills were suspended in mid-air as a letter-writer checked a name or sentence, but it did not take long for the sound of scratching to start up once more. Deeds for land, marriage contracts stipulating the dowry of a young girl, the wholesale of a crop, complaints of wrongdoing: whatever was being committed to the written history of the city it was not only the words that conveyed the meaning. The scribes took pride in their work, seeing themselves more as artists than mere channels of communication. They had mastered the Maghrebi script, spent their lives perfecting dots, lines and curls until their fingers were raw and permanently stained brown. Today they may be committing the sale of a harvest of wheat to paper, but tomorrow they could be called to the palace to transcribe a royal order or to a mosque to copy the Qu'ran for a wealthy benefactor. Then they would reap the rewards of their craftsmanship in this life and for eternity.

Yusuf stood at the top of the street looking down at the activity. He did not know quite where to begin. The prospect of approaching each letter-writer and requesting a sample of his work, having to explain over and over again with fabricated reasons left him demoralized. They would question him, look at him curiously and ask why he did not come with an official letter from the makhzan explaining his presence. They could refuse, demanding he leave and return with evidence giving him the authority to demand they submit their craft to a silly experiment.

A spoken oath meant nothing here. While in the Sharia courts swearing on the Qu'ran with witnesses present could restore a person's property or compensate blood with money, in the Street of Scribes people did not trust words flung into the air. What if God was not listening on that particular day, too busy instructing his angels to scribble down the sins being committed in the city? If there was a Street of Scribes in heaven, no doubt the letter-writers there worked through the night to keep on top of the paperwork. No, these craftsmen knew the value of the written word, how it was a witness when the testimony of men failed and their bodies gave up their oath.

Yusuf considered a different option. Somewhere in the unfathomable abyss that was the makhzan records there was a ledger of all official scribes operating in Marrakesh. He could seek it out, demand those on the list present themselves to him with a sample of their writing.

But he knew locating the list – let alone gaining the right decree from the right authority – could take weeks if not months and would draw the attention of the whole cohort of makhzan officials working within the city. Farook had insisted on drawing as little attention as possible to their work. This resulted in Yusuf standing in the early February sun looking like a fool among Marrakesh's more educated residents.

He would become a laughing stock, mocked behind his back for his audacity. He had to think of a reason strong enough to compel the scribes. Perhaps a second breakfast would do the trick. That way he would have more time to think up a good enough reason and besides a half empty stomach was just a distraction to the creative process.

He turned back and walked up the street until he came across an eating establishment. Sitting down he ordered breakfast. Soon after an unwashed looking boy placed hot bread, two fried eggs sprinkled with salt and cumin and a bowl of green olives swimming in olive oil in front of him. He returned moments later with a pot of tea.

Yusuf wet his lips and tucked into his breakfast, resentful of the miserly offerings presented to him earlier that morning by his wife. She was a good woman all in all, and tended to his needs before he even knew what they were. But there was a time in the month, which rolled in like a Saharan wind and lingered like an unwelcome guest, when he found himself spending more time outside the house than in. He would never understand women. They were ruled by a different moon. His long years of marriage had taught him it was best to not even try, let it pass and order would eventually be restored.

As he sat bemoaning his fate, the issue of gaining samples of writing drifted to the outer reaches of his thoughts. Just as he filled his mouth with a handful of bread dipped in egg yolk, a slap caused him to choke until he had no choice but to swallow it whole. He squinted up at the person responsible for this near-death experience.

'Si Yusuf, what brings you to the Street of Scribes? Are you on official business?' Ibrahim asked as he took a seat opposite him.

'You could say that,' Yusuf grumbled.

'If you need a letter written why not come to me?' he asked, with a click of offence in his voice.

An extra glass was brought to the table and mint tea poured out.

Yusuf thought about it. He had known Ibrahim for a long time, even struck up a friendship of sorts. He was an official scribe who had done well for himself, taking on an apprentice at his shop further down the street. He had used Ibrahim for various official duties. He recalled the time when a dispute over land between a Muslim and Jewish resident had ended in the Sharia courts and how Ibrahim had faithfully attested to the Jewish man's documented claim, resulting in the judge ordering the Muslim to return the land to its rightful owner. He could be trusted, both for his written and spoken word.

Perhaps Ibrahim could be of assistance. What that assistance might look like was unclear, but he knew the scribes better than Yusuf and they trusted him as a colleague. Yusuf swallowed his last piece of bread and washed it down with the dregs of tea remaining in his glass.

He waved Ibrahim to lean in and explained the situation, warning him of the need for discretion. Once started, he found he could not hold back the details and enjoyed the opportunity to offload his frustrations to an enthralled ear. Ibrahim listened attentively, smart enough to not ask questions and accept the story as told. He rubbed his hand over his thin beard in concentration.

'The scribes will not submit samples, Si Yusuf, especially if they think it might implicate them in a possible crime,' he said, stating the obvious.

Yusuf nodded in agreement. Ibrahim arrived at the same dead end quickly enough. Farook had set him an impossible task.

'I have it,' Ibrahim said with enthusiasm, slapping Yusuf once more on the back. Yusuf heaved forward, his turban almost falling onto the greasy plates. This backslapping was quite improper, particularly in public. Regardless, Ibrahim had a plan, which was more than he could say for himself.

'Si Yusuf, return after lunch and I will have more samples of writing waiting for you than you can carry,' announced Ibrahim.

Yusuf waited with bated breath for an explanation but none came. Acting as though they were complicit in a secret project on the orders of the Sultan himself, Ibrahim tapped his nose and winked. Slapping Yusuf on his back one final time for good measure, he left, charging towards his shop with a determination which caused passers-by to step aside.

What had he done? What would Ibrahim do? A temperamental wife, Farook's expectations and now Ibrahim, a civilian loaded with information and a plan that would probably end in catastrophe: Yusuf felt caught in a trap of his own making. He pushed the breakfast plates away from him and called for the bill. Nothing could be done, he told himself. He had no choice but to return later that day and if Ibrahim was up to no good, he would soon teach him the consequences.

He paid for his breakfast, feeling bloated with worry, and gradually made his way home, hoping his wife had withdrawn from her seclusion and begun preparing lunch.

19

Sugar trade

On returning home, Yusuf found his wife hidden away in the upstairs rooms, while the children played unsupervised in the small courtyard. Patting them on their heads as his passed, he made his way to the living area and settled on the divan. Over the years he managed to build his family a modest house, two rooms downstairs with a small kitchen and two rooms upstairs. The walls were untiled, white-washed with minimal awnings. He hoped one day to tile them in Fez fashion, but that was a long way off. His position in the government drew a tiny salary that was often suspended during times of financial difficulty and only recently instituted. The current suspension was in its fourth month with no end in sight. Of course, officials did not get rich from their salaries. Their position was an obligation to the Sultan and by default to God. Money was made through bribery and acquiring trade contracts through the right connections. But Yusuf did not have the stomach for hustle. He held a small licence for the local distribution of sugar, which brought in a comfortable income. But the sugar trade was suffering from malicious rumours. That rebellious Mohammed al-Kattani and his Sufi order had been spreading rumours for years that the British made sugar using pig's blood. The idea was ridiculous of course, but the Kattaniyya's were smart enough to know what resonated with the un-lettered man on the street. Tell them the British were hooking the population on a white substance to create an export trade and their eyes would glaze over. Tell them that it contained pig's blood and they would rush to wash their mouths out before heading to the mosque to pray for repentance.

Blast those Sufi orders and their meddling with affairs of the state. Why the Sultan didn't just order the arrest of al-Kattani was beyond Yusuf's comprehension. If the state took action perhaps he could one day afford to take his family to Mogador as he had promised his wife when they first married. Until then, he had no choice but to suffer her moods in silence.

He unfurled his turban and laid it on the divan, rubbing his hair free. 'All provision is from Allah,' he muttered to himself.

What was the point of worry? There were no guarantees in life, no such thing as security. The wealthy could lose it all with a wrong word placed in the right ear and the poor would continue to grumble. In Morocco, the son of a black slave could crawl out of the harem to stand behind the new Sultan pointing to where he should sign one day and the next find his family flung to the street with nothing but their babies on their backs. What was the point of the struggle? Without doubt, gratitude was better than greed.

He rewrapped his turban around his head. He considered for a moment calling his wife down to fix some tea, but decided it would be easier to stop at a shop on the way back to the Street of Scribes. He would visit Ibrahim and then make his way to Farook to confess all. Surely the man would understand. He seemed a reasonable fellow, not subject to flares of anger and rage, unlike others in the makhzan. Whatever damage Ibrahim had created, they could fix it together. If not, Yusuf would tell Farook exactly what he thought of their investigation and the amount of time they were wasting going over those letters instead of just rounding everyone up and waiting until they were ready to speak. They all eventually spoke. The sooner they closed the case the sooner he could go back to building his sugar trade … the sooner his wife would smile again.

Finding Ibrahim in his shop, Yusuf reluctantly entered. Ibrahim dropped his quill and jumped up from his seat. Instructing his apprentice to fetch tea, he winked at Yusuf continuing his earlier charade. Yusuf stifled a groan in his throat.

'Twenty samples, Si Yusuf,' Ibrahim announced with a broad beam across his face, 'and more coming. Others have promised to give me samples by close of shop.'

Yusuf took the bundle of parchments. He struggled to form a sentence.

'How did you collect so many so quickly?'

'Do not worry yourself with trivialities not worthy of your station, Si Yusuf,' Ibrahim replied. 'Let's just say a bit of healthy competition soon gets these scoundrels scribbling. They are a lazy lot, but tell them a big commission is heading this way and the city runs out of ink in minutes. They all think their words are worth ten times their weight in gold.' Ibrahim winked once more.

That will show his wife and Farook. Yusuf was as smart as the next man; perhaps even more intelligent than most.

Recalling his earlier fears, he uttered a pray of gratitude. *God gives and God takes away … and then He gives again.*

20

Perverse proverbs

'What is this?' asked Farook, pointing at one of the samples of writing lying on his desk.

Yusuf read it.

The tears of a whore are hidden behind the door.

He felt himself blush instantly. He stammered, and searched his mind for an explanation. If he had only taken the time to go through the samples before making his way to Farook.

'It's a very well-known proverb, Si Farook, from the Djebala people in the north, I think. Perhaps you know it. It means we regret our sins in private,' he offered in a meek voice.

'I know what it is, Si Yusuf, and what it means. But why did the scribe write it?' Farook asked.

Yusuf found himself asking that very same question. Farook picked up another.

'And this?' he asked, looking at Yusuf.

A little nod is enough from the wise, a donkey needs a fist.

'It … It means the intelligent …'

'Si Yusuf, I know the meaning, but why did you ask the scribe to write this specifically?'

This was not good. Whatever story Ibrahim concocted to get the scribes to submit samples; it was not good. Yusuf picked up another sample and read it.

He stayed the night in the marshes; in the morning he was a frog.

Perhaps this was some kind of elaborate joke, and the letter writers were collaborating to make a fool of him. Perhaps Ibrahim thought it entertaining to collect proverbs that included profanity and insult as a way of mocking the makhzan. This was official business, his work connected to a chain of commands that stemmed from the Sultan himself. He could have the whole street closed in twenty-four hours and their guild shut down indefinitely.

Perhaps twenty-four hours was an exaggeration, well, in fact, closing the street was probably impossible. The city would go into meltdown. But, he could make Ibrahim's life a living hell … somehow.

Flicking through the samples and seeing they were all much the same, Yusuf felt his rage begin to bubble.

'If a man puts a cord around his neck, God will provide someone to pull it,' Farook read aloud, the hint of a smile playing at the corner of his lips. That one certainly rang true.

'If the Sultan declares that noon is night, behold the stars,' he continued.

By the time Yusuf was finished with Ibrahim, the man would see nothing but stars.

'I have had enough,' Yusuf fumed. 'Let's compare the handwriting and be done with it. These scribes like to think themselves poets. I will make them rue the day–'

'Relax, Yusuf. Calm yourself. The words do not matter, it is their style we must concern ourselves with.' Yusuf looked poised to retort but Farook's smile disarmed him. He gathered the samples together, counting thirty-three in total. They spread the love letters on the desk, looking over them and then taking a sample from the top of the pile they carefully examined them for similarities. To the untrained eye the Arabic script looked the same. But, of course this was not the case. The scribes enjoyed leaving their unique mark on the script, writing beauty into the trade of the mundane and the complaints of the masses. An hour and a half later and the work was complete drawing them no closer to the identity of Assiya's lover.

'Si Farook, I must say I do not know why we went to the trouble. I think we both knew the letters were unlikely to have been written by a registered scribe,' grumbled Yusuf. Being unproductive while on the job was one thing, but being ridiculed was quite another.

'We must confirm our suspicions, Si Yusuf,' Farook lectured. 'It may seem we have gained nothing from the exercise, but in fact we have gained much. We have eliminated thirty-three scribes from our immediate investigations.'

Yusuf was in no mood for such a lecture.

'Tell me, what about the scribes who did not submit samples or the hundreds of people who are lettered and living in the city? It seems to me we have eliminated individuals who were never suspects in the first place.'

Farook gathered the samples and tucked them away in his desk draw. Of course Yusuf was correct in his assessment. It felt like nothing had been achieved. But this was police work, as he understood it. It was not an exact science and behind every tiny step forward were hours and hours of work that did nothing but eliminate possibilities. The process of discovery had to be complemented by a process of exclusion. Perhaps if a police force were eventually instituted in the country, a trained police force of course, investigations such as this would not feel so wasteful. Farook could have a team of officers exploring multiple enquiries simultaneously. He could delegate lines of investigation based on the competence of each officer; no stone would go unturned to get to the truth of a case.

Until then it was up to him and Yusuf to refine procedure, ensure they did not botch the enquiry, and be methodical in their approach.

No leaps of judgment, but every turn of thought accounted for. And no jumps into action that only led to more victims with no real certainty regarding the criminal or the reliability of his confession.

'Perhaps I may make a suggestion,' Farook began gently, knowing what he was about to say would only exasperate Yusuf's bad mood. 'We must be meticulous in our work, even if on the surface it seems to be long-winded and unnecessary. In future, it would be best to standardize the samples. Perhaps provide a script you want the scribes to write.'

If he thought for a moment Yusuf would return to the Street of Scribes he was sadly mistaken. Yusuf doubted he would be able to show his face there for a while. No, if Farook wanted more samples or standardized samples, or whatever else, he could do it himself.

'Tell me Si Farook, while I was going from one scribe to another collecting samples were you here at the funduq reviewing the speaking pictures?' he asked, pointing at the wall.

Farook smiled. 'Partly,' he said. 'I also looked into the case of Leila. You recall, 18 years old and missing since September last year.'

Yusuf nodded as they made their way over to the wall.

'I spoke to her younger brother. They visited Jemaa el-Fnaa in the early evening. It was still daylight. The boy said he listened to the storyteller and when it was finished he could not find his sister. He returned home expecting to find her there, but she has not been seen since.'

'We already know this, Si Farook, see it is written here on the wall,' Yusuf remarked, jabbing to the speaking pictures.

'Yes we do, but now we know what it means,' Farook rebutted.

Yusuf shrugged, losing interest in the conversation as he mulled over the humiliations he had endured since Farook's arrival; the Qadi, the scribes and Farook's barking of orders as though Yusuf was nothing but his houseboy.

'Leila disappeared from the middle of Jemaa el-Fnaa in early evening. Maryam visited the French doctor in the mellah in broad daylight and never returned home. Assiya visited the hammam in the afternoon, again broad daylight, but did not return home. And finally Souad went on some errands in …'

'Broad daylight,' Yusuf concluded.

'It means, Si Yusuf, that they could not have been attacked without witnesses or people intervening.'

'They ran away,' confirmed Yusuf, for the sake of politeness. Was this not what he had suggested at the very beginning?

'I find it hard to believe Maryam abandoned her children, or Souad at 15, was confident enough to leave the city walls for somewhere else. I believe they all knew their assailant and that they all have something in common, in the form of a person.' Farook paused for a moment.

'The French doctor mentioned an interesting detail. He said Maryam arrived at his clinic wearing heavy jewellery under her malhaf. He seemed to think this was normal attire. It seems to me perhaps she was meeting someone after her appointment and wanted to look her best. So, I also checked this detail with Leila's family and she left the house wearing her finest clothes.'

Yusuf took a moment to process the implication. Maryam had removed her outer clothes in front of a man … a Christian one at that. The scandal. Did these women have no shame? They had forsaken their families and their honour for wickedness.

'You mean to suggest robbery was the motive behind their disappearance? But, in that case what does Maryam's jewellery or Leila's clothes have to do with the love letters?'

'Perhaps nothing and perhaps robbery had something to do with it. It simply helps in confirming our theory that the women knew their assailant and went on their own volition. The jewellery and clothes imply a desire to please indicating it is likely to be a man they went to meet. The link to the letters will become clear later, but what if the lover is the same man for all of them?'

'What do we do now?'

'I will find a way to speak to Assiya's mother once more. Perhaps she knows who the lover is. His name begins with K, we can start from there.'

They were chasing ghosts with nothing but the initial of a first name.

Then it hit Yusuf. Why had he not thought of it before? The answer sat staring him in the face and if he hadn't been consumed with pointless exercises he might have seen it sooner.

'I must leave, Si Farook. I have an errand I must run.'

Yusuf quickly gathered his clothes. Farook watched from in front of the speaking pictures.

'Si Yusuf, your work with the scribes was very good. It has helped immensely, but we must take small steps, not rush ahead.'

The advice fell on deaf ears.

21

Accomplices to death

He touched her youthful skin and caressed her soft cheeks. Their blush was already beginning to fade, but she was not yet cold. He observed her face, the outline of her naturally arched eyebrows, large almond shaped-eyes, now closed, and her petite mouth. She seemed to be frowning; perhaps her final thought was a question she did not live long enough to have answered. He massaged her temple and tried to release the crease so that she looked more at peace. It was important she was at peace and any questions she might have died with would soon be answered in her absence.

As each one of them slipped into unconsciousness he liked to talk to them, explain his reasons and their life purpose. It was important they understood and saw the beauty in their sacrifice, otherwise their soul would not depart. It would stay in this world to haunt him; he had learnt that difficult lesson.

He could see for some the logic was difficult to fathom. Though their bodies were paralyzed by the time he detected resistance in their eyes. He could not help but feel resentment towards the ones who refused to accept. They silently accepted so much adversity in their lives. Their sex determined their life trajectory from the moment they were born, and yet they would not accept their sacrifice. Perhaps through his work their combined hopeless existence could mean something. In those moments when his angered flared he said a quiet prayer for their souls. *To God we belong and to Him we shall return.*

In others he saw gratitude. If they could speak they would say thank you. They didn't have to. He understood and in that moment, when he comforted them through their last breaths, the divine appeared. They were not victims. They were accomplices.

He thought about the story of Ibrahim in the Qu'ran. God, in His wisdom, had prevented Ibrahim from fulfilling what he believed a divine command. He had saved Ibrahim's son Ishmael from sacrifice. Though a prophet, Ibrahim was not made for the act of killing, his spirit not strong enough to bear the guilt. But guilt was a worldly emotion that would, as with all things, pass with death. And then the gardens of paradise would open to those willing to submit to divine will; resentments removed from the chest, hunger from the stomach and wrists adorned with bracelets of gold.

God had not stopped him. God, if anything, had facilitated his work and presented him girls one after the other, desperate for meaning. They had come so easily, so willingly, it was as though in the end the choice was made for him. He remembered each of them although the number was large. He recalled every one. He had ways of recording their place in his assembly. And those whose spirits lingered he tolerated as part of his daily life. He felt them watching from the corner of the room while he slept, caught them following him in the market. He tried to accept their presence with benevolence, realizing that God would reveal the reasons why they lingered when the moment was right.

He touched the silver jewellery adorning the girl's neck. It was cheap, weighing nothing, and displaying no craftsmanship. It didn't matter. She looked her finest at her moment of death and would go to the next world at her most beautiful. He lifted her head gently and pulled her long light brown hair from beneath her. He brushed it through with his fingers and laid it on her right shoulder. Picking up a clay bowl he meticulously laced white jasmine bulbs through her hair so that she wore a crown of flowers. They would blossom in her grave and release a fragrance to sweeten her sleep. He stood up and stumbled in the dark. He pushed the large piece of furniture to the back wall and began to dig. He worked through the night collecting the dirt in even piles around the grave. Standing in the grave, he measured its depth. Trial and error had taught him the smell would appear quickly if the grave was too shallow.

Hearing the sound of birds bringing in the encroaching dawn, he picked up his pace. He climbed out of the grave and went over to the body. Touching her face once more he felt coldness had set in. Lifting her small frame, her weight no more than that of a little child, he carried her to the grave and placed her in. Next, he covered her with dirt, starting at her feet, all the while reciting prayers of peace. He worked his way up her body and just before covering her face removed her necklace and placed it in his pocket. When he had finished he stomped across the floor, flattening and wiping the earth of any evidence and then heaved the furniture back to its place to stand over the corpse.

She was just a corpse now. The spark that had danced behind her eyes when they had met in the garden was gone. Her spirit had transcended the physical realm. He found his book and wrote down her name on the list. He lingered on the name above hers.

Latifa was a good girl, but showed fear at the end and so he could not but help feel disappointed when her time came.

As he patted the dust from his clothes he heard the distant sound of the dawn call to prayer. He retreated to the back of his house to complete his ablutions. Seeing that the neighbourhood was still sleeping, very few of the men having the discipline or fear for the first prayer. He left the alleyway and walked to the mosque three streets down.

22

A father's burden

Farook stared down at the couscous floating in a bowl of soured milk. It was as though time had rewound to his first days in the city. Only now he knew too well its streets and corners, its moods and obsessions. There were days when he felt trapped in an asylum: the walls constructed to contain the lunacy, but also sustaining it.

The city inhabitants seemed to drink from the same water fountain. If the mood in the market was jovial then it seeped through the alleyways, into the mosques and madrasas, kitchens and living rooms until the sound of laughter and play followed a person throughout the course of their day. Traders would add a few extra potatoes to a customer's basket; eateries would feed beggars loitering at their doors; and the sound of uninhibited laughter would tumble from the rooftops. But, if the mood was downcast then fights would break out over the price of a few tomatoes; children would be smacked for their impertinence; and the city bakeries would turn into battlegrounds, all etiquette forgotten as the young jostled with the old for bread.

The lack of rain meant the atmosphere in the city was far from jovial. All joy had been burnt off by the midday sun. People walked about looking up at the sky, bumping into each other and cursing beneath their breath. Some of the men toiling land beyond the walls congregated nightly in forests to pray for rain. Perhaps they thought by standing in unison with the trees Mother Nature would take pity. Their prayers went unanswered and so they returned to their farms to pick the locusts off their crops one by one. Mothers rationed their milk. They breast-fed their new-borns only when the cloth soaked in sugary water for their babies to suckle no longer pacified. A rumour spread in the north of the city that there was a shortage of onions and the price soared in the south. People pushed and spat to buy whatever was left in the market to pickle in vinegar or salt and store for harder times.

Farook took a sip from the bowl and placed it down. The heat was building, and with it tempers. He had walked passed Assiya's family home twice that morning and sat down certain, despite no evidence, that his very presence would be enough to entice the mother out. Intuition was not a feeling in the pit of the stomach that went unexplained, a mysterious sense or ability that sat just beyond our consciousness. It was cerebral, it was being alert to the world around you, absorbing information, digesting it and then making a decision without the need to consciously rationalize the reason. That's why he sat waiting for Assiya's mother to make an appearance. Because a logic he had not yet unravelled told him his presence in the neighbourhood was already known and not completely unwanted.

He watched a beggar with a cane, rattling a tin pot. People pushed past him, turning to curse his ancestors as the waft of his unwashed body hit them in the face. The beggar stopped in the middle of the street, his eyes locked on Farook. Farook pushed his bowl of couscous towards him and the man sprang forward with a youth concealed by his layers of rags. As the beggar stood gulping from the bowl, Farook noticed the young boy with the copper hair approach. Ah, the neighbourhood informer. The boy was a trader like everyone else in the city. Except he traded information, a produce always in demand and not subject to the whims of passing clouds.

Farook stood up and followed the boy. He had no idea where they were going, but it did not worry him. He was being called and that meant a step closer.

They reached Assiya's house, the door hanging slightly off its hinges. Farook hesitated for a moment wondering if his intuition had failed him, before gently knocking. The boy disappeared around a corner. A man with thick eyebrows and a long beard answered.

'Come in.'

Farook stepped into the house and followed the man through to an interior room.

'Why are you watching my house again?'

He had not expected the father to take his bait. This was a far better outcome than he could hope for. This was something he could work with.

'I wanted to speak to you about Assiya,' Farook explained, bowing slightly.

'And were you not told we wanted nothing to do with your investigation? You spoke to my wife in the market and the whole neighbourhood gossiped about nothing else for weeks. Is it not bad enough that our reputation has already been damaged because of my daugh… Assiya?'

'I apologize for any distress I caused you,' Farook offered. 'I assure you my intention was never to bring dishonour to your family. I am of the opinion that the truth will set a person free. I understand the burden of shame, but if it cripples our ability to do the right thing it is a weight we should remove from our society and our backs. Finding out what happened to Assiya is the right thing to do, for her if no one else.'

'You have honourable principles, but it is only when you are truly tested that your real values emerge. Hardship teaches us what we are truly capable of and unfortunately I do not have the luxury of keeping opinion. What you say does not change the fact that my daughter dishonoured us and by doing so destroyed any hopes we may have had as a family.'

'And if I swore to be discreet?' asked Farook. 'Surely, as a family you want to know what happened to her?'

'What difference would knowing make?'

The truth was he couldn't say if it would make a difference. Perhaps it was naïve to think an explanation would ease suffering, shame and ruin, as though simply by knowing why a person could better withstand the consequences. There were no procedures he could refer to as an offering of reassurance, there were no guarantees the answers would placate the anger or fill the hollowness. His only guarantee was his mind: the way it functioned, it's obsession for answers.

'I don't know if it would make a difference,' he admitted.

The father nodded in understanding.

'Girls are a burden on a father. From the moment she is born you worry. You know you will have to feed and clothe her, ensure her safety and pray that one day a man will marry her, treat her well, and lessen your burden. And if she is ruined she stays with you into old age. A boy, you can send out to work, to run errands. From a young age he can bring something into the house. If you have the financial ability you can educate him in the madrasa or in a trade and perhaps one day he can lift his family out of misery. Not girls.'

Was it any wonder Assiya had searched out comfort in the arms of a lover? Was it so hard to believe Souad might have switched paths in search of another life? Perhaps they realized the chains of their confinement were located in the eyes of others and not around their ankles. Was it fair to judge them so harshly for their willingness to risk everything after coming to the realization that really they had already lost? Assiya had been propelled forward by a dream based in her heart and just as she gathered the courage to pursue it someone had stolen

114

it from her chest. The unfairness of it was what compelled Farook, the need to uncover the bureaucracy of injustice, to pull it apart and expose it for what it truly was.

'Whether Assiya is alive or dead, she is dead to me,' the father said, interrupting Farook's thoughts. 'Death is better for her. Whatever her sins she can answer to Allah, but she would not be able to return to this house and live a normal life. No one will marry her and I would not be able to look at her after what she has done to us. We will most likely leave Marrakesh, I do not know to where.'

'What if I promise to do all I can to restore both your honour and hers? Perhaps then you will not have to leave the city and the dignity you once knew will be restored. All I ask is that you allow me to continue investigating her disappearance.'

The father sat silently for a moment pondering Farook's promise. Eventually, he retrieved a parcel from beneath the divan and handed it to Farook.

'There can be no return. The only path is forward,' he said. 'My wife is a clever woman. Assiya visited the hammam every Monday afternoon. One afternoon she returned with her hair dry. It was enough for my wife to realize she had gone somewhere else. Not wanting to worry me she waited until the following Monday and followed her to a garden. When the girl returned home my wife confronted her. We confined her to the house, not that we had to. She did not get out of bed for days. My wife may be clever, but she is also weak. She suggested we locate the man and marry Assiya to him. It would protect us from any shame. Perhaps that would have been the best solution in the end.'

'Why did you not do that?'

'Because she disappeared. She woke one morning and convinced her mother to let her visit the hammam after having not washed for a week. My wife, in her naïvety, agreed. I was not at home and we never saw her again. We found the letters that evening, hidden amongst her bedding. There was no way of knowing who the man was or who

115

might have assisted Assiya in writing to him. I made some enquiries, but I was afraid of drawing to much attention.'

Farook tucked the parcel of letters under his arm.

'You made a promise, Si Farook,' warned the father. 'A promise I will compel you to keep. Perhaps our honour can never be restored, but maybe answers will ease my wife's guilt.'

* * *

Yusuf left the Qadi's house and walked towards home. The conversation had been difficult. The judge tested Yusuf with enigmatic questions: creating ditches for him to clamber out of and fields of silence to cross. Yusuf stuck to his story and did not change his version, despite the sweat building on his neck. In the end, the decision was made and the directive given. It was not like the judge was unfamiliar with giving such a directive, it was a daily occurrence and announced for less worthy infractions. Qadi Abdullah always ate a hearty lunch and slept through the night.

Yusuf had already chosen his men, filling his mind with the logistics of what lay ahead. He was a good organizer. It was one of his talents. Once the decision had been made there was little value in the person ordered to execute it debating its validity. The Sharifian dynasty came from the bloodline of the Prophet, and the Sultan was a direct descendant, after all. What was done by empire and in its name was the will of God, divine in its purpose and mysterious in its action. Rebellion to God's authority on earth was rebellion to God Himself.

Yusuf's other talent was following orders.

PART TWO

23

Bastinado

He heard the slap before he felt it. The whistle echoed off the stone walls so that it continued to ring in his ears long after the sting had faded from his cheek. He tasted blood in his mouth. He could feel the men around him waiting, waiting for him to gather himself so they could slap him once more. He counted the days by the frequency of his beatings. One always came before breakfast and the next soon after the mid-afternoon prayer, which was just audible in his cell. And then the long night, the sunset and evening prayers would come and go and any minute the doors could be flung open and he would be surrounded by nothing but shadows. He slept a shallow sleep, his eyes occasionally snapping open in the blindfold.

His last image was of being dragged through the street, and seeing faces that he knew well gasping as he passed. It kept appearing to him from the darkness as though he was there in his body and yet not – a moment of clarity, a reason to go on.

He was no longer sure of time; his confinement could have been three days or three weeks. He only became aware of it when the long periods of darkness were shattered by the bright light of pain. His arms had been tied behind his back and the stiffness had set in so thoroughly he could no longer feel them. His feet were bound, the only thing keeping him upright being the wooden post behind him.

'Again,' came a voice from near the door.

He shook his head in order to clear his blood-filled ears. The voice was familiar, maybe he had heard it so many times now it had become a part of his memory or maybe it came from another place.

Another slap disrupted his concentration, the sound whizzing through the air. His body lurched sideways, his left shoulder and head slamming into the floor. He stayed in the foetal position; it offered him an absurd moment of serenity in which he wept like a child yearning for his mother's breast. Strong arms lifted him up and placed him against the post.

Would this end?

At first he was confused and asked the men repeatedly why he was there. Their silence lingered as his question fell on deaf ears. They continued to stand over him, their menace needing no words. And then he fell silent, saving his energy for what was to come. They hadn't really asked him anything; they just beat him relentlessly. But mostly they slapped him. He wanted to know why. If he knew the reason, he could tolerate the pain.

He slumped down. Pink spittle escaped from his mouth and fell on his soiled clothes.

'I swear to you on the head of our Prophet I have done nothing wrong,' he whimpered. He sucked in his breath, as though hoping to suck back the words.

'Stop!', instructed the same voice. 'Give him water.'

A clay jug was brought to his mouth and he gulped at it desperately. The liquid coursed through his body like a flash of light.

He didn't want to die, not here. He began to sob. One of the men sneered. He didn't care anymore. The opinion of others lost all of its

120

importance when facing death. Whatever he had done, he did not deserve this.

The man near the door stepped forward and crouched in front of him so that they were eye-to-eye. He gathered his remaining sobs and looked at him through his blindfold.

'Where is she? What did you do to her?'

The prisoner frowned trying to link the questions to a specific person. If they told him who she was maybe he could at least try to answer the question.

His shop flashed in front of him. The voice had come from his shop. Was it a customer?

'You are dextrous with the meat cleaver. Did she refuse your advances, your proposal for marriage? Is that why you killed her? What did you do with the body?'

And then it all made sense.

They killed murderers. They tortured and crucified them in the square. He felt his trousers wet as he lost control of his bladder and he began to cry once more. A pool of urine formed beneath him and it ran towards the man.

Yusuf stood up and moved away from the butcher, just beyond the line of urine. He nodded to one of the prison guards and he stepped forward to deliver a punch to the butcher's gut which relieved his victim's bowels. Yusuf stepped further back, holding his nose.

The butcher fell silent, and his head hung loosely in front of him. They waited for a while to see if he would regain consciousness on his own. He didn't. One of the guards emptied a bucket of dirty water over his head. He awoke slowly, looking around as though hoping he was already in his grave.

'Bastinado!' called Yusuf to a guard standing by the door.

Anything but the bastinado.

They said after the bastinado a man would confess to anything and never walk the same way again. You could tell those who had undergone the torture by the way they stumbled along the street, with their feet shattered and spirit broken.

The butcher raised himself to his knees and begged, he begged for his life, searching out Yusuf's sandals to kiss.

'Please, please, Si Yusuf. I have done nothing wrong.'

'Did you write love letters to Assiya? Sign them with your initial K?'

The butcher shook his head furiously, confused by the new name. He could just about keep account of sales, let alone write a letter.

'I admit that sometimes Souad would come into my shop and sit and talk with me. I would give her extra meat on those occasions. I admit I touched her once, but just her hand. I stroked her hand once and that was it. I regretted my mistake straight away. May your children prosper, Si Yusuf, may a mosque be built in your name …'

Yusuf looked at the man shaking and sobbing. It always happened this way; they always resisted at first, took the pain and then gave something up. It was a negotiation of sorts. Now, theoretically he should let the man rest. He had after all just confessed an immorality. But there was more. If he stopped now perhaps the butcher would clam up and it would take longer to get the full confession. They always gave their full confession.

'I said bastinado,' Yusuf shouted as he left the dungeon.

24

The salt

'Si Farook, a message just arrived for you.'

Farook held his hand over his face to protect himself from the light. The proprietor stepped into the room and closed the door. He continued in a hushed voice, 'The Pasha, Si Farook, the Pasha of Marrakesh has requested your company at his residence in an hour. A young boy just arrived with the message.'

What could the Governor of Marrakesh want with him at this time of the morning? The proprietor waited for a response.

'I will bring you some hot water for your ablutions,' he said, before leaving for the kitchen. Farook closed the door behind him. He stood in the middle of the room, observing the stillness.

The Pasha of Marrakesh, Hajj Abdeslam al-Wazy, had a reputation for his strict personal adherence to religion. Within the confines of his home he observed all the religious rites and in the public sphere he was considered a formidable authority. Within the makhzan gossip mill he was known to have his tentacles in every trade, including, some said, the production of counterfeit coins through his

brother-in-law. It was also said his spies operated in every neighbourhood of the city, the Pasha knew what had happened in a
particular district before the residents. No doubt, through his spy
network he had followed Farook's presence in the city.

Something had happened, and it was something related to his case.
The fact that he was being called to the Pasha told him he was the
last to know. He suspected it had something to do with Yusuf. The
man had disappeared since their last meeting. Local makhzan machinations must have kicked into overdrive. But what had instigated it?
How had it travelled all the way up to the Pasha?

He dressed quickly and while waiting for the proprietor to return
he went over to his desk and took out the bundle of Assiya's letters to
her lover, which, for some reason he would likely never learn, she had
written but never given to the man she loved. He had compared them
to the scribes and even to those written by her lover. They were in a
different hand. Someone in the city had written them for her. It was
very possible someone knew what happened to Assiya in her last days
before her disappearance.

The proprietor stepped back into the room. He poured warm water
into a basin and Farook rinsed his mouth and washed his face. He
helped Farook into his selham and brushed it down. He went over to
the corner of the room and picked up Farook's shoes.

'I have slippers that will fit you, Si Farook.'

Farook shook his head. The proprietor reluctantly placed the shoes
in front of him. He hesitated a moment while he bent down.

'Please speak,' said Farook encouragingly.

The proprietor stood up right. 'I ... was ... I was at the Street of
Scribes the day before yesterday on some personal business. They are
all talking about the women you are searching for. The rumour is girls
of marriageable age are being molested and killed in their beds while
their families sleep. They are saying there is a monster on the loose
in the city or perhaps even a gang of men taking advantage of young
women. Some of them are claiming the makhzan is fully aware of the

situation, but refusing to do anything about it because the perpetuator is from an influential family.'

So, Yusuf had opened his mouth to the scribes. Craftsmen and their guilds were a threat to order in the country's cities. Stories of the tribulations they caused reached even the palace and in some cases the Sultan himself had to intervene. Riots, revolts, strikes, petitions, intrigue and fear mongering; they were willing to resort to almost anything to achieve any economic concession from the makhzan. At least now Farook understood why Yusuf was avoiding him.

'Thank you for telling me. Is there anything else?'

The proprietor shook his head reluctantly. 'Just that the city is awash with rumour. I heard on the other side of the city that they have already caught the man and he has confessed all. Apparently they are holding him in the prison.'

'Who is he?' Farook rushed to put on his shoes.

"I … I do not know. They say his screams can be heard beyond the prison walls. They used the bastinado and the salt on him,' he continued.

'The salt?' Farook straightened up and looked at the proprietor.

'Yes, first they beat the soles of his feet until it was almost impossible to walk, and then the salt … They cut open the palm of the hands and then fill the wounds with salt. They then bury the fingers into the wound and bound the hand with wet sheepskin. When it all dries the hands are useless stumps.' The man stopped talking. The description alone was enough to make him feel faint.

'And these are rumours you say or do you have confirmation of them?'

'I heard it from a reliable source, but I have not had it verified,' replied the proprietor. He shook his head in disbelief. He had lived in the city his entire life, spent his childhood playing in its warren of alleyways. It was changing so fast and the future seemed more uncertain than it had ever seemed before. He lowered his head, and melancholy replaced his usual upbeat mood.

'What is to become of us, Si Farook? There was a time when people feared the Sultan, who in turn feared God on their behalf and this kept each of our excesses in check. Nov   is we have all been overcome with an unhealthy lust for life   ruption, forgetting that one day we will all become dust.'

Farook patted the proprietor gently on h   'We are indeed in the midst of difficult times and all each of u   is keep our own morality. We only answer for ourselves in the

The proprietor nodded. Farook's words   l only a mild comfort.

'Thank you for telling me,' Farook said as he   or the door.

The proprietor looked into his face. His eyes   e those of a child fearing the dark night and spirits that lurk in   'Anything, Si Farook. I am at your service. I took an oath   d look after you.'

25

Ten days

Taking long strides, Farook marched through the alleyways and exited at Jemaa el-Fnaa, heading south. The Pasha lived near Bab Agnaou within the confines of the Kasbah walls, as did most makhzan officials of high standing. As he walked through the near-empty square a flash of blue in a sea of red caught his eye. A group of men were sitting in a circle on the floor. In the middle of the circle a wood fire burned, upon which sat a steaming battered kettle. They all wore the same electric blue thobe and head wrapping. Farook looked at their dark faces washed with indigo. The Blue Men of the Sahara. They were a nomadic tribe roaming freely across the Sahara who disregarded the lines men drew in sand. One of the men raised his glass to Farook in offering. Farook politely declined.

What was the Saharan tribe doing in the city? They would not enter the gates unless invited to do so by the Sultan, which could only mean he had some use for them. Whatever was bubbling in the city seemed beyond Farook's authority to know. In many respects he preferred it that way and wished the lines between his work and the political intrigues of court were kept by all, but they rarely were. If only he were left alone to undertake his investigations without being subject to political instability he was sure it would not be long before he developed a procedure to be proud of. Instead, he was forced to push back against the ambitions of others, as he was, without doubt, going to have to do with the Pasha. Worse still, it seemed it was because of those instabilities that he was called upon at all.

At the doors of the Kasbah he presented himself and was escorted to the Pasha's palace. The palace was as grand as the Sultan's holiday homes dotted across the country. Farook was in no mood to take note of the details.

He entered the cavernous reception room to find the Pasha waiting for his arrival. He was tall with a speed in his movements that told of a man who always got what he wanted. He turned to Farook as the other men in the room quietly left and they both bent forward. They lightly kissed each other's shoulders and shook hands in greeting. As Farook took his seat opposite the Pasha on a low divan, he noticed Yusuf loitering in the corner.

'Sit down, Si Yusuf,' invited the Pasha.

Farook waited, trying to refrain from judgment and conclusions. The situation would reveal itself.

The Pasha opened the conversation. 'It is with great honour we receive you in our city, Si Farook. I was made aware of your presence and your reputation reached our walls before you. I am so glad, with the help of your colleague here,' indicating Yusuf, 'you have not disappointed us.'

A servant entered the room. He was a grown man wearing a red jabador outfit. The harem trousers hung loosely between his strong thighs and the matching red shirt fell just over the waist line. He served mint tea in delicate glasses with sweet pastries. Farook accepted the tea and a small pastry. As was custom, the Pasha waited for Farook to take a sip. Instead, Farook bit into the pastry. Frowning, the Pasha took a sip from his glass.

'The honour is mine, Hajj al-Warzy,' replied Farook. 'I must admit I was surprised by your invitation this morning. I have been in the city for over a month and had humbly hoped to meet you sooner.'

'I thought it best to allow you time to settle, Si Farook, and it appears you did more than that. You have successfully captured the culprit in no time at all.'

Farook looked over at Yusuf. So, the second rumour was true. Whatever Yusuf had been up to since their last meeting, and for whatever reasons, the man had at best used his own naïve initiative and at worst sabotaged the case. Farook had underestimated what he was capable of and more than anything his stupidity.

'And who is he? The culprit I mean,' asked Farook, turning back to the Pasha.

'His name is Khalid al-Gazzar,' replied Yusuf. 'He is a butcher from the Riad Zitoun el-Kheddim neighborhood.'

So, he had gone after the butcher. It was not surprising; he was the easiest target after all.

'The man is innocent,' Farook said, speaking to the Pasha and ignoring Yusuf entirely.

The Pasha looked at Farook anew. His reputation did indeed precede him, defying orders, ignoring hierarchy, overconfident and generally thinking himself indestructible because his was in favour. The Pasha smirked.

'But, Si Farook, he has admitted to the crime and signed a written confession.'

Farook did not fancy explaining the unreliability of confessions extracted through torture to the Pasha or Yusuf. The entire justice system would collapse if it were not for torture and to challenge a confession was to challenge the system.

'The case is closed, Si Farook. We must move on. As you know the country is battling many enemies both external and internal. Even Mother Nature seems to have turned against us. I am grateful to you both for resolving this situation before it had to be reported to the

Sultan's brother, Moulay Hafid. The Caliph of Marrakesh has many pressing issues as the Sultan's representative in the city and it would be irresponsible to trouble him with a small case of some missing women. I will of course be reporting your fine work to the highest authorities.'

'And the bodies?'

A flash of irritation crossed the Pasha's otherwise serene face. 'You mean the bodies of the missing women I suppose.' He flicked his hand towards Yusuf. 'Give him a few more days,' he said, 'and I am sure the butcher will explain what he did with them.'

'Without the bodies we have no proof. The man is innocent,' Farook persisted.

The Pasha smiled.

'Perhaps he chopped them up and sold them to the city during these times of great hunger.' He looked over at Yusuf. 'And then there would be no bodies or need for evidence.' He turned back to Farook. 'Do you have an alternative theory?'

Farook paused for a moment. The Marrakesh authorities were plotting. They were up to something. Was there something about these women they wanted to conceal? Could someone have wanted them dead? Or did this have nothing to do with the women? Was their disappearance nothing more than an opportunity to execute an ambition a while in the making?

The Pasha waited for Farook.

'I have made a recent breakthrough in the case,' Farook said, ending the silence. 'It would be an outrage if proven, with evidence, that we have the wrong man.'

The Pasha adjusted in his seat. 'What breakthrough?'

'Some letters.'

The Pasha leaned back into his cushion. 'Ah, the letters. Yes, I have heard all about them. You mean the letters from Assiya's lover of course. I suspect you would need another six months to get to the bottom of them and I doubt you have six months. A new season will be coming and the Sultan will be calling his advisors to Fez.' He laughed.

'I would say ten days,' retorted Farook.

The Pasha rested his arm on his raised knee. He gazed at Farook with a paternal smile.

'So be it,' he snapped, clapping his hands together. Yusuf jumped in his seat. 'In ten days you will report back to me'

'And the butcher?'

'We have a man in custody who has confessed to the crimes. He will stay in our custody until you report to me. Don't worry, Si Farook, we will take good care of him.'

Farook stood to leave.

'Si Farook,' the Pasha called him back, 'you will continue to work with Yusuf. He has much to learn from your fine work and it would be a shame for us not to benefit from your talent once you leave the city … Ten days it is.'

* * *

left the Pasha's house and walked towards Bab al-Rubb. He xpanse in front of him. could see farmers turning the dry sun-baked soil. A wide dirt track led out towards the beautiful Eureka Valley. Men on carts dragged scared donkeys, and other men on horses passed him, entering the city for perhaps their first time. Beyond the farmland the Atlas Mountains rose, its peaks coated in snow. They were so formidable, unbreakable. They were the only constant in this country of shape-shifters, uncompromising and eternal in their testimony. There was no way over or around them, only through. The mountain chose your path, not you. Farook stared down the dirt track. Every road led to the unknown, every journey to a new realization. Some men were crippled by fear, seeking shelter in predictability; others counted each step as a lesson.

He turned to return to his funduq and found Yusuf standing behind him.

'I did only as I was instructed,' Yusuf said in defence of an accusation not yet levied.

Farook resisted the urge to grab him, to shout into his face how disappointing he was. 'You are nothing but a pawn,' he replied in as calm a voice as he could muster. 'And so is that butcher. The distance between you and him is not that great, but the difference is you have blood on your hands and he does not.'

'If I have blood on my hands than so does the Sultan,' Yusuf flared.

'Then God damn us all,' replied Farook as he walked away.

26

A white flag of surrender

The headache was one of the worst Farook had ever experienced. He had returned from the Pasha's house and lay on his bed massaging his temples to release the pressure. He was in an awful predicament. He needed intelligence. The hardest part of being a foreigner in Marrakesh was that he was not tapped into an information source. No one whispered in his ear. He had thought Yusuf would be a good source of intelligence, but the man did not have the stomach for it. Try as he might, Yusuf was not built to withstand the conspiracies of court and government. The passion to fight it did not appeal to him in the way it appealed to Farook and the desire to benefit from it was not matched by the needed quickness of mind. He could not be trusted again. His only source of information was the funduq proprietor. He doubted the man had the connections to reveal what the Marrakesh authorities were up to.

The answer lay in the case, not government theatre. A man could get lost in the maze of makhzan machinations in search of a single clue. But the letters offered something solid. And he was ahead of the

Pasha and his associates; they did not know he had the letters Assiya wrote to her lover.

He had ten days.

He decided to visit the hammam, perhaps the hot steam would clear his head. Besides, if you wanted to know the mood of a city there were certain places you went to: the mosque; the water fountains; the public bakeries and of course the public baths.

He made his way to the hammam. A white rag flapped at the door as though the building and its occupants were in surrender. Seeing it, he stepped inside, glad his impulsive decision had coincided with male timings for the public bath. If it were women's hour, the flag would be flapping red in a fierce statement of defiance.

Once inside he undressed, wrapping a thin linen cloth around his waist. He handed his clothes to the hammam supervisor.

'Would you like a scrub?' the supervisor asked.

Farook nodded.

He entered the first steam room, a long rectangular hall with domes in the ceiling letting in hexagons of light. He walked to the end and through a door into another identical room. The temperature rose considerably and he loitered to give his body time to adjust. He moved to the third room, the steam hitting his skin, the ceiling dripping with condensation. The room fell silent for a moment. He found an empty wall and sat down. Through the mist, men sat gathered in twos and threes, some on their own. Their conversations picked up volume once more as they continued to scrub their bodies down to the very bone. Farook listened leaning his head against the way and closing his eyes. They were mostly complaining about their wives, their crops or bad trade. Within the grumblings he heard the palace mentioned in whispers, references made to the Sultan's extravagance and the outlandish demands of his harem.

As his body began to perspire, a thin layer of sweat and steam resting on his skin, he tried to block out the chatter. He thought of Tangier. A crisp air would be blowing in from the Mediterranean and the sea would be rough at this time of year. Clouds would gather over the city and burst with sustenance and then the sun would fight through and smile down on its subjects. The foreign legions would be filled with talk of the coming spring, camping and hunting trips to organise, picnics on the slopes of the surrounding mountains and new arrivals from Europe.

As he recalled the long evenings spent in conversation with foreign diplomats and merchants and mornings spent in writing, the sound of broken Arabic ruptured his memories. Nothing more than a murmur at first, but the sound of Arabic spoken through a foreign throat travelled through the steam trapped in the room. He had been followed and the culprit was easy enough to determine. He knew the man would not be able to resist the temptation to seek him out and so he waited with eyes closed.

When he opened them, a silence had descended and he saw that most of the other men in the room had left, except for a young boy sitting in a far corner scrubbing at his feet and the doctor standing over him.

'Monsieur al-Alami, what a pleasure to see you again.'

The doctor adjusted his loincloth and sat down next to Farook.

'I am not one for public baths,' the doctor continued. 'The steam is of course a great cleanser and I come only for that, but they leave much to be desired by way of hygiene. My house boy insisted this is the best one in the city for cleanliness and I must say he is right.'

'You made the right choice, Dr Delacroix.'

The doctor was one of those men who liked the sound of his own voice and stopped listening the moment he stopped hearing it. It was best to let him speak. Farook listened to his request for assistance on securing city authority approval for his clinic again. If only he knew how impossible that would be. Despite the doctor's opinion of himself and Farook, neither had the leverage to influence city officials on anything.

'The Blue Men, Mr Farook. They are roaming this city posing a great risk to foreign residents. Why, just last night I had to draw my pistol on a group of them as I rode past. I have tried repeatedly to meet with the Pasha to explain my fears. I must say it is most fortunate that I meet you here today. I represent the concerns of the twenty European residents of Marrakesh. Our safety in these troubling times is of upmost importance. We make great sacrifices to be here and work for the betterment of the country, yet live in constant fear we may be lynched on the streets.'

What would become of Morocco? Would she muster her meagre resources and navigate herself towards a self-determined future or would she sit on the dinner table like a stuffed goat, waiting to be carved by a dozen sharpened knives? Whatever was brewing within the city walls it was unlikely to have anything to do with the girls. But, the girls were being used to incite fear and he had to stop that. If he closed the investigation he would eliminate the patsy. More than that, he had taken an oath. He had promised to restore Assiya's honour.

Between the European residents and their sense of entitlement and the Moroccan lust for power and wealth, the country would be deprived of all its blessings. Its own bounty would be distributed and squirreled away in foreign banks or private treasuries hidden in the Kasbahs dotting the countryside, while the population fought for the last sacks of wheat.

While under the constant scrutiny of a pack of hyenas nobody in Morocco seemed to fully grasp the gravity of the situation, too absorbed in the hunt. They were willing to risk sovereignty and exploit the country's weakest, most vulnerable inhabitants, as they clambered for political gain. Farook was not interested in fighting for a piece of the çarcass, only in who held the death weapon and how to muscle it from their hands.

'The Tuareg are guests of the Sultan, Dr Delacroix, as are you,' Farook stated.

'Mr Farook, I took you for a modern man, one who understands the value of good relations with Europe and justice. This afternoon I was writing a letter to a French newspaper to describe the condition of European residents in Marrakesh and seeing you here, I thought perhaps divine intervention had provided me with a more diplomatic solution. It seems I was wrong.'

'You see me well, Dr Delacroix. I *am* a man who understands the value of justice, but justice belongs to no one.'

Arabs were all the same, they knew only violence, thought Dr Delacroix. His short time in Jerusalem and now Marrakesh had taught him that. Even when you gave them a more peaceful path, medical clinics, schools, roads, they still chose to fight. The civilized world had no choice but to resort to using the same language, the same methods again and again until the blasted race accepted the inevitability of progress.

Farook watched the doctor leave.

Seeing the hammam assistant enter the room, he called him over. The man sat behind Farook and began scrubbing with a hemp glove.

Farook lent forward and closed his eyes again. He picked up his last thought on the case.

Assiya.

He would not allow them to sidetrack his work again.

He would follow the evidence.

He would locate her lover and the person who wrote her letters.

27

An heir

The Pasha of Marrakesh lay on his divan in his family room, leaning on his right elbow. His legs were stretched out across the length of the mattress. His large calloused feet poked out from his white house trousers. He rubbed them together absentmindedly. Flecks of dead skin fell onto the luxurious hand-woven carpet gifted to him by an Eastern merchant many years ago. In front of him sat a bowl of fruit on a silver tray from which he occasionally plucked a tart strawberry which he popped into his mouth. He grimaced at each bite, as the sourness hit his tongue. The drought had even interrupted his love of eating from his garden.

His head was bare, exposing a sprawling bald patch with a few stray hairs standing to attention. They had somehow survived the onslaught of old age and responsibility and he held a secret affection for them and their will to go on. They were like the last soldiers of an army refusing to retreat. He rubbed his hand across his bald patch, recalling younger days when his thick dark curls would excite his wife so that she would grab a fistful and pull his face towards hers.

Now, she barely looked at him or he at her. The sight was too startling for both of them. Life was cruel to the body. It led you to believe all was well until suddenly one day you woke up and found the raising of five children displayed in rolls of fat and loose skin; the building of a family legacy etched across your forehead; and the management of a city in the stoop of your shoulders. And just when you think your job is done, you must create an heir.

He was not complaining. God forbid.

Old age had many blessings, and he knew them all, but its one failing was a fear of death.

The world had changed. What it meant to be young had changed, bringing in an era marked by confusion and rebellion. There was a time when a man would observe what God had given him and raise his cupped hands to the sky in gratitude. Now, men raised begging bowls, never satisfied and always wanting more. At least that was the case with his oldest son. They had spoiled him. That was their mistake.

If the Pasha didn't act soon his son would find himself working under the authority of imbeciles like Yusuf al-Mahdi. Because of that fool the Pasha had lost face. It was only because of Yusuf's long-standing relationship with the Qadi that he had been given an audience. If the Pasha had known he was a complete moron, he would have verified his version of events.

If he continued to keep the butcher prisoner, thus perpetuating the now undeniable lie that it was he who was responsible for the missing women, he would lose more face. If he revealed the new information he had just received, Farook al-Alami would walk about this city like he owned it.

That man from Tangier was nothing but a traitor. He represented Europe creeping into Moroccan affairs, sly with a native face but disloyal heart. He thought he could change Morocco with modernity and he wore that opinion with pride, confident in those shoes. He was an insult to the traditions of this land and its religion.

Someone should explain history to the man. It was the Moors who took those very ideas to Europe through Andalusia, civilizing the Christian land and bringing them enlightenment, while they pleasured their sisters and farm animals. Yet this Farook seemed to ignore all that, under some delusion that morphing into a European would somehow make him more of a man. The Pasha understood why Farook al-Alami was close to the Sultan. They were cut from the same cloth, and it was imported.

The Pasha was an interior man. He was not made from water but rock. His horizons were marked by mountains to overcome and shifting sand dunes to traverse, not flat oceans as far as the eye can see.

One of old age's blessings was hope. He hoped he would go quietly in his sleep, watched over by his wife and son. He had fought all his life. He was tired, but he would take up his sword again to halt the sacrilege of his city one more time, a city once filled with the sound of God's ninety-nine names being chanted from every mosque and madrasa.

But all that was to come. The immediate problem was more pressing. Somehow, he had found himself wedged between a fool and an upstart. The Qadi and his hunting dog were wrong after all, which meant Farook al-Alami was right, and the Pasha did not want him, of all people, to be right. Reports from the prison indicated the butcher was not in a good way. A fever had taken him, leaving him shivering in a pool of sweat in his dark cell. If he died it would only make things worse.

Perhaps his mind was beginning to fail him after all. It was one thing to forget where he had placed his house slippers, but quite another to be fooled into treachery. He counted the slow decay of the mind as another curse of old age.

'*La hawa wa la quwwata illa bi Allah*,' he muttered to himself under his breath. Truly, there is no power or strength except through God. He only hoped God would discharge his power through him so he could undo this riddle he found himself tangled in untouched by the vulgarity of conspiracy, for the sake of his son.

28

The assembly of the dead

The door was bolted. A rotting plank of wood ran across the middle of it. He could hear her shuffling around in the room, her small feet dragging across the earthen floor, tracking from one end of the room to another with no particular purpose. The sound of her defiance infuriated him. He wanted to charge into the room and shout into her face to sit still. He wanted to intimidate her into silence. But he knew it would be pointless.

She had known him so long that she knew what he was capable of. She could predict his moods. She would look at him with those empty eyes, as though she was completely oblivious to what was going on.

He had saved her, pulled her out of the gutter with his own hands and still she was ungrateful, unloving. She would be the last to join his assembly.

Yet, there were moments when he could tell she enjoyed it too. She liked the risk: relishing in the excitement of danger, holding her breath in anticipation of where it might end.

He reached into a large chest in front of him and removed a necklace. Placing it to his nose and inhaling deeply, he recalled its owner. He repeated the action over and over with each item he pulled from the chest, inhaling and placing it around him in a circle. It was as though they were there in spirit battling for his attention. He quieted each of them, telling them to wait their turn — they too would speak.

He looked at each item — a trinket, piece of clothing, a lock of hair — and recalled each girl in chronological order. He retold their final moments as though he were an imam reciting a Qu'ranic story to a congregation of children. He tried to ease their spirit when they protested, explaining they were part of a special order of women who would also be remembered in history. He had given them immortality. And if they were to ever be forgotten, one day someone somewhere would uncover their lives to speak of their strength and purpose.

But they were refusing to listen. Their chattering crowded his ears. 'Quiet!' he bellowed.

He needed to think; this was not the time for words of comfort.

The makhzan had taken a sudden interest in his assembly. They were searching for ghosts and he held in his custody the traces they left upon their departure.

They were investigating his girls via two paths, the man from the north, and through the Pasha's palace. He knew which of the two he wanted to meet. The man from Tangier intrigued him. He was certain they had much in common. But not yet. He was not ready. Thankfully, he had been left in peace.

Except for the smell. The smell was becoming harder and harder to mask.

'The garden,' whispered Latifa.

He looked at her silver necklace. She had lingered behind, he knew she would do the moment he detected horror in her eyes as she took her last breath.

'You are in a better place that most, Latifa,' he explained.

She sulked for a while before persisting. Her voice was soft, locked forever in innocence. 'I am lonely.'

Perhaps she had a point. He could move some of them to the garden. The earlier ones were nothing but bones. It would free up space and he could treat the graves with lime and salt. It meant he would have to dig up the entire floor and rearrange his entire assembly. It would take him a whole night, maybe longer.

He would also have to keep her happy or she would fuss about and meekly complain about the disruption. He took a yellow kaftan from the circle and inhaled its perfume. He recalled its owner. Assiya. She enjoyed the chase more than the others. She knew she was courting danger and held no delusions, but at the last moment she forced his hand. The stupid girl really thought her life was her own.

He was angry he would have to part with the kaftan. The girl brought a negative energy to the assembly with her accusations of foul play, but that did not mean she was not welcome. Despite her complaints, she belonged in the assembly, offered comfort to the others, and knew his moods well enough to usher silence amongst when it was needed.

He folded the house dress. Perhaps a break from the group would do her good. He would get back the garment eventually and return it to its rightful place.

29

The other two

Farook sat under an olive tree in Koutoubia Public Garden reading a newspaper. The mosque's minaret rose a short distance away. Its presence was felt across the city. He sat away from the spot where Assiya's mother had seen her daughter. It seemed they had hidden their love in the open. The minaret offered a protective shade.

He knew it was a long shot, but if visiting the spot on the day and time she would meet her lover satisfied nothing but his curiosity then it would be worth it. Besides, he knew the ways of some men. They were capable of transitioning from one love to another smoothly without emotional turmoil or wallowing in the places of their previous devotion. He carried under his selham the letters. This is what detectives did was it not? They waited and observed, took in details of a scene and made sense of them and then tested the accuracy of their conclusions against reality.

The garden was almost empty: a few men leaving the mosque and heading home, after reclining in a shallow sleep in the corners of its prayer halls; a child wandering aimlessly towards the square; and birds chirping in the tree tops.

He glanced down at his paper to take in the headline. The Algeciras Conference was still making front-page news. It reported a concession here, a compromise there, until there was nothing left to bargain for, except perhaps the retention of pomp and ceremony for it's own sake. Farook hoped something of Morocco would survive the inevitable; whatever survived would be their only weapon. Whatever attempts to halt European influence had been devised too late. What was the point of attempting to save a dying companion after watching him bleed out on the ground for a whole morning? Farook didn't care ght for nothing but their apathetic. Their silence complicit in the tyranny of greed. The makhzan could collapse tomorrow and he would quietly celebrate. It was a parasitic disease which was eating the country from the inside. It was not the makhzan that would save the country. It was impossible to colonise the soul if the soul believed in something other than the body it occupied. Whatever happened to the country, the people had no choice but to reincarnate.

He looked up from the newspaper, pulled his attention away from events unfolding in the north, and watched as a young man sat under a citrus tree. He looked morose. He sat cross-legged resting his chin in his hand. He pulled at blades of grass and discarded them looking up occasionally to watch people pass. Was he waiting for someone?

Farook thought back to the description Assiya's mother had given. There seemed to be a resemblance to the young man in front of him, but there was nothing particularly unique that separated him from other men loitering aimlessly through the city. Farook continued to watch him for a while as he pulled at the blades of grass and discarded them. The melancholy surrounding the man made Farook wonder further. Could it be him? There really was only one way to find out.

Farook stood up and made his way over to the man.

He stood over him, blocking the sun and casting the man in shadow. The young man looked up at Farook in surprise.

'I would like to talk to you about Assiya,' Farook said.

The man hesitated a moment. A flash of panic crossed his delicate features. He stood up slowly and glanced at the mosque as though contemplating escaping to its prayer halls to claim sanctuary from the law.

Seeing some softness in Farook's eyes he reconsidered his first instinct to flee. 'Have you found her?'

Farook shook his head. He pulled out the letters from under his arm and handed them to him. He watched as the young man read them. The man was unable to hide his emotions.

'Are you going to arrest me?' he asked.

'No,' stated Farook. 'But you will tell me everything. Every detail, from the very beginning to the last time you saw her.'

The man bowed his head and nodded.

'I wanted to marry her,' he said, looking into Farook's eyes. 'She just disappeared one day and stopped meeting me. She told me it had to end, but gave no reason. I looked for her everywhere and if it weren't for my mother's warnings I would have visited her father. I still come here occasionally, though it brings my mother great distress. But perhaps one day she will come back. Do you think that might be possible?'

Farook looked at the young man carefully, wondering if he would ever find Assiya.

He shook his head. 'I doubt it very much.'

* * *

Yusuf felt a constriction in his chest. Perhaps his heart was packing in. He wouldn't blame it, it was already rotten. He thought of the butcher released from the city prison and returned to his wife and children. He did not feel guilt. Why should he carry the burden of guilt when he was not responsible for acts of state, even if they were executed through his hands? He did feel regret.

In all his years as a makhzan official he had never betrayed a colleague. Yet he had betrayed Farook al-Alami easily enough, the only man he worked for who took him seriously. *Whoever strays from the path of prudence will come to rest in a company of the dead,* Farook had once told him. Apparently it was a proverb from Europe. Yusuf had dismissed the meaning at the time, more interested in knowing the extent of Farook's travels in the continent. Now, it made complete sense. He was living proof of its truth. He had strayed from prudence by suspending his better judgment and common sense because of pride. And look where it had got him. He felt the only company he deserved was that of the dead. Now, he was a slave to the Pasha – there only to do his bidding – while Farook ignored him. Would this be his legacy?

Perhaps death was a welcome release from not just his humiliation, but also that of his ancestors and heirs. Whatever power his father had managed to scrape together from nothing, Yusuf had squandered in minutes. His family legacy would end abruptly with him: a low achiever. If Farook would only give him the time of day, Yusuf could explain his reasons and perhaps he would eventually work with him again. He knew it was a pointless exercise that would only end in more humiliation. What mattered to a man like Farook al-Alami was not grovelling and submission, but loyalty and honesty. Yusuf had shown he possessed neither.

Besides, the Pasha's instructions were clear. Yusuf was now to avoid Farook, despite earlier being told to work with him. Instead, he was to investigate two new reports of missing girls. He could not fathom there were now six girls missing from the city. What was he supposed to do? How could he find these two missing girls without the assistance of Farook? He was like a kitten whose eyes had been poked out and whiskers cut off by the neighbourhood children, thrown to the alleyways to survive.

The initial interviews with the families only served to prove Farook's theories right. One of the girls had even drugged her parents with a sleeping potion to escape the house, and taken her mother's worthless jewellery with her. Wherever they were going, they wanted to look their best.

Since then he had hit a dead-end. He spent the whole day brooding in his living room, dismissing his wife's attempts at conversation and snapping at his children. He wondered what Farook was doing and if he had made any headway with the love letters. Perhaps Farook already knew about the two missing girls or had the lover in his sight. Yusuf sighed. He had pitted himself against Farook unwittingly. He felt his chest contract and grabbed at his jellaba. The only way was forward, but he could not see through the fog of his own self-pity.

30

Petitions

Farook strode through the souk, his dark selham flapping behind him and his shoes making slight clicking sounds as the heel met cobbled streets. It was late morning, the market in full swing before lunch. The sky was overcast, a light grey just visible beyond the palm leaf coverings. The promise of rain seemed to have filled the city with renewed spirit, a burst of hope breaking through the prism of resigned hunger. Just an hour of rain could save the harvest, could deliver the city from the edge of starvation.

From further in the market, a blind man approached Farook. His back was stooped and his clothes nothing but rags. To add to his misery, his feet were twisted in reverse so that he walked on the front of his ankles. Farook had seen the deformity before. It was one from which people could at least make a pitiful living. As the man passed, shuffling awkwardly with no sight to guide his way, and no firm footing to keep him on it, Farook pressed a coin into his palm.

'God will make your path easy, remove your obstacles in the form of friend and foe, and bring you to triumph in this life and the next,' the blind man called to his faceless benefactor. Farook turned back to look at him. If only all it took was a battered coin.

He continued through the souk, aware that the tanneries were somewhere to his left. The smell travelled along the walls of the narrow alleyways and lacerated his nostrils. He walked further along and turned right finding himself in the blacksmithing section. The craftsmen were hard at work with beardless apprentices with the hands of old men, assisting the bending of metal. The sound of grunts and iron hammered into shapes reverberated in his ears. He picked up his pace so as to escape as quickly as possible. The lover had told him all he knew, like a sinner desperate for absolution. It was a craftsman who helped Assiya, someone she knew and trusted. She kept the identity from her lover, using it to tease him and provoke jealousy.

Farook now had to retrace Yusuf's steps, and to speak to the people he had spoken to at the beginning. He could not trust what the man had told him. There was little point in trying to speak to the butcher. Even if he were granted access, anything the man said after the trauma of his confinement would be of little value. He would probably invent crimes to confess to if there was a chance his hands and mind could be restored.

The lover was innocent, trapped by a hopeless infatuation. He had loved Assiya and still did. Perhaps one day he would recover from her disappearance, but until then he would sit under the citrus tree in wait for her. The punishment for his crime of loving a woman forbidden to him seemed unnecessarily harsh and one he might never stop suffering.

There was one other man he needed to speak to and hoped he would be at his shop. Farook turned a corner and walked into a narrow street. He had not been there before, the silence of the city a new sound to adjust to. As he passed he heard the traders whisper to each other, a barely audible narrative following him along his journey. It felt like a single pair of eyes was watching him.

'Si Farook,' he heard a man call.

Searching for the voice he recognized no one from the row of blank faces. A man cleared his throat from his right. Farook turned to look at him. The man slapped Farook on the shoulder.

Astounded by the imposition, Farook stepped back and waited for him to dare to speak.

'Ibrahim,' he stated.

Seeing no recognition in Farook's eyes, he stumbled on.

'It is very worrying news, Si Farook, very worrying times. Six girls. Two reported in the last few days. It is terrible, terrible ...' Ibrahim trailed off.

Farook remained silent, processing the new information.

'Si Yusuf informed me, you see. I assisted him in the early days of your investigation. He spoke very highly of you.'

Farook raised an eyebrow.

Ibrahim began to wish he had never approached Farook. He willed himself to stop talking. But he had to say more in order to extract himself from the conversation, a one-way conversation as it turned out, that he should have never started.

'Twelve years old, the latest one. Only twelve years old. It is just a terrible situation.'

'What were the circumstances around their disappearance?'

Relieved to have gotten a response, Ibrahim rushed on.

'Yusuf and I are old friends, old ... old ... friends. He trusts me with his life, why even his children's lives. We met for breakfast only a few days ago. He told me every ...'

Farook waited patiently for the details, but Ibrahim stopped mid-sentence. Farook felt someone tugging at his selham. Looking down he saw Mohammed, the kitchen boy pulling at his clothes.

'The proprietor told me to find you,' he said breathlessly. 'There is an emergency. You must come straight away.'

They reached the alleyway of his funduq. Mohammed ran in front of him the whole time. A commotion ahead drew his attention and outside his funduq he saw a crowd gathered. They nudged at each other. Some of the men pushed the women to the back as they shouldered their way to be as close to the funduq door as possible. He approached the crowd. The young boy squeezed between the many legs to get to the door. The group silenced their curses and parted for his passage. They were a mix of people, some in rags, others with tailored jellabas and clean turbans. They stood behind him, collectively holding their breath. He could feel their eyes boring into the back of his head, expectation silencing them.

'Who is there? Go away or I will call the … the …' came the voice of the proprietor from the other side, the panic put a pitch in his voice that would pull every stray animal in the city to his door.

'Farook al-Alami,' he said.

The group erupted into pandemonium. He turned to find them reaching for him. Some grabbed his selham, others grabbed his hand to kiss it, and the women in the back smacked their faces and cried out in ululations of public grief, calling his name. 'Si Farook, Si Farook, help us please. May God protect you and extend your life,' they called.

The door opened and he felt a whoosh as he was pulled inside. The proprietor quickly bolted the door, checking it twice just in case. He stood between Farook and the door, baring his teeth like a guard dog ready to die for his owner.

'What is the meaning of this?' asked Farook, pointing to the door.

'Petitions, Si Farook,' the proprietor stated, taking Farook by the elbow and leading him to the internal courtyard. Mohammed stood in the corner, biting his nails.

'Don't just stand there boy. Bring the man some coffee,' the proprietor yelled at him. The boy scurried to the kitchen, disappearing into the darkness.

'Petitions for what?'

'Si Farook, the city is in chaos. It is all anyone is speaking of and your name is being mentioned every time the rumour is circu-

152

lated. It is no longer safe for you in Marrakesh. They could have ripped you from limb to limb out there. Have you ever seen a mob in action?'

'They didn't want to kill me. They wanted my help,' Farook explained.

'And have you never heard of mobs ripping off the hand giving them bread? When the fever catches, they themselves forget the reasons.'

'What are they petitioning for?' he asked again. A huge bang on the door made the proprietor jump out of his jellaba.

'Missing women. They are all claiming women are missing from their family. They want your help,' explained the proprietor.

'How many are out there?'

'I cannot be sure. Perhaps fifteen, perhaps twenty. It started after you left. First one person, then another and then they began to gather.'

'Are they genuine?'

'I do not know … No … I do not think so. Not all of them anyway. One man claims he awoke this morning to find his mother missing. I asked how old she was and he said perhaps seventy. I asked when the last time she left the house alone was. He said three years ago and yet this morning he woke and she was not in her bed. I suspect many of them think they can extract blood money from the makhzan. Who is to know if the women they claim are missing even exist, but they think the makhzan will pay some sort of compensation. I don't know Si Farook, I just don't know. My door, Si Farook, and heart, I don't know if they can take the banging.'

The proprietor was clearly experiencing either some kind of shock or delight. He could not quite decide which it was. Either way, he turned out to be useful just by the fact that he willing answered all of Farook's questions.

Patting him on the shoulder, Farook smiled.

'Do not worry. We will remove them and all will return to normal.'

'But how, Si Farook? Now you are trapped in here they will camp out there till you reappear. I have a business to run and I cannot let you leave. I am sworn to protect you, but my heart …'

'You must go out to them,' instructed Farook.

The proprietor looked up at him in panic.

'I … I … I cannot. They might rip me apart.'

'Of course you can. I have much work to do and must continue with the investigation. I am running out of time. Go out to them and speak to them with kindness. Listen to their pleas; gather their complaints. Then tell them Farook al-Alami hears their petitions but before he can listen to them individually they must be lodged officially with the makhzan. Tell them the man to lodge them with is Yusuf al-Mahdi and inform them of his address. Explain to them he has been informed and is ready to record all their complaints.'

The proprietor gave a meek smile; failing to appreciate the twist of cunning Farook had just delivered.

'But is he aware …' the proprietor trailed off. Realizing Farook's plan, he lifted his shoulders high as though delivering a message from the Sultan himself and headed towards the door.

31

The promise of absolution

The clouds from the previous day had not yet burst, but their very appearance above the city swung the mood from desperate to hopeful. Yet the skies over Marrakesh were testing the inhabitants, teasing but also draining their enthusiasm. The clouds gathered and then dispersed, making promises and breaking them just as quickly. It brought some to the brink of apostasy. What kind of God took people to the edge of despair till they grovelled, then gave them a reason to rejoice only to sweep the sky clean of any hope? Was this a divine joke? As new clouds gathered the residents of Marrakesh looked up to the sky once more and implored it to show mercy. They had no choice but to plead, finding themselves caught between cynicism and the surrender to a stronger power.

Farook pushed the door open and entered the shop. It had an unusual smell, the muggy promise of a cleansing downpour not penetrating its interior. A nauseating stench of disease mixed with rotting leather assaulted the nostrils. It ran deep as though embedded in the walls themselves. The shop would have to be razed to the ground to eliminate the odour, the frankincense a mere afterthought that did nothing but add insult to injury. Hajj Mesfewi stopped mending a brown slipper and looked over from behind the counter.

'Farook al-Alami,' he said with not a hint of surprise. 'I have been expecting you.'

'Why so?' asked Farook as he stepped towards the counter. People always gave away more than they intended in the moments of a first meeting.

'Well, I knew eventually you would pay me a visit. It's unfathomable that a man of your standards and intelligence would take the word of a man like Yusuf al-Mahdi.'

He looked at Farook's Italian shoes.

'May I inspect them? You can understand why a man in my profession would want to.'

Farook hesitated for a moment. The request was not only unusual but audacious. He entertained the cobbler's request and removed his shoes. Hajj Mesfewi rushed from behind the counter to place a bed of reeds at his feet. Farook stepped onto it and passed them to him.

'There is a strange smell in here,' Farook said, as he watched the cobbler return to his position.

'Dead skin,' he mumbled, his attention absorbed by the shoes.

Looking up, he smiled at Farook. 'Leather. It is not handled with the love it deserves here, unlike in Europe. Our treatment methods are not as sophisticated.'

The cobbler returned to inspecting the shoes, turning them in his hand and peering into them. He placed them on the counter admiring them and traced his finger across the sides.

'The beauty of this shoe, Si Farook, is that it is cut from one piece of leather. There is minimal stitching, very little interference,' he said. 'You see – the skin is hardly damaged.'

Farook stepped closer to the counter.

'Yes, it is perhaps what makes them unique.'

'Exactly,' the cobbler's voice raised in excitement. 'Each pair is unique yet cut from the same cloth. Europe appreciates beauty, Si Farook, and knows how to preserve it in a way Morocco does not, I regret to say.'

Farook nodded, taking the shoes from the counter.

'What is beauty, Hajj Mohammed? Surely, it is a subjective judgment,' Farook asked.

'I agree. Beauty takes many forms, Si Farook.' The cobbler watched closely as Farook put the shoes back on his feet. 'Innocence is beauty, but the moment it is lost is also beautiful. Strangely, your shoes remind me of that.'

'How so?' asked Farook.

'Only in the way the leather is preserved in its finest moment. It has been skinned from the calf at the perfect moment and treated with the love and respect it deserves.'

Farook met the cobbler's eye. There was no fear there. He seemed to be enjoying their conversation like a man might enjoy a conversation struck up with a stranger in the market about the most benign of subjects. Yet they both knew why Farook was there.

'What are they like to walk in?' asked the cobbler. 'Would it be an imposition to suggest I put them on my feet? If they fit, of course.'

'You would like to walk in my shoes?'

'That would be conceited of me. I meant only that I would like to feel my feet in them.'

Farook ignored his request.

'I would like to inspect your ledger,' he stated.

'So, Si Yusuf informed you of the ledger.' He scanned the shop, lifting shoes and looking under them. 'Give me one moment.'

He retreated to the back room.

Farook stood in the middle of the shop alone. He looked over the shelves and walls, noting a Berber chest in a corner. He walked over to the chest and inspected it. The lock was rusty and would not take much to break.

The number of women missing was most probably higher than his last count. The likelihood was that some of the petitioners were legitimate in their claims. Let Yusuf sort them. Starting with a new case would only consume time: visiting the family, verifying their account, pursuing leads. It would take days if not weeks to get to where he was now. Besides, the proprietor had already gathered significant information about the petitions from the crowd outside the funduq the previous day.

He bent forward to test the lock, pulling at it with mild force. The door behind him banged shut. He straightened up to find the cobbler watching him.

'Unfortunately, I cannot find it. My mother is out running some errands. She tidied the shop yesterday evening and seems to have hidden it.'

'Why would she hide it?'

Farook moved back towards the workbench.

'It's her memory, Si Farook. It is not what it used to be.'

'And the chest - what is in that?'

'Oh, just things my mother likes to collect. She keeps the key around her neck at all times.'

'Tell me, does the name "Assiya" mean anything to you?' he asked.

'She was the wife of the Pharaoh and surrogate mother to the Prophet Moses – may peace and blessings be on him. In tradition she is known for her beauty and sacrifice for the religion of God. She will be among the first women to enter paradise. That is the only Assiya I am aware of.'

'You are a religious man, Hajj Mohammed,' observed Farook.

'I have faith, Si Farook. I believe in a higher power. Faith does not require evidence, only belief in the mercy of God.'

'Yes, but it is evidence that shores up conviction. I will return and when I do I will insist on seeing your ledger.'

The cobbler showed Farook to the door. Farook stepped out into the alleyway, the sky above once more promising absolution. He had to follow the cobbler, find someone to monitor his movements ... someone he could trust. If Yusuf were not so stupid or untrustworthy, he would be the perfect man for the job. But Farook was alone in the city, there was no man within its walls he could put his faith in.

32

Too much for one man

Yusuf sat alone and cursed Farook and the makhzan with every foul word he could bring himself to muster.

It had been four days since the meeting with the Pasha. He had six days left to resolve the case or six days to prevent Farook from solving it. Perhaps they would reduce him to a market inspector, spending his days checking traders were not frisking customers out of a tomato here or a cucumber there on their weighing scales. He couldn't think of a more miserable existence and shuddered at the humiliation it would bring. And now he was being forced to retreat to his living room, instructing his wife to not answer the door to anyone.

The first lot had arrived the previous afternoon, all sixteen of them. He was taken aback when he saw them all at his door, but soon realized how it had come to be. Farook had played a smart trick and with a cunning he wanted more than anything not to admire. He was stalled by the mob of people, processing them like goats being sold at the livestock market. He couldn't turn them away. He sat and listened to each of their complaints, making false gestures of concern, taking the most basic of notes in a ledger and then shooing them off, their faces tear-stained by either onion juice rubbed into their eyes just before entering or genuine grief. By petition number five he found a sly way of separating the false claims from the potentially true ones – most were false. Calling his wife from behind the curtain, she brought him a mashaf. This would put the fear of God into them and for those who had no fear of God, fear of an undisclosed comeuppance.

After listening to the report, he would place the Qu'ran in their right hand and tell them to make an oath of truthhood warning if they were found to be lying then the punishment that began in this life would follow them to the next.

It worked. Some changed manner completely and abruptly. Their animated grief was quickly replaced with saccharine smiles and quick exits. Others persisted, even going so far as taking the oath. On further questioning their stories collapsed and they left feeling Yusuf's wrath in their very bones and worried they might not even make it home to kiss their children one final time. To be sure he should have thrown one of the liars into the dungeon overnight, as a deterrent to anyone else thinking they just discovered a get-rich quick scheme. By evening, seven more people joined the mob and he began again, warning them of the temporal and eternal consequences of taking a false oath on the Qu'ran.

Then there were those who persisted, who grabbed the holy book from his hand and pledged their oath from their heart, kissing the mashaf and soaking it with their salty tears. Their daughter, sister or wife was missing. It was the truth to them and no amount of warning or fear would deter their telling of it. Six of the twenty-three who made a petition persisted in their claim; six more women missing, doubling the number overnight.

Thankfully, no one came the following morning. Perhaps news circulated he was taking oaths and so they stayed away, or the city's liars and tricksters had been exhausted. Most likely, the pouring rain kept them in their homes. He quietly celebrated the clouds. Their sudden burst had cleared the air which had become suffocating with dust and deceit.

He looked at the six pieces of paper in front of him, each with the most basic of information. He thought of asking his wife to bring him some egg white. Perhaps he could stick the papers on the wall and create his own talking drawings, or whatever it was Farook called them. But he didn't. He couldn't be bothered. What difference would it make if they were at eye level or spread across the carpet, the situation remained a riddle.

He read their names again: Breem, 17 years old, missing since December 1905; Lubna, 14 years old, missing since August 1905; Dunya, 23 years old, missing since June 1905; Marwa, 14 years old, missing since September 1905; Warda, 21 years old, missing since July 1905; and Malika, 18 years old, missing since January 1906.

Nothing … No lead and no reason to get up and face the world: just a list of names, ages and dates with nothing connecting them. He was a fool, completely clueless. Add the names to the confirmed six and he was now investigating the disappearance of twelve girls. It was too much for one man. Without any doubt he truly was a fool. There was only one way to salvage the situation. The only suitable medicine for over-ambition was humility.

He called his wife and told her what he needed. She looked at him with concern, worried that her husband had finally lost his mind.

'The rain,' she explained, as though the sound of it did not somehow reach his ears.

'Woman, bring me my selham and do not worry about the rain. And bring me a gas lantern.'

She retreated to the back of the house. If he fell sick it would rest on her to listen to his complaints in the middle of the night that death was finally upon him.

Collecting the scattered papers, he stood up and tucked them into his house trousers. Next he threw his jellaba on and took the selham from his wife, who stood there watching him, unimpressed. He placed it over his shoulders. He felt the weight of its thick fabric on his back, but knew it would only protect him from the downpour up to a point. Wrapping his white turban overhead, he lifted the hood of his jellaba and selham and placed them neatly over it.

At the door he slipped his yellow baboush slippers on his feet and braced himself. Looking at his wife one final time, who stood there denying him the encouragement he so craved, he took a long breath and stepped out, holding the gas lantern in his hand.

33

The taste of home

Outside the sky was grey with the growing rumbles of thunder. The alleyways quickly filled with rain water, as there was nowhere for it to drain. He only hoped the city's basic sewage system would not burst, the filth and rats of the city pouring over his feet.

He ran as fast as he could, paying no attention to what was ahead of him, not that he could see further than a few metres before him. The city was deserted. Shops remained closed for the evening, doors and windows were firmly shut, as the residents had no desire to act as barriers between the rain and the earth. Aside from the occasional mule leaning against a wall in complete submission to its fate, the rain dripping from its nostrils, he saw no other living creature. It took a long time to arrive at the funduq. The need for extra caution slowed his progress. He skipped over or around pools of muddy water, and just before reaching the door, thinking the worst was over, he walked straight into an ankle deep puddle. Shaking his foot free, he banged on the door and waited. He could feel the proprietor's presence on the other side, breathing quietly and listening for who it might be.

'Open the door, makhzan official,' he bellowed into the wooden door.

The door opened slightly and he pushed through, not waiting for an invitation.

'Where is he?'

'Out,' said the proprietor, taking a few seconds to recognize Yusuf in his bedraggled state.

'Really – in this weather?' Yusuf asked, in no mood for procrastination or deceit.

'Well, you are out.'

Yusuf scowled at him and walked into the middle of the courtyard, allowing the rain to drench him once more.

'Farook al-Alami,' he called up to the first floor.

He got no response.

'Si Farook, I know you are there. I will stand here until you agree to talk to me.'

Still nothing. Yusuf crossed his arms and parted his feet ready for a long wait.

The proprietor darted behind him and ran up the stairs. Standing outside Farook's door, he knocked gently and entered. Farook stood by the fireplace observing the flames dance in front of him. He rubbed his hands together, a thick woven blanket over his shoulders.

'Si Yusuf is in the courtyard and refusing to leave until you speak with him.' His funduq had not seen this much drama since a mule crushed a tradesman in his sleep the summer before.

'I heard,' said Farook, the flames drawing him further and further into the fluidity of their dance.

'He will catch his death,' said the proprietor.

'Leave him there.'

'But, Si Farook …'

'I said leave him,' Farook interrupted, as he continued to warm his hands.

Fifteen minutes passed. Yusuf refused the proprietor's invitation to stand in the kitchen against the burning coal stove or to remove his selham so it could be dried. His teeth began to chatter and his knees jolted about in their sockets. The rain seeped through to his very core, drenching his clothes completely and leaving his skin wet through. He would definitely fall ill.

He began to feel stupid, thinking perhaps he should listen to his wife more often instead of acting on impulse. But it was too late now. There was no retreat. He would stand there until Farook showed mercy or he died. The decision was no longer his to make, leaving would be to admit defeat. It felt mildly liberating standing in the rain waiting for an unknown fate. He didn't have to fight; he just had to endure.

Looking through the raindrops that fell like bloated tears, he saw Farook's door slightly ajar. It was fully closed earlier. He took it as all the sign he needed and headed towards the staircase.

Yusuf entered the room, closing the door quietly and found Farook with his back to him still facing the fire.

'Undress, dry yourself and put on that jellaba. Wrap the blanket around you and come and stand next to the fire,' Farook instructed, not turning to look at him.

Yusuf did as he was told, locking his jaw tight so Farook could not hear the chattering of his teeth. Eventually, he came to stand next to Farook thinking a glass of mint tea would heat him up perfectly. As though reading his mind, Farook bent into the fire and retrieved a kettle. He poured two glasses, handing one to Yusuf and took a sip from the other. Yusuf stifled a gasp.

'You … You do not drink mint tea,' he exclaimed.

Perhaps Farook also felt the predicament they were both in and had relinquished his love for Europe. Farook looked at him and gave a smile, one filled with information withheld.

'I only drink it when it rains,' he said in a quiet voice, turning back to the fire.

When he left his house and faced the storm Yusuf had a plan of what he would say, how he would be. He would explain his quandary; show his weakness for ill-considered decisions and the mess they often got him in. And he hoped Farook would take pity and recognize that he was not a leader but someone who was happy just to abide. But the conversation was not transpiring according to that plan. It took Farook exactly three minutes to disarm him of his will through the offering of undeserved companionship.

'But why only in the rain?' asked Yusuf.

Farook paused for a moment, lost in the fire once more.

'It reminds me of a time,' Farook began. 'The first time I was in London. It rained so heavily for days and days that there was hardly any sunlight. You could go for a week without seeing any sun: the sky permanently grey and overcast. It felt like you were living under some impending doom.'

Yusuf knew exactly what that felt like. It was, in fact, exactly how he had felt since being assigned to the missing women. The sensation that he was caught in a tragedy that was both compelling and destructive: its outcome unknown and wholly unpredictable. Farook continued, engrossed in the traction of the memory.

'I spent days in my lodgings looking out of the window at the biting cold, the heavy raindrops battering the glass that protected me from its force. The people there are used to it, hordes of them rushing by to go here or there on some errand that would serve no meaningful purpose in the end. It makes you wonder what it is all for. I often asked myself why we even bother. We all die and eventually become dust. What do we hope to achieve by chasing life? A legacy? Eventually we will all be forgotten.'

He paused to look at Yusuf and noticed his shivering. Yusuf remained silent, wondering how long it would take for him to be forgotten after his death. Perhaps his grandchildren would tell their children about him, but beyond that his life would become another human story amongst the millions that go unrecorded. His moments of joy, pain, fear and acceptance would become nothing but insignificant details lost in the story of Man. The thought was comforting because it freed him from desire. Perhaps a quiet life was not such a bad thing. But quiet was not an option in Marrakesh. Survival meant struggle and, despite his mood, the urge to do more than survive burnt strong. His failure was an insult to his father's sacrifices, a moment in the history of his lineage squandered by stupidity. Farook interrupted his thoughts to continue.

'On those days I stood by the window and watched them and the horse and carriages trotting by. And I made some tea that I brought with me. I sipped it slowly, relishing the sweetness of home.'

Yusuf did not take Farook as a man inflicted with nostalgia. He appeared the complete opposite, a man obsessed with the future, modernity and the promise it held. It was difficult to imagine him vulnerable and unsure of who he was.

'It reminded me of Tangier. The taste took me back to the Mediterranean on a windy, but bright day. But it also reminded me of how far from home I really was, how I might never get back. I knew if I ever returned I would be a changed man and that it was only upon my return that my journey would truly begin. It is a hard lesson to accept that the person you are when you begin a journey is not the person you will be when you return and yet the place you left is the same with the same expectations of you.'

'What were you doing in London?' Yusuf ventured to ask, the sound of the city's name resting uncomfortably in his ear.

'I was there on the order of the Sultan,' Farook stated with a feigned authority.

'For how long?'

'Six months. I returned again for a further four months a year later. I drink mint tea only when it rains to remember what it is like to be a stranger in the world and in your own skin.'

Farook drained his cup and moved away from the fire. Yusuf stood in his place, adrift. Farook truly was a stranger to the world. Where did he fit? He did not belong here and yet he did not belong any-where else. For all his reserve, his confidence, perhaps Farook was as lost as the rest of them. Was it possible he also experienced fear and doubt like normal men? Yusuf stretched his hand towards the fire as though hoping to pull out the answers to his questions from its fading flames.

'Why are you here?' Farook asked from behind Yusuf's back.

'There are six more girls missing,' Yusuf said, knowing if the Qadi or Pasha learnt of his betrayal at the very least his career would be over.

'Does that include Latifa and the twelve-year old?'

He may be a stranger, thought Yusuf, but he has friends.

'No it doesn't. Including them makes ...'

'Twelve,' Farook finished for him. 'And why are you telling me?'

He had collected himself, once again distant and impenetrable. Yusuf cleared his throat.

'I thought we could work together. Perhaps we can put what hap-pened behind us and find out what happened to these women; give their families some peace.'

Farook laughed, walking back to stand next to Yusuf. He took an iron rod from the wall and stoked the fire back to life.

'Tell me, has the makhzan no leads? Are they so desperate they sent you in the rain like a wet alleyway cat hoping for shelter?'

'No, I came on my own volition. If they knew I was here then I would lose my position,' Yusuf said, rubbing the sting of the accusa-tion from his face.

'Si Yusuf, you should leave. Take the jellaba and blanket. You can have them returned later. And please know when we meet again one of us will have the answers to the questions that keep the other awake at night.'

Yusuf removed the blanket from his back and threw his damp selham over his shoulders. He withdrew the notes from his house trousers and placed them on the desk.

'Si Farook, I once thought perhaps we could be friends and the prospect brought me much joy. I have learnt a great deal from you and believe you are not a vindictive man. A man can do nothing but learn from his mistakes and if he is incapable of that at the very least he can admit he is a fool. I have been a fool. If you ever need a friend, I am here in Marrakesh. I am at your service.'

He walked out into the driving rain.

34

Jihad of the tongue

The ram horn blew early the next day. It made a continuous piercing sound which reverberated across the city. It yanked the city's residents from their dreams and installed a sense of dread as they jumped out of their beds and rushed to make their ablutions. It continued to blow most of the morning, sending women into a panic as they gathered their children about them and men out of their homes to congregate on local corners. By breakfast, street criers and armed men accompanied the sound of the horn. The guards took up positions at the city doors, inspecting donkey-drawn carts and people as they passed under ornate archways. They patrolled in twos, ready to react to any suspicious or deviant behaviour. People rushed past them. Their heads were kept low and their mouths shut.

The city criers took up strategic positions on corners and in market places and called their news to the people, telling them where they were to gather. They repeated their calls over and over until their voices were hoarse and the message had reached every household. Rumours circulated. Was the city coming under attack from an unruly tribe? Had its day of retribution finally come? Had the Sultan died? Why was the entire city being called to the Koutoubia? And then men and women began to walk towards the mosque, the centre of official absolution.

The mosque quickly filled. Men occupied every inch of floor space except that behind the screen reserved for those women bold enough to enter. The gathered crowd spilled out into the gardens surrounding the mosque, some seated under trees and others standing and looking up at the minaret in all its stature.

People continued to gather from every corner of the city, amassing as though woken from a collective dream, marching in one direction to face the eternal consequences of their humanity. When the mosque was filled to capacity, hundreds of people stood shoulder-to-shoulder to offer an initial prayer. Crowds began to congregate in Jemaa el-Fnaa, waiting for the news to spread down the line until it reached them like a whisper passed from one man to another, until the final message contained only traces of its origins. Farook stood at the back of the prayer room, watching the men take their positions next to each other, all facing Mecca, the most holy of cities. He saw Yusuf in the second row behind the Pasha and the old Qadi. The Pasha turned, momentarily catching Farook's eye.

The adhan was sounded. The call to prayer reached the mass of people and silenced them all, alleviating their fears with reassurance that there was always a more powerful authority than one's current oppressor.

> *God is the Greatest,*
> *I acknowledge there is no deity but God,*
> *I acknowledge Mohammed is the Messenger of God,*
> *Hasten to prayer,*
> *Hasten to success …*

The muaddin continued in his sweet melodious voice, which emanated from the top of the minaret to comfort the weary and attract the stubborn. The city residents offered a short prayer, two cycles of the pre-scribed movements. They raised their hands to their shoulders, palms forward, and placed them down again by their sides. They bent forward in unison, hands on their knees now, and then stood upright once more. They bent their knees to the floor and placed their foreheads to the ground, sat up, bent forward once more, and repeated the cycle. All the while they whispered private prayers to God at each change of position: heal my sick child; bring me wealth; secure my harvest; find me a wife; bring me an heir; bring my enemy to justice; grant me paradise; expand my mother's grave. The demands were endless. It was only because the God they prayed to was the Satisfier of All Needs, the Possessor of All Strength, the Generous and the Hearer of All, that they continued in the hope that one day their prayers would be answered.

Farook joined in the congregation, moving his body mechanically, but he had no prayer to offer. This was not what the prayer was about: to ask, plead and beg – to trade blind submission for services ren-dered. No one questioned why the prayer was as it was, or why it was so physical if all that mattered were the incantations uttered. For Farook the prayer was about silencing our demands on the world; it was an individual or collective meditation, which had been hijacked by opportunists who thought of God as there to satisfy their every whim, like the head of a complex network of angels whom he sent scurrying to answer every call. He hated blind faith: the narrow mind willing to accept anything as truth as long as it ended in the satisfaction of every mundane desire born from a meaningless existence. Yet, real intelli-gence and competence were frowned upon. A man able to devise his own course to step into the unknown with only the certainty of his own agency was an affront to the All-Powerful.

As the prayer came to its end the men uttered salutations of peace to the angels who were sat upon their shoulders. The crowd lingered in its position. They waited. They were not called to the mosque simply to offer supplementary prayers. They all looked toward the pulpit to see who might appear.

From the front row a figure made his way to the front, accompanied by two servants. He took the three steps to the platform in long strides and looked out onto the crowd. He was a man built for the stage or maybe the stage had been built for him. He looked out at the congregation as though it belonged to him. Through a simple command he could send ripples of joy or fear, and through a wave of the hand he could change the fate of every man and woman gathered. Murmurings broke the silence as the congregation beheld their Caliph. They called out in salutations of peace and invoked God's blessings. His well-kept beard framed his broad face and his pale skin spoke of evenings spent planning the future in dark rooms during nights in whispered prayers. He raised his large hands for silence. The sound of blessings faded like the cries of a sated child. He extended the silence, looking over his congregation with a paternal smile.

'*B-ismi-llāhi r-Rahmāni r-Rahīm*,' he began in a raspy voice. 'In the name of God, the Most Gracious, the Most Merciful. I stand here as Caliph, the Guardian of this majestic city. May God preserve it and His representative Moulay Abd al-Aziz, the Commander of the Believers and Sultan of this blessed land – may his reign be long and his heirs prosper. I call you here today as your father to warn you. Heed my warning; protect yourselves and your families. Our enemies are many and conspire together for our downfall. Beware of the enemy from without and the one within. Look about you and inside you and fight your enemy through jihad. Enjoin good and forbid evil. And remember, there are multiple jihads: that of the sword, the hand and the tongue. The latter is the weakest of the three. And then there is jihad al-nafs against oneself, the hardest of them all. If you cannot enjoin good and forbid evil with your hand or your tongue then at the very least fight it in your heart. Purify your hearts through prayer and charity and find your reward waiting for you with God, the All Seeing. And protect your women. They are your covering as you are theirs and the Prophet – may God send prayers and peace upon him – enjoined the best amongst us are those who are good to their wives. And if you feel they are unsafe then do not let them out of their homes.

This brings me to a present danger: a sickness which has taken hold in our hearts and our homes. You have heard the rumours; tongues are loose and words come easy. I stand before you today to separate truth from falsehood. As of count this morning, fourteen of our female companions have been confirmed missing. We as men have failed to protect what God has made us responsible for. We have let down the weak amongst us and cannot call ourselves men. While the Sultan – may his reign be long – sits in Fez fighting our external enemies with his tongue, I, protecting this Abode of Peace, stand before you ready to crucify the enemy from within. Protect yourselves and protect your families and rest well knowing I oversee this great city and will return it to security. All power is from God. Peace and the blessings of God be upon you.'

Caliph Moulay Hafid stopped and descended the pulpit as the congregation once more broke into murmuring, their supplications were replaced by commentary and questions. An imam stepped forward to offer a prayer. The crowd raised their cupped hands and poured the blessings over their faces. Farook watched a man from the back row stand quickly and exit the mosque. The cobbler. He seemed in a rush and if it were not for the crowd gathering at the doors and grabbing at loaves of bread being distributed he would have followed him.

35

Offers of friendship

Farook left the mosque playing the sermon over in his mind. Two more girls missing, the number was increasing by the day. Who knew where the number might stand tomorrow? The spree of disappearances was impossible to investigate alone and he had no way of knowing how long the women were missing for, the order of their disappearance, or if any connection between them had been established. There was not enough time in the day or competent officials in the makhzan. Yusuf's notes helped. They offered further detail and he was grateful to Yusuf for that. From the notes he was able to determine women and young girls had been disappearing from the city since the summer of 1905. The pleas of the family had previously been ignored. It could only mean the culprit knew Marrakesh well and that he was a long-term resident. It also meant the missing women could not be far. They could not have been taken beyond its walls. The logistics of removing them from the city and chances of being noticed were too high.

Why was the makhzan only now treating the case as a priority? What purpose did the Caliph hope to serve in his speech? It was well known Moulay Hafid coveted the throne, but would he dare turn against his brother during these difficult times? The Sultan was weak and surely internal instability would only weaken him more.

Perhaps it was naïve of Farook to think the Caliph would wait until the Sultan had regained his strength before seeking to overthrow him. It was the perfect time to strike, and to create an internal crisis so that he found himself battling threats on different fronts. It was after all why he had been sent to the city in the first place, and yet he feared he was failing in his task.

And where did this leave his investigation? Did it even matter who the culprit was anymore? The fear and excitement would catch alight and in the rising heat people would demand blood. It would not matter to them from whom it flowed as long as it flowed. The families would not get their answers. They would be expected to find comfort in the punishment of an innocent man: a sacrificial body whose suffering would bear testament to justice.

Farook left the mosque and marched through Jemaa el-Fnaa. Walking through the crowds, lingering to take the opportunity to draw wild conclusions based on nothing but conjecture, he could feel their excitement pulsing down the alleyways. Men held their daughter's hands tightly as they took them home as if expecting them to be snatched from their very grip. Doors would be locked, windows bolted. Potential suspects free to roam, while potential victims were confined to inside for their own safety.

He would not allow it. If it were the last thing he did for the young Sultan he would put a stop to the conspiracy. The country would not implode because the Marrakesh authorities were willing to exploit those already downtrodden to serve their own agenda.

He felt someone pull at his sleeve and turned ready for a confrontation. A man, his face concealed, leaned towards him. 'Follow me,' he whispered.

The man darted into an alleyway and Farook followed until they reached a dead end. The man turned towards him and removed his hood.

'Dr Delacroix,' Farook was taken aback, shocked to see him in Moroccan attire.

'Disguise,' the doctor said, looking up as if a mob of people were about to jump from the rooftops at any moment and attack. 'You heard the Caliph, it is not safe … especially for us foreigners. He practically encouraged the city to attack us. We are retreating to the mellah. The Jewish quarter is the safest place for us.'

Farook was in no mood for such self-absorption.

'I think the women of this city are in danger, Dr Delacroix. The Caliph made no mention of foreign residents.'

'We have women among us too. You heard what he just said, whipping the men into a frenzy, talking about internal and external enemies. Everyone knows what Moulay Hafid is after and it seems you have provided the perfect pretext.'

Farook could not help but agree with him for once. He had unwittingly handed the Caliph the kindle to start his fire.

'You must help us,' said the doctor. His eyes bulged from their sockets as they darted in all directions. Stepping past Farook, he looked out of the dead end, turned and handed him a letter. 'You must have this delivered to the Sultan or to your friends in Tangier. We cannot get any mail out. The Pasha confiscates it at the gates or sends a tribe's man to retrieve it when it is on the road. He has spies everywhere, Mr Farook. This city will turn to violence.'

Farook took the letter, the wax seal unbroken and tucked it beneath his cloak. He almost felt sorry for the doctor. The Caliph's words had found their listener and the doctor would spend the rest of his time in Marrakesh looking over his shoulder, if he ever dared leave the mellah that is.

'The Sultan will protect you Dr Delacroix. Stay in the mellah if that is where you feel safe. I will see what I can do.'

The doctor bowed to Farook and put his right hand on his chest. Blushing as he realized that perhaps he had taken his false persona a little too far, he lifted his hood and turned to leave the dead end.

He paused for a moment, 'Mr Farook,' he called. 'Have you any new information about the lady you visited me about?'

Farook shook his head.

'I often think about what might have happened to her. If I had only known then I would have been more observant. Perhaps I might have then been some help to you.'

'You helped more than you realize,' Farook replied.

The doctor smiled softly, exposing his discoloured teeth.

'France is your friend and if you were to ever require her assistance then you need only call,' the doctor said.

Turning around, he slipped back into the throng of people.

In less than twenty-four hours two people had offered him their friendship: Yusuf and now the doctor. He hoped that, whatever was to come, he would not have to depend on either of those offerings.

PART THREE

36

The one with no name

He threw her to the ground and stood panting, watching over her to make sure she did not move. His heart pounded against his ribs and he took deep breaths to calm it. The decision had been so impulsive, so unlike him.

Usually, he liked to take his time and select his victims carefully to ensure they fitted with his assembly. It was no good if the next girl destroyed the energy in the circle with her rebellion. He had learnt that lesson already from Assiya. They had to be willing to be part of the history he was making or at least submit in the final moment.

But time was something he was running out of. The city would soon collapse into chaos and every action would suddenly become more perilous. He had to finish his work and he was so close. When the true number was revealed they would marvel at his capacity to move in the shadows of the city, undetected for so long. He would become legend. His work would be told to children as warning about evil, and retold in the circles of Jemaa el-Fnaa for the men to shudder at, their faces lit by candlelight and admiration.

He went back to the door and checked it was locked, making sure there was no way of seeing in. Then he stepped over the still frame of the girl and checked the interior door. He put his ear to the rotting wood. Nothing. He could not hear that woman shuffling about in the next room, or her wheezing. It gave him relief that she was still for once. Perhaps she was curled up in the far corner of the room, as she liked to do, and had fallen asleep. Regardless, the peace lifted his optimism and diluted the adrenalin pumping through his blood.

He returned to stand over the girl. Despite it being a rash decision – he had grabbed her without even checking if someone was watching – there was something in the way she looked at him as they crossed paths which told him she wanted it too.

Looking down at her, he thought of the Caliph and his message. The makhzan was responding in exactly the way he had hoped. They were a bunch of fools, incapable of a single decision without an external trigger. They knew only how to react, much like a dog reacts to his master, doing his bidding and waiting for punishment or reward. They would get their punishment, and he his reward. And when it happened the sweetest part would be they delivered their own downfall with their very own hands.

Except Farook al-Alami. He was no fool. He had watched him in the mosque, observed his false prayers and his attentive eyes, always learning. Had their eyes met momentarily? He caught glimpses of him bending in insincere humility and lifting his palms to the sky in faked gratitude. He found his intrigue about the man deepening further still. They seemed alike in many ways. They both stood outside the circle, watching the pack as its members devoured each other for scraps, congratulating themselves for being alive. Al-Alami was different; his lack of tolerance for Man was obvious. Like him, he had enough self-respect to know better than to spend his life grovelling. At some point, Farook decided to get up off his knees and stand upright. And since then he never bent his knees to a man and when he bent them to

184

God, he did so in the knowledge that the only God worth bowing to was the one who lived through you.

It was true. They were alike and they wanted the same thing. The only difference was their methods. Al-Alami still operated under the delusion he could change the system from within. He would eventually learn how pointless that was; leave him to his delusions. They would soon shatter at his feet and be trampled upon by less worthy men. He would soon show the man from Tangier just how much his hopes were based on a fantasy made up of nostalgia for a nation that never really existed. One had to be capable of great evil to effect great good.

* * *

The girl twitched. Her arm reached out from beneath her torso. He saw her fingers begin to scratch at the floor. She was gaining consciousness. He frowned at what he was about to do. Poison was the better method; there was no blood. He preferred to lull them into a sense of security, watch them take a sip of the drink he lovingly put in their hand, and then observe the truth dawn on them as the poison began to take hold. There was a point of realisation where for a moment they were caught on the cusp of lucidity and intoxication, which he searched desperately for in their eyes. When he saw it, he thought he might die with them.

But there was no time for that. He went to the corner of the room and picked up the heavy rock he had taken from the garden. At the time he wasn't quite sure why he took it. Something just told him to. And now the reason revealed itself. He smiled to himself, pleased with how fate had colluded with him in his plans but held back her reasons to do so.

Turning the rock over in his hands, he found that the girl had pulled herself up to a sit against the wall. Her veil hung limply around her neck, tugged away from her gasping mouth. She couldn't be older than thirteen. God had played his part. All he had to do was trust. She was perfect, unable to conceive of the evil in this world.

Looking up at him, her face twisted, her mouth ready to let out a piercing scream. It died in her throat as he raised the rock to the ceiling and dropped it on her head. Her body collapsed into a heap as though someone had cut the puppet strings that had held her upright her whole life. A stream of blood trickled down her face and stained the floor. Her eyes bursting with the full knowledge of her mortality only a moment ago were now devoid of any vitality. He nudged the body gently to make sure and felt no reflex. If she wasn't dead, she would wake to find herself buried, and discover a fear reserved for the very few who experience such horror.

Looking around him, he felt a pang of guilt. He had promised one of the girls company. But the situation was impossible. She would have to wait and find solace in the scent of jasmine. There was no way he could move the body of the girl in front of him. He had to bury her here. And yet that too was problematic. He could already hear Assiya beneath him grumbling her complaints, waking the others so that their protests might eventually wake the whole city. He looked at the door. The second room had enough space for him to start from zero. Ambition was what killed most men; his number had already been decided by others and he reminded himself just how close he was. But he needed more space for the one lying on the floor and those to come.

From the silence in the next room, he suspected she was asleep in the back. He would have to get her out before he could move the body in to bury it. The girls were unsightly to her. Perhaps she thought her feigned ignorance would protect her from God's punishment, that somehow on the Day of Reckoning she would be able to convince this all-seeing being she held so tightly too that she did not know what she walked over. She was a fool like the others. Her religion was food for her ignorance. She knew and enjoyed the benefits. He saw the change in her walk when she wore the yellow kaftan for the first time. A confidence had come over her that he had not seen for many years. And still she showed ingratitude, not appreciating the sacrifice both he and his assembly had made in giving her the kaftan. Perhaps it was time she earned her rewards instead of fearing her punishments.

He approached the door and waited for a moment with his ear to it once more. Still he heard no sound. He fought to pull the door open, it's swollen wood clinging to the warped frame. The room was empty; the bedding folded neatly in the corner and the floor swept. Panic began to bubble in the pit of his stomach, but he restrained it. He knew her; she would return. She always returned, loyal to the end. He quickly went back into the first room and picked up the dead weight. He only realized when she was already in his arms that he would never know this one's name.

37

The field of man's actions

Yusuf nodded his head rhythmically. He hoped it would have a calming effect on the Pasha. If not, then at least it might buy him more time to think. He nodded in agreement to everything the Pasha said, despite not really listening to a word of it. Instead he imagined his fate over and over like a recurring nightmare he could not escape. Sometimes, he was banished: his home and belongings confiscated and he and his family left destitute. Other times he was in the dungeons: left to the whims of the men he sent there who spent all day plotting their revenge. Regardless of the scenario, his fall was inevitable. He looked down at his broad stomach wondering how long it would last before deflating from hunger, and if somewhere within it he had the strength for what was to come.

The Pasha paced in front of him, smacking his hands together and raving at the walls. He ranted about how he would take every man down with him, leave no one standing and burn the city to the ground rather than go quietly. He relived his youth, transforming his past corruption into glory, and his privilege into sacrifice for his people.

'That man will not destroy me, not destroy what I have built,' he yelled.

Yusuf looked on. He was preoccupied, wondering how long it would take for him to lose control of his bladder, and if, like the butcher, his bowels would soon follow.

'We must write to the Sultan to warn him of the enemy that shares his blood.'

Yusuf nodded. Perhaps the Sultan could save them, providing he could save himself.

'He is a scheming son of …' the Pasha stopped. It was foolish to sharpen the knife before placing it in the adversary's hand. 'What do you suggest? I listened to you and that old fool, the Qadi. Tell me, what should we do?'

Yusuf was roused from his nightmare, just before a guard had been about to force his face into his own faeces, laughing heartily while he choked on the stench.

'A letter to the Sultan may help. We could warn him of Moulay Hafid's … his brother's scheming,' he suggested, wondering when the written word had ever saved anyone.

'But it is impossible. Moulay Hafid knows of every letter leaving this city and if it falls into his hands we will never see the sun again. I will not spend my last days in a dungeon with you for company.'

Yusuf nodded. He was glad of the Pasha's ability to foretell every danger.

'Perhaps we are in no real danger. It is unlikely Moulay Hafid will act against you when you are appointed by the Sultan,' mused Yusuf.

It was the turn of the Pasha to nod. He stopped in front of Yusuf and smiled broadly.

'You are right. He would not dare. He might be able to whip up fear and chaos, but he can't touch me. I can rally my private army. This city belongs to me and while Moulay Hafid might be playing at chaos in the hope it will topple his brother, it is the Sultan's blood he wants, not mine. Without me, this city would crumble.'

The Pasha concluded his thoughts and stood relieved. He would sleep well after all. That just left Yusuf. He hardly had that kind of protection. He remained sat on the divan looking up at the Pasha, pathetic and desperate.

'I suggest you resovle this case, Si Yusuf. Do whatever it takes, but end this now before it is completely hijacked and along with it your chances of a peaceful death surrounded by your grandchildren. If this escalates it will be you who must live with the consequences, your friend from Tangier is protected but you, my brother, are not.'

Yusuf left the Pasha's house. It was settled: he would die in the misery he had spent years conjuring in the imagination of Marrakesh's residents. He had dug his own grave and a more intelligent man would climb into it and accept his fate. 'Solve the case,' the Pasha had said, which really amounted to 'you are on your own.' When the time came Yusuf knew he would have no allies, no protectors. They would just as easily feed him to the baying crowd as anyone. He was disposable.

His only recourse would be the coins he saved over the years. Perhaps they could buy him and his family time or passage, he would take whichever was offered.

There was no resolving the case. He wasn't even sure of all the women and girls' names, the order in which they disappeared, or even how many were missing. Farook had shunned him. The Qadi was powerless. And the Pasha had made it clear his protection would not extend to Yusuf.

There was a time in a man's life when he stood in the field of his actions and measured his life's work. He saw an abundance of fruit trees which had been planted early to sweeten the bitterness of old age once ripe, or he saw a field marked by the trenches of failure. Yusuf was at that point and he saw only trenches, all abandoned, providing nothing but pits to fall into. He could not go back to cover them and he could not go forward. There was no path without hazard ahead. His only choice was to stand in his place and wait. He could only hope someone would appear and take pity, offer him passage to a meadow unscarred by the recklessness of man.

38

The breaking of men and boys

Horses galloped through Jemaa el-Fnaa, whipping past people and kicking up dust. Riding them were men as strong as their stallions, their faces concealed by head wraps showing nothing but their wild eyes darkened with black charcoal. They carried weapons on their bodies: swords, knives and pistols. Their cloaks billowed behind them, thrashing in the wind their passage created.

The inhabitants of Marrakesh stood with their backs against walls and watched them pass, covering their mouths to prevent swallowing the dust of their own downfall.

People panicked in the souk, stock purchasing whatever provisions they could find: days-old bread, withered salads or animal bones with nothing but fat and sinew attached. Fights broke out at the city water fountains as people pushed and kicked to get to the single pump. Children were assigned the task of returning to the fountains again and again to ensure they had enough water to last them for as long as possible. Men and women did not stop to gossip or update their neighbours on the latest news. The city was already saturated with tales of cosmic proportions. Scuffles broke out between the invaders and residents. Some were brave enough to refuse them a space in their gardens to set camp. They were quickly dealt with: pushed off their land, laughed at and ordered to fetch water and provisions. Doors were bolted and the flat rooftops usually reserved for women were overtaken by the men of the household, who stood guard ready to fight or prevent entry from above. They knelt down peering over low walls into the alleyways at the new arrivals, leaving their women protected behind doors and blind to unfolding events, second-hand witnesses to their own fate. Shops remained closed and by late afternoon the streets were deserted and deathly quiet, except for the sound of camps being set up and the clucking of nervous chickens.

As the sun began to set, the call to prayer rung out across the city and imams stood to lead congregations devoid of supplicants. Their chants echoed through vacuous mosques and returned to them unanswered. By nightfall the city was scattered with campfires which lit up the sky and told of the beginnings of a long sleepless night filled with soothing lullabies to comfort terrified children. Around the campfires men sat sipping sweet tea spiced with zaatar and roasting cubes of meat, which they tore into with their teeth straight from the hot metal skewers, their pistols and swords still strapped to their waists. Their tents stood behind them covered with thick sheepskin, waiting to shroud them after the long journey.

Farook sat in his room listening to the new sounds filling the city. He heard the barrelled laughter of men and the sound of horses sleeping beneath him as they turned and twisted against each other, snorting air through thick nostrils. The funduq was full to capacity with the unexpected guests. He had not left his room all afternoon, but was still able to surmise what was unfolding outside. The kitchen boy brought lunch to his door, tapping gently before entering. Farook had walked the neighbourhood in the morning, but finding his path blocked by panicked residents and laughing tribesmen, he knew it would be another day lost to the city.

He heard the proprietor rushing around the funduq up and down the stairway and across the courtyard working hard to give his patrons no cause for complaint. The funduq residents were threatening in their presence and, though they masked it with polite invitations to join them for tea, the weapons they carried on their hips left no room for doubt.

Farook looked up at the speaking pictures. The original four had practically peeled off the wall. The corners drooped like rabbit ears and the parchment glistened from the crusted egg white. Every time he took one step closer to Assiya, the city pulled him back. Whether it was Yusuf's incompetence, the Qadi's grovelling, the Caliph's ambitions, whatever it was he was relentlessly being denied the opportunity to investigate properly. This was the way; this was how men were broken. The day was wasted.

Around the originals he had stuck new speaking pictures. Most had barely any information: a name and age and not much more. Some were completely blank, reminding him of the official number missing, and of their unregistered existence. Fourteen in total, though the number could have gone up. If it had, he would be the last to know.

The names of the women stood out to him. There were so many … perhaps too many to remember: Breem, Lubna, Dunya, Marwa, Warda, Leila, Maryam, Souad and Assiya. And then there were the nameless, the twelve-year-old and all the others whose families had come forward to assert their daughter's existence. The value of their lives was shown by the number of tears shed.

Meaningless.

Their names and their lives were all meaningless. The women did not matter and their end mattered less. As though their bodies being hijacked by society was not bad enough, their very existence was nothing more than a currency, a counterfeit coin used to buy power. For what end? So that one brother could take the seat of another and rule with the same self-engrossed naïvety. He would have no part of it, and yet he had no way of stopping it or extracting himself from the unfolding spectacle.

'Master,' he heard a timid voice call.

He turned to find the kitchen boy standing by the door. He had not heard him enter, lost in the darkness of his thoughts.

'Yes, Mohammed,' he said gently. 'What can I do for you?'

The boy looked older, wiser then when Farook first entered the city. He held himself with a straighter back and looked Farook directly in the eye.

'Take me with you.' The boy's words revealed the maturity of his attitude as a farce.

'Take you with me where?' asked Farook.

'To Tangier. You will leave now, no?'

'Why would you think that?' Farook asked. 'I will leave when my work is done here.'

'The Glaoui have come from the High Atlas … They have sent their private army into the city. They are camped in every corner and the tribesmen are already harassing residents. I heard a gunshot early this morning.'

This sound would follow him into his dreams and force him out of them too, Farook thought for a moment.

'Come stand beside me,' he said.

The boy moved cautiously towards Farook.

Placing his hands on his shoulders, Farook looked him deep in the eyes for a long while before speaking. He was still a child, helpless, and with nothing but his thoughts of the future, which could both sooth and make him suffer.

'You have nothing to fear. They are here on the invitation of the Caliph of Marrakesh, to protect the city,' he explained, knowing full well his lie. Yes, they were there by invitation of Moulay Hafid, but not to protect it. To occupy and show the Caliph's might to his brother. There was little point in explaining this to the young boy. It would only distress him further. Farook saw that his words did little to comfort the child and he berated the world for its cruelty. But he knew it would be wrong to fill the boy with a hope he could not later deliver.

'But the Pasha has also sent his army onto the streets,' said Mohammed.

'All this,' Farook said, thinking of the tribesmen, the city, the funduq, his life, 'will pass. One day you will be a grown man and then you can go wherever you want and be whoever you want. You will only have yourself to answer to.'

Patting Mohammed on the shoulder, Farook knew that once again he told him a lie. The boy's fate was already written; this was how boys were broken.

39

The right moment

Later that evening, Farook stood on the rooftop of the funduq watching the embers of fire burning low across the city. He felt the sense of his self-imposed confinement deeply. He did not care to see the city the way it currently was, crippled with anticipation of what might come next. He may not have warmed to its streets and markets or found companionship amongst its inhabitants, but it did not mean he wanted to see it burnt to the ground.

Lines had been drawn across and through it and though he was no longer certain where he stood, he refused to comply with the new boundaries or remain within the areas safe for those deemed loyal to the right brother. So he chose to stay where he was. The rooftop was the only space still unoccupied, still beyond the reach of the makhzan. It was in many ways sacred ground. It was usually reserved for women but could be occupied by men if it came under threat.

Farook was the only of the funduq's patrons on the rooftop. The others were snoring deeply in their chambers, some tossing and turning. He stood, a lonely spectator to the long night with only the stars for company. He looked up at the night sky marvelling at the stars that dangled over the world like lanterns, witness to every life and every breath for time eternal. The stars would outlast them all, indifferent to the infinite suffering and bursts of joy below.

He stood there for a long while, counting the campfires and estimating the number of men circling each one. The men were stamping their feet with boredom and already missed the Atlas with its snow-capped peaks. They were mountain folk. The alleyways were a prison compared to the open green valleys, and the townhouses were mere shacks against their large Kasbahs, which had walls as impenetrable as their courage and banquet halls large enough to feed an army. It would not take long before their hunger for a hunt caused them to fidget in their tents, forcing them to emerge and start sharpening their swords and cleaning their shotguns.

He thought of Yusuf's betrayal. Perhaps he was too harsh on the man, too unforgiving. Perhaps not. Yusuf's actions towards the butcher were deliberate and merciless. Violence was a curse of human nature and it resulted in nothing but more and more killing until no one quite knew why they killed. Yusuf's actions not only inflicted a suffering honed and perfected through trial and error on an innocent man, but also put the whole city, if not country, in danger. The ripple effects of his actions were evident in the campfires lighting up the city and his inability to look Farook in the eye. Each person lived with the consequences of his actions and Farook felt no obligation to lighten the burden of men who so easily placed the burden of suffering on others.

Only science had the power to break the cycle of violence, not the Sultan concerned with the continuation of empire or a system with little concern for the truth of a God indifferent to the misery of man. Science laid out the case for justice by proving the methodology of a crime: the what, how and why. It measured the criminal act by the sophistication of its execution and mapped its results. From that the right proportion of justice could be allocated, handed out with not a pinch more.

Farook stopped in his thoughts. He knew what needed to be done next. His meeting with the cobbler left little doubt as to his guilt or at the very least the man knew more than he was telling. But even a little doubt was too much.

Assiya had led him to a lettered craftsman.

Souad had led him to the cobbler.

Maryam and the jewellery she wore on the visit to the French doctor had made him think of the wooden chest at the cobbler's shop. Perhaps that held the secret.

He did not need to investigate the other missing girls. Hajj Mesfewi's shop provided ample opportunity for further scrutiny, a crossroad where the stories of the three girls may have intertwined. He had to verify the cobbler's handwriting, inspect the wooden chest for its contents and question him about Souad. But more than anything, he needed evidence. Without hard evidence – evidence he could touch, smell, measure and trace – justice would remain aloof with oppression waiting in the shadows to take its place.

Perhaps the cobbler had already destroyed the ledger and emptied the chest. Why wouldn't he destroy the evidence, when he knew it was that which Farook wanted so badly?

Farook thought back to his time in London when he would listen to heated discussions in tearooms about the Whitechapel Crimes, even so many years after they had finally stopped. It was as though the killer, Jack the Ripper they called him, wanted to be caught. He left the gruesome evidence of his crimes out in the street, even mocking the police with letters. There was glory in recognition, not in the taking of secrets to the grave. The cobbler, or whoever he was protecting, did not want to be forgotten, he wanted to be written into the history of the city. The effort was too consistent, the numbers too high, and it could only mean the motive was more than the satisfaction of a twisted psychosis. He was orchestrating a macabre theatre in which he was the main actor on the stage. How could it be appreciated without a captive audience and props to demonstrate the extent of his intelligence?

Farook turned his face away from the campfires and walked towards the staircase. If only it was as simple as returning to the cobbler to demand he hand over the ledger and open the wooden chest. If he did, and even if he proved his suspicions, to whom would he hand the man over?

The Caliph? He would hang the culprit in public, all part of destabilizing his brother's seat on the throne.

The Pasha? He would discreetly hand him over to his army for them to rip his body and feed to the masses in defiance of the Caliph, emerging as triumphant over the city.

The Qadi? He would squander the opportunity to learn about the workings of an unusual mind by throwing him in the dungeon to rot.

And what about Yusuf? He would simply hand him over to the authority most explicit in its threats or promises.

Nothing would be achieved, no progress made. Farook was just another cog in the machine which churned out affliction on the city. For all his commitment to identify the criminal through physical evidence, that very evidence could be used to warrant other heinous crimes. It was true, science had the power to provide proof for good and lay out the case for justice, but it was also capable of rationalizing great evil. He would not sharpen the knife with which they would use to stab justice in the back. If it meant waiting for the right moment, until the situation in the city calmed so be it. He just needed to determine where Yusuf was with the case and what the cobbler was up to. His eyes found the half-closed door and the steps leading down to the funduq rooms. He knew just the person to gather that information.

40

A traitor to the Sultan

The Pasha stood holding two letters. One was sealed and the other ripped open, the red wax seal appeared like crusted blood around a jagged cut. Yusuf sat in the same position as usual, growing increasingly panicked at his involvement in the Pasha's plotting. If the Pasha called him to his palace than Yusuf appeared like a genie, ready to fulfil his every whim and ask no questions.

Despite the Pasha's earlier warning, Yusuf's investigation into the missing girls had practically been brought to a complete stop. Instead, he had spent the last few days running around the city, delivering messages to the Pasha's allies, and returning with observations for the old man. In a way, he could not complain. If he were left to investigate the girls he would be at a complete loss as to what to do and quickly expose his incompetence.

He had not seen Farook since their last meeting and was grateful for that too. Farook was alone in the city now, alienated from the authorities and with no local support. Though Yusuf secretly held on to the hope that he would get to the bottom of the missing women, in reality he had absolutely no idea how to go about doing so and suspected Farook was way ahead of him. He shouldn't have given him the notes about the other missing girls. It was another stupid decision, a moment of weakness.

Better that the Pasha keep him busy with menial tasks, at least then he was unable to do more damage. He could deliver on those and as long as he wasn't being asked to singlehandedly discover the girl's whereabouts; he could claim those tasks as reasons for his failure to do so.

He recalled Farook's ramblings about mint tea in the rain and after some distance saw the man as too philosophical for his own good. Yes, it was important to make sense of the world and one's fate and life experiences, but wallowing in emotion was unbecoming of a man. *What is passed is dead*, as his father liked to say. It was important to keep moving forward. Wallowing brought nothing good. If a man wants to drink tea in the sunshine he should drink tea in the sunshine. It was tea, not wine. There was no need to surround it with such profundity. Farook's principles were his greatest weakness. The world was immune to the musings of the soul, and required action and pragmatism, not deliberations about right and wrong. Whatever touchstone a man used to judge his actions, the world gave him a chisel to shape it. Yusuf had learnt that many times and yet somehow he kept making the same mistake.

The Pasha kept reaching under his turban to rub his bald head. He was reflecting, perhaps worried. Yusuf was quickly learning the Pasha's stress indicators and though being in the man's presence still unnerved him, he also fantasized about becoming indispensable after this mess with the Glaoui was over. He saw himself managing a spy network or overseeing the collection of revenue. It was that or escaping the city with whatever he could carry under his arms.

That Berber tribe was trouble. Its leader was capable of an evil planned down to every little detail in pursuit of his ambitions. The biggest mistake the previous Sultan made was giving them the 77-mm Krupp cannon, the only one in the entire country. With it the Glaoui subdued every warlord as far as the eye could see from their Kasbah in the Atlas. They had taken control of every trade route, enriched their treasuries with passage taxes, and now came out in support of Moulay Hafid. Their men were armed to the teeth and thirsty for blood. Their presence in the city soothed no one except the naïve. Despite reassurances coming out of the Caliph's palace, there was no safety in the city.

Only the Pasha seemed to feel safe. He did not appear so concerned about the visitors. He assured Yusuf they would not attack and that Moulay Hafid was not so brazen as to actually resort to violence against his brother. Their presence in the city was sufficient to deliver the message to the Sultan that his power was built on foundations that could be razed at any moment. According to the Pasha, they would eventually pack up their possessions and return to their mountain caves like the animals they were and then the city would return to normal. Yusuf hoped he was right. His wife was losing her nerve, stuck within the confines of the home with nothing to comfort her but chores and wailing children.

The Pasha handed one of the letters to Yusuf. He took it and looked the letter over. Despite the script, he recognized the hand. It was bold and confident, not stumbling as the letters dropped and rose above the lines.

'I cannot read English,' he stated matter-of-factly, returning the letter.

'I had someone translate it for me,' explained the Pasha as he placed the second letter on the side table. 'It was bound for Tangier,' he said, raising an eyebrow. Only God could protect Farook if he were selling secrets to Europe.

The Pasha cleared his throat.

My dear friend,

It has been too long since we last wrote and I hope this letter finds you in good health and spirit. Please send me news of Tangier and our friends. I long to return home and rest my eyes once more on the Mediterranean as it cuts between Europe and Africa, treating both shores as equals.

I have no doubt you are keeping abreast of events in Marrakesh through your network and specifically developments in my investigation, so I will not bore you with details here. Suffice it to say, the situation is bleak and the missing girls practically forgotten in the bedlam of political intrigue and ambition. You would think these girls' insentient beings, their life brought forward to serve the needs of others with no consideration that they too may have thoughts, feelings or, heaven-forbid, an opinion.

Woe to be a woman.

I find myself grateful for the body I was born into, something I have never before considered an advantage, but merely a fact of life. I now better appreciate how this has shaped my place in society, given me opportunity and through a simple thing of physical attribute allowed me to stand in this world with dignity and stature in a way denied to the opposite sex.

I say it once more, woe to be a woman.

I have made progress in the case despite the fact that my methods are misunderstood and mistrusted. Every small step forward has been marred by obstacle. I will not lie by claiming I have not felt defeated at times and my enthusiasm has occasionally evaporated in the growing heat of the spring. My convictions have been tested. But I have remained firm, certain in the knowledge that there is a better way.

Just as I ponder the fate of these girls, I find myself ever more curious of the man responsible for their fate, whatever that may be. I believe them to be dead and that a man, who knows this city well, to be responsible. My desire to discover the facts behind their disappearance is increasingly being overshadowed by an obsession to know the man responsible. It is no longer enough that I know what happened to them, I feel I must also know why. I want to know his history, motives and methods and I only hope that when the time comes the situation allows me to extract that information. You see I must know him, to understand the mind behind the act. If, as I suspect, the girls are dead it is already too late to help them. The most we can do is end the suffering of their families. But the case allows for so much more. We can speak to him and profile him so that in the future we recognize the behaviour for what it is.

I am not informed on studies of the mind or detective work and any education I have is self-taught. However, I cannot help but feel I am walking an unchartered path in Morocco and that emboldens me to test my ideas with practical application. And though this thought empowers me, it also frightens me. I often remind myself that there is much to be learnt from success, but even more from failure.

I have so much I would still like to say, but fear this letter may be intercepted and therefore must be careful with my words. I am confident I will be returning to Tangier soon and when I do I look forward to your warm hospitality and our long evenings of enlightened conversation.

Your friend,
Farook

Neither the Pasha nor Yusuf spoke for a while, both interpreting the letter in their own minds. Yusuf felt slightly embarrassed by its content. Its emotion was too raw and exposed for his sentiments. He cringed at what the Pasha must be thinking. It was humiliating for a man to talk the way Farook had in the letter, sympathizing with the opposite sex in a way that placed blame on man, when it was God who chose, in his wisdom, our place in the world. Of course their lives were hard, but so were men's. They carried the weight of responsibility on their shoulders as soon as the first fluffs of hair showed above their lip. If word got out about this letter, Farook would be humiliated and ridiculed. They might accuse him of blasphemy or acts that went against nature and all things sacred. It would destroy him. Yusuf visibly shuddered at the prospect.

The Pasha had still not spoken, turning the second letter in his hand. Yusuf waited for him to open it. He felt the anticipation in Yusuf's gaze and handed it to him to inspect. It was written in the same script. Yusuf wondered why it had not been opened.

'French,' said the Pasha. 'This was also sent from your friend, destined for Mogador.'

Yusuf looked up, he had not realized Farook was also literate in French.

'It is not from your friend,' continued the Pasha, reading Yusuf's thoughts. 'My informants tell me it is from the French doctor in the mellah. He has barricaded himself in the Jewish quarter along with the other foreign residents fearing for his life.'

Yusuf pondered the ramifications for a moment, blasphemy, perversion and now treason. Was Farook intent on self-destruction?

'Your friend from Tangier is working with the disbelievers,' the Pasha stated, drawing out the final word to imbibe it with as much venom as possible..

The accusation was far more serious than any empathy for women. The Pasha continued in his mindreading taking pleasure in any dregs of respect for Farook crumbling. 'We could throw him in the city prison and leave him to rot for this act alone. The Sultan will disassociate himself and let's see how long it takes the man to eat his imported shoes out of hunger.'

The blood drained from Yusuf's face. Farook had come undone after all. For all his intelligence he had made a fatal error that would see him spend his final days left to die of thirst or insanity – whichever came first. He felt a shudder come over him once more. Perhaps he should warn him, tell him to flee the city tonight. It would of course leave Yusuf in danger, but could he really sit back and watch Farook dragged to the dungeons like a common criminal? Farook, who he had shared endless bowls of couscous with, who despite his faults would not willingly hurt anyone. Was he truly capable of such an atrocity?

The Pasha smiled, no longer concealing his pleasure.

'Do not worry, I have no intention of acting against the man … yet.' His reassurance stopped short of consolation. 'The doctor is a coward. From the moment he entered the city he began his petitions to protect the foreign residents. Demand upon demand for guards and a constant need for assurances. This is probably another of his letters to his father or the French legation whining about the dangers of life in Marrakesh.'

Yusuf was starting to feel confused. Why had the Pasha not just opened the letter and read it, like Farook's?

'You, Si Yusuf, must ensure the letter is delivered unopened to Mogador and quickly.'

'I … I don't think I understand.'

'You don't need to understand, you just need to do. If the French think their people are in danger they will not hesitate to act, they are already looking for a pretext to turn their ships to Casablanca and this could be it.'

'But … But … We don't want them to turn their ships towards Morocco.' Yusuf wondered whose side the Pasha was really on.

'Don't be a fool … Of course we don't. But it will force the Sultan's hand, which is what we want. He will have no choice but to deal with his brother once and for all, and by doing so order will be restored to the city and I can return to my retirement. And my son can return to managing my affairs …" The Pasha paused for a moment, his thoughts returning to his son. The boy was probably still sleeping after whatever shenanigans had taken place the night before.

Yusuf took the opportunity to speak. 'Shall I deliver the letter myself?'

Foreign invasion was probably less treacherous then a perilous journey across lawless land.

The Pasha exhaled heavily. 'Must I explain every minor detail? No, have it delivered. I need you here, but make sure it is put directly into the hand of the person it is intended for and no one else.'

'And Farook al-Alami?'

'Leave him be for the moment. He has no more than two days left to report back to me. He is out of time. When he comes with nothing to show I will instruct him to leave the city by nightfall. As much as I would like to teach that man a lesson, I am not fool enough to do so while he sits under the wing of the Sultan. If he leaves then we will be rid of him for good and I will forward a report on to Fez. It will get there before he does. Let the Sultan deal with him. His imagination is so much more vivid than mine.'

'And what of the girls?'

'Girls?'

'The … missing girls,' Yusuf stuttered.

'Oh, yes. Of course. Them. Once this is over and the Glaoui and that man from Tangier have left the city then you can focus once more on discovering the cause for their disappearance. You have done such a fine job of it so far.' The sarcasm in his tone was subtle, but his smile left no room for doubt.

'Or, if you wish you can re-arrest the butcher. The choice is yours,' the Pasha concluded. He dismissed Yusuf with a wave of his hand.

41

A bundle of bones

The morning air was bright with the signs of an early summer. White storks swooped from their nests atop the city buildings and treetops to spread their strong wings lined with black feathers. They glided overhead looking for scraps for their emancipated offspring. The sound of their young calling for food littered the air with a frantic clicking as they sat impatiently in their conical nests. The nests were deep and large, but empty of provisions, like the baskets carried to market place.

Spring seemed to have already passed. It was just a brief memory except for the incessant clicking, a reminder to the world that new life had been born and came with its own demands. A bloated sun relentless in its punishment replaced the truncated spring which had refused the world its generosity. What little the harvest brought had been claimed by those old and astute enough to know the value of greed.

The streets and alleyways were desolate, despite the sunrise call to prayer which urged the city residents to bow in gratitude to God. They chose to stay in their dreams which were filled with succulent roasted meats and steamed vegetables atop mounds of fluffy couscous, rather than wake to the nightmare of babies crying out in hunger and their own growling stomachs. God had abandoned them. Why should they forsake their dreams for such an ungenerous creator? They prayed in their homes and in their mosques for what felt like an eternity. They pleaded and begged and yet still they continued to be afflicted with one calamity after another, a relentless shower from above that failed in its nourishment of either their land or their souls. 'Patience is half of religion,' the imams fed them with a wooden spoon as though patience satiated hunger while the Sultan and his officials sat on their divans with stomachs that knew no season or drought. So, they lingered in their dreams filling their stomachs with the taste of resentment, spiced with the fortifying flavour of rebellion.

Except for a few – who had long since comprehended that patience was a construct designed to silence the complaints of the poor – the promise of a better life to come appeased their demand for one worth living now. Those men left their homes confident in their own creation and purpose, needing neither mercy nor food to keep them on their path.

He stood outside his door watching the alleyway for any others, who may also be out at this early hour demanding their rewards from this life and leaving to God what the next might bring. He saw no one.

He lifted the bundle and tied it onto his back, a thick woollen blanket gathered and knotted in the middle to hold its unworldly content. He rushed down the alleyway, cursing time and its determined march forward. He had hoped to leave sooner, just after the call to prayer when the sky still cast shadows into the alleyways, but it took longer than expected. Instead, the only shadow was that which he cast with his own body and the bundle on his back, making his form deformed and hunchbacked against the walls. *Perhaps that was best*, he thought to himself as he heaved the bundle further up his back – *hide in plain sight*.

He marched forward, keeping his frame bent to better distribute the weight and he thought about the long sleepless night just passed. He did not even find the time to pat down his jellaba. It was caked in dust and earth. He only hoped if he were to pass anyone they would see him as nothing but a destitute, who carried his worldly belongings out of the city to seek provision on an unmapped road, one that had been formed by the shuffled steps of all the others before him.

He too heard the rumours the city was emptying itself. Many of the visiting tribesmen chose to return to their homes in the mountains, having depleted Marrakesh's resources and hospitality. Some of the residents chose to escape rather than fight. How committed they were to their departures was anyone's guess. The steady stream of pack-laden mules and caravans at the gates suggested they were certain, but the slightest hint of hope or opportunity would have them rushing back.

He stopped for a moment, thinking he heard the shuffling of small feet behind him. He turned, the bundle restricting his movements. He was alone in the alleyway. Looking about, he considered the rumours might be true after all and continued on his journey. As he came into courtyards he saw the residue of previous occupiers: garbage; the stench of horse manure; blackened earth where their fires burnt; and outlines where tents had once stood. He felt relief and allowed his mind to roam back to the previous night. It had been both beautiful and painful and while nerves had left his heart pumping, he had also savoured every moment. It felt like the goodbye he had always craved, but which had been denied to him by history and circumstance. Yet it was circumstance that forced him to act and by the end of the long night he thanked it. Practicality had yielded a gratifying closure; one that he would cherish through whatever came next. He needed only a few more days to complete his work and knew what that meant. It meant he would soon have to answer for his actions. Soon he would join the millions of others who had passed through this world and knew the truth of what lay beyond it. A truth which was denied to those still attached to the mendacity of life. And while that filled him with fear, as the passage would no doubt be painful, it came with sweet anticipation. He could explain it finally. He knew who it must be to, the one who desired to understand his reasons, who might be capable of comprehending his mission.

His assembly had been forgiving, patient and generous through the long night. Even Assiya had silenced her complaints. Perhaps finally understanding that it was already too late, she had found comfort with her companions. That was ultimately what he wanted for her and what he tried to give her. He left her in her stillness and took others instead. Why disturb her when she had finally accepted her place? He recalled his uncle in those long lost days of peace and security. 'Keep your liver clean,' he would say. 'The liver is the centre of emotion and intention is everything. If it is unclean whatever good comes from your actions will not return to you.' His intentions had always been good. While his methods were debatable, he checked himself when the distaste for what he felt compelled to do turned to pleasure. He kept his pleasure in check through self-reproach so as to keep his intentions and liver clean.

Of course, when his scheme was finally exposed then the accusations would fly, much like the white storks above, scattered in all directions. Apostasy, possession by djinn, insanity, pure evil, or all of them together. Only the few would comprehend it. Only Farook al-Alami would see through the lies and desperation to explain it as an anomaly, a bastard act with no relation to the world in which it was born. Al-Alami would understand that his actions were driven by sound thought and good intention and designed to correct the injustice of power.

The results of his labour were already evident. Panic was rising and with it anger. It had burrowed deep into the complex bureaucracies of control within the city. It was not just that the grumbling of empty stomachs seemed more pronounced. The complaints of the poor were as old as the Marrakesh's fountains and the makhzan had ways of appeasing them: sacks of wheat delivered to the most destitute neighbourhoods; the feeding of the homeless in Jemaa el-Fnaa; extra night prayers in the mosques; lambs sacrificed in public spaces and the meat passed to grabbing hands and even the announcement festivals and public entertainment. The cycle repeated itself according to the season and the makhzan had learnt the best way to appease the multiple complaints of the masses was to take the wind out of them, by providing momentary satisfaction or distraction. By the time they awoke from their slumber – induced by full stomachs or late nights of prayer or revelry – they would have forgotten what it was they complained about. Until the season changed and those old resentments returned to swell and ebb once more. It was nature's rhythm and could not be disrupted, only intensified and repeated endlessly, like the life cycle of Man himself.

But the details of each ebb and flow were recorded in history. Their cause and the effect was noted in books which were prized and passed from one keeper to another. The nuances now were the most interesting they had ever been and they were a direct result of his efforts. As he walked towards his destination, the weight of the bundle sitting heavy on his back, he could not help but smile at what had already been achieved. The Pasha sat in his palace tasting the same fear as those of the men whose backs he broke to build it. Men like his uncle. His tribe had always been loyal to the Sultan and submissive to his divinity. The one time they resisted they were met with a violence which stamped their blood into the ground and out of the annals of time. Surrounded by a paraphernalia of power that offered him little comfort now, the Pasha sat worrying about the posterity of his life and plotting to undermine the Caliph. The city could come to war. The whole country could be embroiled in internal fighting, late to realize that the real enemy was the one from within, the corrupt and diseased liver of this once pure nation. It was already happening.

And the Caliph. What of him?

Moulay Hafid furthered his scheme more than anyone else and openly acknowledged its significance on the pulpit of the Koutoubia

Mosque. In a backhanded compliment, the Caliph used his assembly to exacerbate the city's state of fear and then flexed his army in his brother's face. He did not once anticipate his work would play such a significant role in the cannibalism of those hungry for power, only that it would magnify the rottenness of the banquet. Once more, he felt a surge of gratitude for the invisible hand that worked with him and not against him. He was on a noble cause.

He felt the muscles in his cheeks ache, realizing his grin had spread wide across his face. He was not far from the garden. Once at the end of this street he would turn left to see the wall demarcating the Jewish cemetery. He looked up at the way ahead and his smile dropped from his face. Ahead stood a group of four men dressed in blue. They carried their weapons for everyone to see and concealed their faces behind a veil. How stupid of him to let down his guard. They watched as he hesitated. They silenced their chatter and waited for him to cross their path.

He had no choice but to pass them. If he turned back their curiosity would only be confirmed. They would chase after him to find out what he was hiding, to quell their boredom, if nothing else.

He continued on, adding a low prayer to his steps in the hope they would see only a man short of a sane mind or a wandering marabout short of a home. As he got closer, the stench of their unwashed bodies filled his nostrils and he resisted the urge to gag. They watched as he passed. Their bodies had frozen as though hunting game in the desert. Only their eyes followed him. They drew their impressions from the frown crossing his forehead; the dust covering his clothes; his mumbling; and the weight of the bundle on his back.

They remained silent. As he passed he felt a trickle of relief.

'What do you have there?' One of the men asked to his back, his tongue was as foreign to this city as his clothes. He stopped. He had exposed himself and his mission to unnecessary risks lately and perhaps now fate had finally abandoned him to face the consequences alone. He could drop the bundle and run away from the men to the nearest gate. He could exit the city and abandon his plans or he could turn and face them, fight them if he had to. He knew he would never run; it was not an option.

He turned to them, lifting the bundle on his back and tightening his grip around the knot. 'Stale bread for my chickens,' he replied, lowering his eyes to their feet in false humility and hoping they would not hear the rattling of the sack's contents.

'Bring some here,' ordered the same man, the leader of the four. 'We have not eaten since last night.'

He struggled to find a suitable response. His mind went blank, unable to conjure a way out.

'It's stale,' was all he managed to say.

The man shifted his weight and menacingly touched the blade strapped to his hip. Then he slapped his friend's shoulder and let out a booming laugh.

'You think we care about a bit of staleness? We are desert folk.' He smacked his chest in pride. 'Our stomachs were built for hardship.' The other three men grinned toothlessly in agreement.

'Now hand me some bread,' he said, the smile had left his face as quickly as it appeared. The other men stepped towards him.

Only divine intervention would save him now. Fate would either fulfil her part of the agreement or he would find out he had made a deal with the devil. If they opened the bundle it would all be over, his assembly scattered across the alleyway.

'I … I can bring you some fresh bread from the baker. If you just let me deliver this load I will return with bread still steaming,' he stuttered. He should have said he was delivering supplies to his master, perhaps indicating his master to be a wealthy man of influence.

'You son of a whore,' the man bellowed. He took pleasure in the signs of fear in his victim. 'If I say give me bread you give me bread. Don't you know we are here by invitation of the Sultan? Do you wish to defy your Lord by refusing to feed his guests?'

The other three men nodded, stifling their laughter.

215

'You city folk are an ungrateful bunch of heathens. You know no hardship or survival. You can all rot from disease as far as I care.' He made to grab the bundle.

Taking a step back and gripping the knot even tighter, he prepared himself for the beating that would come, perhaps a beating that would propel him into the next world where he could meet fate and ask her why she tricked him so.

He felt his stomach churn from sick disappointment and the bile rise to his throat. His chest constricted and forced him to lean forward. He opened his mouth to gasp for breath. Had the beating already started? Why were the men stepping away?

He tasted the bile as it filled his mouth and then it projected out splattering the leader's face and clothes with a green slime. His friends stepped further back in horror as they watched a man they all feared flap his hands in panic.

'Bring me a cloth,' he screamed. A dirty rag was handed to him and he wiped his face frantically.

'I have been sick,' he muttered, feeling the weight of the bundle still steady on his back. He wiped the green vomit from his mouth with his sleeve.

They all stopped and looked at him anew, his dirty clothes, his stoop and earlier mumbling. Perhaps destitute, perhaps diseased, either way his stale bread no longer held the appeal of earlier. He looked at them with pathetic eyes. Could it be fate had not abandoned him after all? Had fate remained inactive for but a moment only to test his resolve and to then take control of his body to deliver him from his predicament?

42

Salt in her hair

That stork would die today. If nothing else were achieved, she would kill that stork sitting atop her house and roast it for dinner. At least then she might be able to serve some meat to her husband and children and stop having to listen to their complaints of hunger, as though she didn't have her own to suppress. The only one who never complained was her daughter Assiya. Like the apothecaries in their laboratories dotted around the city, her daughter had always found a cure for every affliction. Except, unlike them, she was not full of false promises. The poor girl learnt early there was no such thing as miracles, only patience.

Men and children, they were the same. They had no resilience and drew the whole world into their misery. She had spent her entire life bent forward in service to either men or children, remaining silent, stifling her complaints though they were no less real. And now that stork with its clicking offspring woke her every morning at the crack of dawn to interrupt her already restless sleep. As though it was not bad enough that she had to watch her children wither in front of her very eyes – their frail bodies looked like they would break in half from the slightest bump – she now had this constant reminder that their lives were as pathetic and insignificant as the chicks in the nest above her, their right to survival no more legitimate.

She secretly hoped Assiya had run away and not come to the horrible end being suggested by the neighbours. Her husband could say what he liked about honour and shame, but honour satisfied male egos not empty stomachs. Lying awake with her husband snoring in his deep slumber beside her and the children scattered around the floor, she imagined her daughter in Mogador or Tangier, the salt catching in her hair. In her fantasy, Assiya was sat on the shore with her hair flowing free. The sea wind caught her thick black locks and sent them in every direction. Assiya would remove her hair from her face so she could look out on the open expanse of the Atlantic, her aspirations reaching as far as the horizon.

She did not care what they said about her daughter; let them whisper that she was a vixen, witch or whore. Their words could not touch her now, whatever her fate. Cursed beings, women were trapped by their bodies from the moment they were born to the moment they died. If a woman rebelled, she was labelled and shunned. Rebellion came in many forms, but after the first minuscule sign of it then a young girl was forever watched in fear she may shame a man, but only in the eyes of other men and complicit women. Whatever God thought mattered less.

And if she complied her fate was even worse. Doomed to bring child after child into the world, feed and clean and worry about them, serve her husband and never dare raise her eyes or voice to the injustice of it all until the day came for her body to give up its strength and she died in either childbirth or resignation. At no point during her ordeal did anyone consider for a moment she may be capable of something more or perhaps they feared just that. If women were taught to read and write only the Almighty knows what rights they might discover in the holy text, and only then would every man truly know female strength.

Assiya had always been strong, a rebellious streak ran through her from the moment she learnt to grab her mother's breast and draw it to her mouth. She had decided at a very young age, before she could even sit up, that she would do as she willed and though often it led to smacks from her father and sobs into her mother's chest, in her young mind it was the price you paid for freedom. Not freedom of the body, the female form was acquisitioned from the moment the midwife parted the screaming baby's leg: claimed and promised to someone else. It was freedom of the mind Assiya had always fought for and despite her fears of what might have happened to her daughter's body in her quest, she decided to believe her spirit was free.

Lifting herself from the raised mattress, she stepped over the sleeping forms of her children and went into the other room. Looking around her, she saw how much needed doing. The floor sweeping, the bedding and blankets that her family continued to sleep in in the next room taken to the roof to be beaten and aired, the water fetched from the fountain, the dough prepared and taken to the public oven, breakfast, the dishes, the room in which they slept swept and aired and then the few vegetables left in the basket in the corner peeled and chopped to make the broth to accompany the bread. And then she would have to think about what she would feed them in the evening. There would be no meat today, despite her plans for the stork. If Assiya were here she would have crawled from her corner in the next room and quietly helped her mother with her chores, offering comforting companionship through her silence.

Looking down at herself, her mother saw her dishevelled state. Her housedress was crinkled and fraying at the seams. She touched her hair and felt the knots and grease in it from not having visited the hammam for so long. She felt unclean and old. Her spent youth was marked by the early lines across her face and hands cracked and hard.

She went over to the corner of the room and took an earthenware jar from a nook in the wall. She shook it and felt the few contents clink against each other. They were the only coins left from the meagre savings she managed over the last year from the household income. If her husband did not bring home something today then tomorrow they would all go hungry. She needed to wash desperately. The smell of her stale sweat lingered around her. But she also needed food for the evening. If she left it to the late morning, the prices in the market might drop a little as the sellers tried to rid themselves of the rotting vegetables. But there was also the chance there would be nothing left.

Deciding there was nothing to do until her husband awoke, she busied herself with the list of chores. The disappearance of her daughter had had an adverse effect on her freedom of movement. Her husband ordered her to keep her appearance in public to a minimum to show some humility in the face of the scandal. Now, with the added public panic and makhzan order to keep women in doors she had not left the house in days.

She grabbed her hair and pulled at it in frustration. The pain cut through the weight on her heart. She kept pulling, enjoying the feeling of resistance in her scalp and the breaking of individual hairs as they came loose in her hand. She stifled a wail, so desperate to scream out and bang her head against the walls, to smack her face repeatedly.

Instead, she covered her mouth with her hand and sobbed into it. Suppressing her gasps for air, she sobbed with her whole body shuddering as each wave overcame her, not sure which of her many afflictions she was grieving for. Hearing a sound from the other room, she quickly straightened her back and wiped her face of tears.

The curtain, frayed like her housedress, parted and her husband stepped into the room, his loose trousers gathered around his groin. Rubbing his eyes, he looked at his wife as though beholding her for the first time on their wedding night, uncertain and nervous.

'Why are you up so early?'

She lashed out at his question.

'Because I am damned to be a woman.'

Her husband looked around the room in search of a reason for her outburst. 'The children need to eat,' she complained, knowing the ticking of his mind and the conclusions he had just drawn. A host of reasons for her behaviour were crowding his mind and not one of them pointed in his direction. He rubbed the sleep from his eyes, regretting having succumbed to curiosity and leaving the comfort of his mattress.

'I will go to the market later and see what there is.'

'No!' she screamed. Her protestation died in her throat. It was as if it was the first time in their married life she had used the word.

'I will go. If I do not leave this house I will kill someone.'

He shrugged his consent, unable to find the strength to argue.

'Fine, but not now. The market will not have opened and the streets will be deserted except for criminals and vagabonds. Make do with what you have and go later in the day.' He turned back and retreated into the next room to step back into his dreams. His wife returned to her choked sobs and thoughts of Assiya with salt in her hair.

43

A female presence

The room was smothered in darkness with only a thin line of grey light coming through the crack between the floor and the bedroom door. Farook lay awake counting the time since the call to prayer. The melody had woken him a few hours earlier and since then he had stayed on his back staring up at the barely visible wooden beams above.

He wanted to jump out of the covers and begin his day. He was never one to linger in bed, unless a vivid dream kept him there. When that happened, he liked to take a moment to locate the origins of the dream in a thought, sight or experience in the real world. Understanding its origin in order to dispel its myth.

But he could not recall his dreams of the previous night, if there had been any at all. Yet something kept him firmly rooted in his position, like a weight on his chest not heavy enough to choke his breathing but impossible to ignore. A presence was the only way he could think to describe it. He tried to locate the source as he felt the pressure pin him further into his hard mattress.

He did not believe in djinn or ghosts. He thought the existence of a mischievous species made from fire to spread trouble and havoc from some invisible realm was a convenient belief that kept man ignorant of the world and subservient to a version of reality based in nothing but myth and superstition. Almost anything and everything was blamed on djinn. If a man, close to the end of his years, left the wife who had suffered him throughout her youth to marry a young maid, the djinn were blamed. The young maid must have conjured malicious spirits to whisper into his ear as he slept to win his heart and property. If a woman bore female child after female child and never a male, it was nothing physical, but the outcome of a deal her enemy must have struck with an evil spirit to deny her husband an heir. Behind every calamity sat a djinn manipulating cosmic powers for entertainment or bribery. The djinn stories most people had grown up with provided an easy cover for human fallacy and a way of denying responsibility for choices made.

Persistent, he thought, *definitely a female presence.*

He resisted his thoughts, uncomfortable with the idea of believing there was actually a female energy in the room, but the stillness unnerved him. It was strong and patient. It was calm, as though it had all the time in the world to wait for him to accept this new reality. He closed his eyes and breathed deeply into his chest, hoping to dislodge the troubling mood it left him with. Taking a few breaths, making each longer than the last, a feeling, as vivid as one of his rare dreams overcame him.

The missing girls were people. They were people like him, with feelings and hopes, good days and bad.

The details of their lives were part of a mystery that consumed him since arriving in the city. He felt empathy for their families and a paternal sadness for their wretched lives. But his motivation to discover what happened to them was cerebral and fed by an obsession to get to the truth. He reminded himself they were not just a series of facts and discoveries to make sense of, but whole people with fears and aspirations.

Assiya had aspirations, hopes for a life filled with laughter and love. She still did. They all did. Her rebellion against social rules of propriety had resonated with him from the very beginning and he couldn't help but feel he knew the girl, though he had never seen her face. It was that of a fighter. This seemed clearer to him now than before. The confidence in her letters to her lover, her boldness and her determination to pursue the yearnings of her young heart made her seem more real to him than the others. She seemed like a person who perhaps he had much in common with. She was most likely dead, but her hopes had not rotted with her corpse. Somehow she was still fighting.

He opened his eyes and found the pressure on his chest had softened. Farook rose from his bed slowly, straightened his nightclothes and made his way to the door. Opening the door he stepped out onto the balcony and looked down into the funduq's interior courtyard. He looked for the young kitchen boy in his usual position curled up in a corner, but could not see him. Perhaps he was already in the kitchen stoking the fire to cater to the demands of the funduq patrons, their numbers thinning, much to the disappointment of the proprietor.

The city would soon wake too and begin its cycle, a routine established by the first settlers in the region – no doubt a few men traversing the mountains in their caravan, pitching their tents in search of water. Then the Almoravid dynasty came and built high walls from the earth up to demarcate the line between nature and man, wilderness and civilization. It was an unforgiving city, with commerce in its blood. Every life could be quantified, a value attached to it depending on how much it took from the communal pot. Looking down once more, he saw the kitchen boy enter the courtyard from the front door. Farook looked at him quizzically. The boy nodded and went towards the kitchen.

Farook returned to his room. It felt vacant, the earlier presence had fled. Perhaps it had just been a figment of the imagination, conjured as he wavered between sleep and consciousness. He rubbed his fingers against his ribs, creating an echo of the pressure that had held him to his bed, certain that the constriction of his chest wasn't merely a figment of his dream-addled imagination.

He went to the speaking pictures and, hesitating, took them down one by one. Without haste, he folded them and placed them on his desk next to the love letters. He would take them back to Tangier and file them. One day perhaps he would look at them again, but they were no longer needed. He would act on his wits now, not his mind. He loitered for a while, waiting for the kitchen boy. There was no rush. A lurking sense of imminence, a foreboding that very soon it would all come together, told him he was doing the right thing. The presence in his room earlier that morning urged him forward. Yet he hoped he was not losing his mind and was not being lead, like his first day in the city, into a dead end. Intuition would have to be his guide.

Mohammed tapped on the door and entered, quietly closing it behind him. His face was flushed red and his eyes bright with information.

'What do you have to report?' Farook asked him. He saw in front of him a man, aged by experience but trapped in the body of a child. He spoke to that man.

The boy tried to speak with authority, raising his chest and meeting Farook in his eye.

'He hasn't left his house for a day. After his last visit to the Pasha he called a messenger to the house. I followed the messenger and he set off on the road to Mogador. I haven't seen him since.'

Farook nodded. Yusuf was too busy facilitating the Pasha's plans. The missing girls were probably the last thing on his mind.

'And the other one?'

Despite his illiteracy and the fact that he could not even say from which village he came, the young boy in front of him had an intelligence and work ethic that surpassed most makhzan officials.

'I followed him this morning,' he started. His speech speeded up so that Farook had to place his hand on his shoulder to calm him.

225

Smiling, the boy continued. 'I thought he was going to the mosque, but he carried a bundle on his back.'

'Where did he go?'

'I don't know. He was stopped by a group of men in blue and I was too scared to pass them. They let him continue on his journey but I had to go back.'

Farook nodded, patting Mohammed on his back.

Mohammed lowered his head. 'I am sorry for my lack of courage, master.'

'You did a great job, Mohammed. You were right to go back. If you are in danger you always retreat, do you understand?'

Mohammed nodded gently.

'Tell me,' Farook asked, 'if you were to guess where he was going in the city, where would it be?'

Pausing for a moment, Mohammed retraced his steps. It was a part of the city he did not know well. But, of course the wall, everyone knew the wall.

'He was heading towards the mellah. He was stopped just before the Jewish cemetery.'

'So you would say he was going to the Jewish quarter?'

'No,' said Mohammed. 'The gates are closed at that time and they are not letting anyone in at present anyway. There are private gardens not far from there. If I were to guess, I would say he was going there.'

Farook paused for a moment. So he has a private garden.

'Mohammed,' said Farook. 'Prepare the water for my ablutions. It is time I complete my work here.'

44

A yellow housedress

Assiya's mother cursed herself for choosing today to leave the house and fight her husband's reservations. The late morning heat beat down on her as she made her way through the market as the sweat drops trickled down her back and gathered beneath her malhaf. She should have been more selective with the timing of her ultimatum. She should have waited until a fresh breeze came in from the desert to lift the stench of garbage and unwashed bodies from the city streets. Like her, the inhabitants seemed to have given up on bathing and the air, normally filled with the scent of spices and musk from the various stalls, carried an odour of neglect and decay. It smelt like rot.

The market seemed so empty, devoid of produce and people to buy them. It was only the week before that the city's population had swelled in number as the tribesmen from the surrounding mountains and desert camped in every available spot awaiting further instruction. Though there were enough of them around to still feel their menacing presence, the numbers had dwindled. The inhabitants – those who dared to venture out – lurked. They seemed to be moving in a slumber, delaying every step as though they had no destination in particular to reach. She always thought of Marrakesh as resilient, defiant in the face of what God, nature and man rendered on her. But everyone seemed so defeated. Just as she found the strength to fight, the battle was lost.

What would become of them? Would it ever return to the way it was? Perhaps for the city, but never for her. She knew that already. She may never find out what happened to her daughter, but she already felt the pangs of grief from the loss and knew they would remain with her, a worthy acquaintance to accompany her through the monotony of hardship.

Stopping at a cart piled with fresh chamomile flowers, she lifted a stem and placed it to her nose. It was devoid of scent. The emptiness in her nostrils confirmed the lifelessness in the small yellow buds. She placed it back onto the cart and caught the disappointment in the seller's eyes. Shrugging her shoulders she continued through the market.

She stopped at a few sellers to inspect their vegetables laid out on nothing but the bare ground. Taking her time, she walked deeper into the market until she found a cart with decent enough produce, the cart owner joyless with empty eyes. She examined each vegetable pile carefully until she had acquired a sufficient amount, feeling his vacant eyes observe her indifferently. Handing them to the seller, she watched him silently weigh them on his rusted scales. She did not recognize him and looking around saw a number of faces she had not seen before. The regular market stall holders were nowhere to be seen.

The seller clicked his tongue to draw her attention and indicated the amount. Realizing she did not have enough, she began to remove a few from the scales. Her embarrassment was apparent in the mild tremor of her hands. The seller looked her up and down with what she thought was disdain, as though she was buying so little. Gathering the vegetables in her basket she handed him the remainder of her money. He looked at the two battered coins in her outstretched hand longingly. And then, as though overcome with benevolence, smiled and shook his head, his eyes alive with sudden warmth.

Feeling caught between the desire to reject the charity and an over-whelming relief that she could feed the children again tomorrow, she resolved to retrace her steps and purchase some chamomile from the previous cart owner to correct her lack of trust in God. She picked up her basket and thanked the man for the produce and the lesson, before beginning her return journey home.

Pausing for a moment, she changed her mind. Why the rush? The prospect of once more being confined to the two narrow rooms of her home was depressing. She would walk a bit further, stretch her legs and enjoy the freedom, however short-lived it might be.

So she continued. She adopted the same slow pace as everyone else and found unexpected pleasure in the stifling heat. Stopping here and there to inspect produce she had no intention of purchasing, she nod-ded at the unfamiliar cart owners. Some nodded back, while others looked right through her.

As the vegetables on display gave way to other merchandise she turned a corner, finally seeing a familiar face ahead. Making her way through the thin crowd, who, like her, carried their last remaining coins with intent to spend them wisely, she stopped and knelt down to come eye level with the lady. Between them sat a pile of musty and tattered clothes, unsold and gathering dust.

'Anything new, my dear friend?' she asked.

The woman looked through her cataracts eyes and after a delayed recognition, they embraced in warm greeting.

'Where have you been?' her old friend responded.

She shrugged, grateful for an opportunity to talk to someone other than her children or husband.

'Ha,' retorted the woman in understanding. 'One day when you are old and almost blind like me it will become easier. How is your family?'

'Well, thank God.'

'Ha,' the woman blurted once more. It was her favourite way to begin any sentence. 'The God you thank is a man and, while we may have many things to thank them for, what they give is only what they want you to have. It's what they deny us that is so precious.'

She nodded in agreement. Why should she be denied anything?

'So, anything new?' she asked again in a humorous tone.

The old woman shook her head. 'Nothing. In times like these clothes do not sell and I barely eat. But what need does an old woman have with food?'

She felt the sadness begin to descend on her once more and in a bid to delay it made ready to leave.

'I must go. The children are waiting.'

The old woman nodded.

'Actually, I do have something new,' she recalled.

Assiya's mother knelt back down, anything to forestall the return home. The old lady felt the clothes on her right with her aged hands until she happened on the item she had in mind. Reaching beneath a pile of what looked like useless cut-offs she withdrew a yellow garment.

'This came in just a few days ago. It was a bit dusty but it's in good condition.'

She took the garment from the old lady and opened it up. It was a yellow house kaftan.

The earth lurched beneath her. Instinctively, she pulled the garment to her face and inhaled deeply, her mind not quite comprehending what her senses were telling it. She looked at the garment again in disbelief and then once more brought it to her nose to inhale. Beyond the smell of earth and another person's body odour she picked up a hint of the sweet scent of Assiya. She held the garment to her face while breathing in, not sure if her nose was deceiving her. But she knew the scent well from the years spent sniffing Assiya's neck and arms when she was younger: a game of intimacy she played with all her children. And though the colour had faded, she knew the dress, had watched her daughter put it on and proudly parade around the house. It could not be hers. It just couldn't be. She looked at the patterning to be sure.

'Where did you get this from?' She shook the kaftan in front of the old woman's unseeing eyes. Her voice quivered over every word. 'Where?'

The woman stuttered. 'A la ... lady brought it to me only a few days ago. I paid a good price. Why? What has come over you?'

'Which lady? Tell me which lady.' She couldn't control her voice.

The woman paused, fearful of where this sudden panic might lead and what she could be dragged into.

'I ... I don't know. I don't remember. I want no trouble from you or anyone else.' Retracting the familiarity they shared only moments ago, she snatched the housedress from her and returned it to the pile. Assiya's mother grabbed the old lady by the shoulders and shook her violently.

'You're lying!' People around them stopped to watch. Time froze in the alleyway: bundles of parsley held in front of noses; a broom suspended in a store owner's hand that moments ago he was using to sweep the ground; a child with his finger up his nose and his mother's hand inches from his face as she was about to smack it away. Ignoring the attention, the adrenalin rushed through every vein of her body and her mind crowded with a host of thoughts.

'You're lying,' she screamed again. 'Tell me who she was or I swear by God I will report you to the makhzan. Who was she?'

The old lady went frail from the shaking and lowered her head in physical exhaustion.

'Take it if you want it. I won't charge you. Just take it and leave me in peace.'

She took her last coins from under her malhaf and shoved them into the old lady's hands. 'Tell me who brought this to you,' she begged. 'For the sake of my children and all that is good, just tell me.' Tears swelled in her eyes. The adrenalin receded to leave behind nothing but the dreams she once had for her daughter, now broken. The old woman looked up at her friend and placed a comforting hand on her arm. With that one gesture the spell was broken: the man at the herb cart continued to sniff the parsley; the storekeeper returned to sweeping the floor; the mother smacked her son's hand away from his nose. The old lady spoke gently to her friend, rubbing her arm to relieve a pain beyond the reach of physical touch.

'I bought it from a woman that comes by sometimes. She lives not too far from here,' she explained. Assiya's mother listened in surprise as the clothes seller described her and realized that she knew exactly who she was and had even once long ago sent her daughter there on an errand.

45

Four choices

Grabbing the yellow kaftan and shoving it in her basket, she stood up and ran out of the market until she reached Jemaa el-Fnaa. She stopped in the middle of the square and spun around oblivious to the people watching as they passed. She breathed heavily against her veil and searched for a path to take. There were too many to decide from.

She spun towards the direction of home. If she went home her husband would take control of the situation. He would order her to prepare lunch while he went out getting to the truth about a daughter he had already forgotten or he might bury the housedress in the back of the wardrobe and pretend it had never found its way home. And yet if she didn't go home … Well, it was impossible to predict how far his anger would stretch or how long it might last. Any freedom she might enjoy would be the first sacrifice as he sought to reclaim his honour. What was freedom anyway, when everywhere you turned you saw the vacant spot your daughter left behind?

She could go directly to the woman and wave the housedress in her face demanding answers. If she refused her questions she would stand there the whole day and night into the following morning striking her face and wailing until the whole city came to demand an explanation. She would not leave until something was done. But what if she wasn't there or refused to even answer the door? She would be ignored, as another person littering the streets of the city, driven to insanity by desperation.

She began to shake with fear and frustration. Uncontrollable tears rolled down her face and wet her veil. *My Assiya. My darling Assiya, what did they do to you?* She stifled a sob, but if it were up to her she would throw herself on the ground and rip at her clothes and skin. *I cannot grieve for you. They won't even give me that.* She wiped her eyes and breathed deeply, calming her cries. She looked around the square. A few people turned to look back at her after noticing her state, but most took no real interest. The square had hosted stranger sights.

She should report it directly to the makhzan. It would be better that way. She could not be accused of making a scene or defying decency. They would not be able to ignore her. The whole city was talking about nothing else; the Caliph himself had mentioned it in the mosque or so she was told. They were as desperate for answers as she was. That Yusuf al-Mahdi would have to listen. His eyes could glaze over when he saw her all he liked but when she gave him the housedress and pressed it into his hands he would have no choice. She didn't like the man. He was no different from all the others, but he was responsible for investigating and was known for getting answers. All that mattered was that he went straight to the woman to find out why she had Assiya's housedress.

She looked north towards the market area and then swung to face the Koutoubia Mosque. The man from Tangier seemed genuine when they had met in the souk. He was the only one who seemed to actually care about what happened to Assiya, who saw her grief. She recalled the accusatory stares of everyone she came across, the attendant at the public bakery ignored her amongst the crowd and the women in the hammam fell silent when she entered. She had failed as a mother and

234

a wife to raise a decent girl and to protect her family honour. But not him. He had not judged her, not looked at her through condescending eyes. There was not even pity in his eyes, only a desire to hear her account of events, hers from her very own lips. He would take her seriously and investigate. She could find him and give him the housedress.

If there was no more courage then she had to find some. It didn't matter how deep she would have to dig. She had to find that last bit of strength and make a choice. She had to take action and not leave it to her husband. Assiya would be her muse.

46

Oaths made and broken

Yusuf was utterly exhausted by the Pasha's constant complaining and scheming. For a man who claimed to be a victim of his position, forced to take decisions that went against his religious beliefs and moral code, he seemed to take great pleasure in plotting the downfall of others. He secretly despised the man. He could not be trusted. He would sell your heart to a sorceress while it was still beating in your chest. And when he wasn't complaining or scheming, he was celebrating his victories. Forced to listen to the Pasha's lengthy descriptions of victimhood, his revengeful designs and grand accounts of triumphs over his enemies, all in one sitting, Yusuf's nerves were in ruin. Worse still, Yusuf was overcome with paranoia. He had not slept through the night for what seemed like forever, waking in a cold sweat and reaching out to find his wife's body just to ensure he was still there and not on some cold, damp dungeon floor. He lost his appetite, something that even physical illness had never diminished in the past. And the Pasha enjoyed it. He relished watching Yusuf's mind crumble before him, played tricks on him, made masked threats and then offered nuggets of comfort just when Yusuf was on the brink of collapse. He was beginning to wonder if physical torture was better than this mental hell.

At first he tried to understand why someone would take such pleasure in doing this to others. A man had to do what he had to do when extracting confessions from criminals, but this was different. It served no purpose except gratification of a perverted mind. But now he didn't care. He didn't want to understand it. He just wanted to get himself as far away from the Pasha as possible.

It was too late of course. There was no way he could extract himself from the vast web of trickery the Pasha wove. He had no choice but to see it through and hope he had sided with the writers of history and not those whose stories they omitted.

He berated himself over and over for capitulating to his weaker self. He was a fool to have ever doubted Farook al-Alami, not just his manner of thinking but his intentions too. Compared to the Pasha, Yusuf realized Farook was a man you could trust with your very life, your family's life. He would never cheat you, not even for all the glory and wealth a man could carry.

He sat in his family room the whole morning; retracing how he had come to the situation he was in. He watched his wife fuss around the house, moving objects and then putting them back in their original place, for, as far as he could tell, no particular reason. He knew his presence unnerved her, and that she preferred it when he left the house early and returned late, but he would be damned if he would voluntarily go to the Pasha's house. The man had not requested his company that morning and he was not about to turn up of his own volition. When he was called, he would go, but until then he intended to hold up in his home and hope the world outside it forgot him.

He played with his children for a while, until they bored him and the frustrations returned. Perhaps he should try to sleep. It was, after all, coming up to that time of day. A nap would at least mean that time would pass without him watching it.

His wife entered the room and stood towering over him with her hands on her wide hips as though observing her children. He hoped against all hope she was not about to unleash one of her episodes that seemed to come more frequently these days.

'There is someone calling for you,' she stated irritably.

'Who, dear?' he asked, in a softer tone.

She threw her hands in the air.

'Do you expect me to know everything as well as do everything? If I did, what use would I have with you?'

Somewhere along the way he had lost control of not just his respect but also his authority both within the makhzan and his home. He would get them both back, if not amongst his peers then God damn it in his family. He just had to figure out the best time to do that, preferably when his wife was in a better mood.

'Can you tell them I am out?'

His wife continued to tower over him, making no attempt to conceal her contempt. Then, as though recalling she had forgotten to lift an arbitrary object from one room and place it in another, she ignored his question and walked away.

Perhaps if he continued to sit there the visitor would just go away. Instead, the knocking got louder and more persistent until it became a constant bang that drummed into his very core. He stood up ready to scare away whoever knocked on his door with threats, as explicit as the situation required. God protect them if it was another petitioner to report another missing girl. They had enough already.

Reaching the front door, he paused for a moment. Perhaps it was Farook, perhaps he had come to seek reconciliation and was banging so loudly because his remorse for what had passed between them was so strong. He laughed at the ridiculousness of the idea. The better option, of course, would be if it were the person responsible for the missing women, breaking down Yusuf's door with his bare fists because the guilt had become too overwhelming and only a confession would relieve him of his sins. This idea made Yusuf laugh even more. No one would be so stupid to confess to a crime before being forced. His utter dependence on fate and the will of others only infuriated him more.

He flung the door open ready to bark his threats. They caught in his throat as he saw before him a woman panting heavily, her malhaf completely dishevelled. He stood stunned for a moment, unsure what to make of the situation. The woman launched into a rapid and erratic explanation.

'What did you say?' His hearing was three sentences behind her speech.

'I said we must find Farook al-Alami. You must come with me now. I looked everywhere for him and asked of his lodging but no one knew.'

Yusuf thought for a moment. Was it possible the winds had finally changed direction to send a sweet breeze of redemption?

'You say you know the woman and where to find her?'

Assiya's mother stood at the doorway, nodding desperately.

'Yes, yes ... We must find your associate and go there at once.'

Farook was a good man, but he was also a marked man. His days in the inner circle were numbered; the Sultan's days may too be numbered. Right and wrong did not secure a person's future.

'My associate is preoccupied for the moment,' he said. The choice between loyalty to Farook and the wrath of the Pasha was no choice at all. 'First I must stop at the house of the Pasha. He will provide guards. You must go home and do not speak of this with anyone. Tell me the location.'

'I will not,' the woman protested. Her voice increased in pitch.

What was happening in this city? The women were developing a defiance that had to be cut short in its youth before it turned into a bitter old hag. He scowled at her, hoping his honed menacing look was enough to instil fear. She glared back at him until he found himself pleading.

'Please, return home to your children and I promise you I will get to the bottom of this. Think what your husband might say if he finds out you came here without his knowledge.'

She paused for a moment. It had been a mistake to come here. She should have continued to search for the man from Tangier. She hesitated a moment, playing with the kaftan in her hands.

'You will inform the Pasha and then both you and your colleague from the north will find out why that woman had my daughter's housedress in her possession?' she asked, her voice calmer.

'Yes,' Yusuf confirmed.

'And will you bring back my daughter's dress? You must take an oath.'

'I swear it by God. I am a man of my word,' Yusuf said, putting a hand on his chest.

Even if she tried to leave now, he would not let her go with the kaftan. It was out of her hands the moment she knocked on his door. She held the kaftan to her nose one more time and then passed it to him, feeling the rough fabric slip through her fingers. Yusuf took it smiling, closed the door and dashed back into the house to dress. She stood there facing the closed door and realized she had made the wrong choice.

47

Work unfinished

Farook stood outside the shop and peered into the small window. He could just make out the workbench at the back of the shop, but there was no sign of life inside. He waited for a while before entering, looking at the buildings along the alleyway and watching the few people passing by. On his first visit he didn't take much notice of the neighbourhood, but now saw it was quite pleasant. There was even colour other than the usual baked red earth of the buildings. Greenery and bright pinks from bougainvillea vines hung over the walls opposite.

He pushed the door open. The room was dim and he stumbled as he entered. The floor was uneven, packed tight in some places and loose in others. There was something different about the shop compared to the last visit. It seemed larger, more spacious, like it had been cleared out. He looked at the far corner of the room and noted the Berber wooden chest was no longer there.

Hajj Mohammed Mesfewi entered from the back room, stopping momentarily on seeing Farook.

'You are early,' he said. 'I am not quite ready.'

'I see no reason for further delay,' said Farook.

'I have not completed my work, Si Farook. I thought you of people would understand that I must finish.'

'What work?'

The cobbler busied himself tidying shoes on the counter. He moved them to the shelves behind him stacking them carefully in pairs.

'Why these shoes – is it not obvious? I must repair all these shoes for my customers otherwise I will become known as unreliable. The cobbler who broke his oaths.'

Farook hesitated for a moment. He looked around the shop. The interior door was slightly ajar and he detected movement in the next room. He tried to look through the gap, but the cobbler closed it abruptly.

'My mother is unwell,' said the cobbler. 'She has not been herself for quite a while now.'

Farook returned to stand in front of the counter. He picked up an orange baboush slipper and inspected it. It was tattered and old, not so much a shoe, more like a glove. Putting the slipper back down, he looked at the cobbler. 'I would like to see your ledger,' he demanded, reaching his hand out in expectation.

The cobbler stopped arranging the shoes around him and nodded in understanding.

'We are very much alike, Si Farook,' he said. 'We want the same things. I have observed you in the city, the way you work, and like me you are driven by good intention. Our methods may be different, but our goals are the same. We both want to better this country.'

'We are nothing alike, Hajj Mohammed,' Farook said, wiping his hands on his selham, as if the very suggestion had muddied him. 'Give me the ledger,' he demanded, anger rising in his throat.

Mesfewi withdrew the ledger from beneath the counter. Before handing it to Farook, he stroked the black leather cover clean of invisible dust. Farook took it and opened to a middle page. He took out one of Assiya's letters and flattened it on the counter. He flicked through the ledger turning pages forward and backwards. Eventually he closed the book. He looked up at the cobbler and found him wearing a smirk.

'I am glad it is you, Si Farook, and not anyone else.'

'The wooden chest,' replied Farook. 'It was here on my last visit. I want to see its contents.' His patience was thinning. The man would not fool him and he would not let him slip away so easily.

'Ah, yes, that is the last heirloom of a previous life. There was a time when the Mesfewi tribe was in favour. We enjoyed all the privileges of court and I was raised within the palace grounds. But nothing lasts forever, Si Farook, as I am sure you know. Ba Ahmed brought in the new Sultan and with that a decay set in which has been eating the heart of this once great nation ever since. My tribe rebelled in 1899. My cousins and uncles – can you believe it – were captured and their heads displayed on spikes at the gates of Fez. They watched from their spikes as my mother and I fled with only the wooden chest and the clothes on our backs through those very gates and made our way to Marrakesh. A whole generation, Si Farook, I can still feel them watching me from their graves. They cannot rest you see until the name is restored in history and justice is done. For every cause there is an effect, every disease a cure, though it may not be known immediately.'

'Where is the wooden chest?'

The cobbler smiled broadly as though entertaining the tantrums of a child.

'It appears you are too late. My mother sold it, Si Farook. Business is not what it once was.'

Farook fought the urge to grab the cobbler. He was not a man of violence, but if there ever was a moment when he felt that it might have some use it was now.

'I understand your frustration, Si Farook, I really do. The handwriting does not match and the chest has gone. You have everything: the culprit, motive but no evidence, no way of knowing for sure. But you must also understand I will finish my work. Nothing will stop that.'

The cobbler took the ledger from Farook's hand and placed it on the counter. He returned to tidying the shoes, behaving as though Farook had already left the shop. Farook stepped away from the counter. He considered his options for a moment and watched the cobbler as he stacked more shoes on the shelves. He had murdered the girls: Assiya, Souad, Leila, Maryam, Breem, Lubna, Dunya, Marwa, Warda and more. There were more, a lot more. How did he kill them? How did he dispose of their bodies? He watched the man at work, his broad back and shoulders, the muscles contorting and relaxing as he moved.

The cobbler turned back and looked startled to see Farook still standing there. He waited expectantly.

'You are a clever man, Hajj Mohammed,' Farook said.

The cobbler bowed his head slightly in appreciation of the compliment.

'I will leave,' continued Farook. 'But I will return later as soon as I have visited your garden. What was it exactly you were carrying there on your back the other morning? Perhaps if I have the whole place dug up we will soon find out.'

The blood drained from the cobbler's face. He struggled for a moment to gather himself, placing the shoes on the counter and clasping his hands together, releasing them and then repeating.

'I did not expect you would have me followed,' he said, composing himself. His eyes darted to the door and then to the ground. 'In hindsight, that was naïve of me. Was it Yusuf al-Mahdi who followed me?'

Farook gave no response.

'I suppose not. I hear you have fallen out.'

A silence descended between them, allowing Mesfewi to collect his thoughts. Nodding to himself he pulled from his jellaba a folded piece of paper and handed it to Farook.

'You will find the proof you need in there, Si Farook. But you must let me finish. I made an oath to my tribe, to the men who lost their lives for this country. Once I am done I will surrender to you and no one else.'

Farook shook his head.

'You will come with me now, Hajj Mohammed. Not later, but right now. Your work is finished. If you come quietly I will make sure you and your mother' – he indicated to the back room – 'will be treated with humanity. If not, I cannot influence what happens next.'

'Please, Si Farook, you must understand that I am not a bad man,' pleaded the cobbler. 'I have done some bad things, but I am not a bad–'

The shop door crashed open silencing the cobbler instantly. He stepped back in panic and whipped his head around to look at the interior door swung partially open in the commotion. The small shop filled with men carrying swords and pistols. They were tall and broad framed and smelt of country air and secret taverns. They made a path from amongst them and Yusuf stepped forward. His eyes met Farook's but he said nothing.

'Take him away,' he instructed the guards.

They barged past Farook and grabbed Mesfewi. He offered little resistance, closing his eyes and surrendering to his fate. Pointing to the interior door, Yusuf instructed the other guards. 'Check the back room and bring the mother too.'

'And shut him up before he dares make a scene,' he called to the guards who were holding Mesfewi outside. Farook heard a thud as Mesfewi fell to the ground. The killer had received his first taste of the punishment he craved so desperately. The other guards passed Farook and kicked the interior door off its frame. Disappearing into the room they soon returned dragging an old woman. She was shaking with fright as if she had just witnessed her own death. They too left the shop, leaving only Yusuf and Farook. It had happened so quickly. Farook stood paralyzed. He held the piece of paper just given to him. Yusuf looked him up and down. Saying nothing, he turned and left the shop.

48

The taste of failure

Farook did not leave the funduq for two days. He saw no point in going outside. Whatever was unfolding on the other side of the funduq walls was beyond his control.

He had thought at the end of the investigation he would feel complete, and that having the answers and evidence would offer him some satisfaction. It didn't. It was not enough. He had failed. It didn't matter that the cobbler confessed to him and placed in his hand the hard evidence he worked so long for, he had lost grip of the situation. The cobbler was in the hands of the city makhzan and they did not care for evidence or a better course of action. They did not care for progress, especially progress that threatened their power. If it took keeping the country in the dark ages in order to retain their grip over it they would do it without a second thought. They would spin the story to their favour, offer the sacrificial lamb to the masses and affirm their sanctimony to the world. Nothing would change and science was not foolproof. He had failed.

On returning from the cobbler's shop he opened the letter handed to him moments before Yusuf appeared and snatched the prospect of progress from beneath him. He read it a dozen times over and compared it to Assiya's letters to her love. They matched. Of course they did. The cobbler was smart. He changed his handwriting for Assiya's letters, but it was her last note to her lover and in it the difficult choice she had to make was laid bare. He wasn't quite sure what depressed him more: the fact that he had solved the case with evidence, but been denied the opportunity to make his point to the authorities and the Sultan or the fact that Assiya had placed so much trust in the cobbler.

He played the conversation with Mesfewi over and over and paused to linger on the end where the cobbler might have explained what he had done with the girls. There was still so much he didn't know; how he killed them, when he started his crimes and what moved him from a desire for revenge to violence. He could not get past that moment and rather than feel angry with Yusuf, he understood his old friend acted in a way most men in his situation would. Yusuf was a cog in the machine and even if he chose a different path the machine would still turn. He felt angry with himself, for his failure. It had all been for nothing.

The proprietor tried to tease Farook out of his room with information he gathered from the funduq guests and his trips into the market. He confirmed the discovery of the bodies under the shop.

He must have groomed Assiya over time, gaining her trust by encouraging her love. He must have selected his victims carefully, stalked them and befriended some and given them the attention they so craved. Perhaps conjecture was all Farook was left with, speculation and guesswork. The only chance of ever fully understanding the cobbler – his motivations and methods – was if he was given the opportunity to speak to him again. But the makhzan would never agree. If he wanted to speak to Mesfewi again, he would have to find a way of doing so himself, without the support of the Marrakesh authorities.

Farook slowly packed the few belongings he brought from Tangier. He gathered his papers and returned them to the leather satchel he took on any long journey. Perhaps returning to Tangier would put a line through the case. He could forget the whole thing and return to anonymity and silent walks along the Mediterranean. But he knew his outstanding questions would follow him along the perilous road north and haunt him late into the evenings. He could not return home unsure of who he would be upon his arrival in Tangier and unclear of who he had become at his departure from Marrakesh. The journey between would be spent in self-reflection, but filled with potholes of self-doubt. He wanted to leave with a firmer footing. Each step towards Tangier might confirm everything more clearly to himself.

The proprietor interrupted his packing often. His voice was shrill as he ran around the courtyard barking orders at the kitchen boy seeping through the cracks in the walls. The funduq was filling once more with guests. It was not lawless tribesmen from the Atlas Mountains taking lodging, but families from the villages surrounding Marrakesh with their children and provisions. Some cooked in their very rooms, stoking small fires over which they boiled lentil soups and broths. The proprietor tentatively visited Farook in his room between attending to his various guests or shouting at them about the smoke and what it would do to his ceilings. He showed a sombre impression Farook had not seen in him before.

On the first day of Farook's self-confinement, the proprietor had almost barged into his room. His excitement had not been tempered by Farook's mood. He described how the cobbler and his mother had been placed in chains and left in cells the night before, and how they were then dragged at first light through the city atop donkeys to the Pasha's house. There the Pasha himself questioned them and when he left the room, unsatisfied with their answers, slaps, kicks and punches rained down on the pair.

Of course, violence was inevitable, but it came with etiquette. It would not do to beat them in front of such a high standing official or

248

stain the tiled floor. When the Pasha returned to the room the questioning would begin again and so it went. Eventually they were carted back to the prison and left to make it through to daybreak or die in the pit of their darkest moment. Farook could only nod at the proprietor. There was nothing unexpected in their treatment.

'Any solidarity or loyalty was lost in the first slap to cross the old woman's face I am told. She turned on her son so quickly and resolutely that it's a wonder she hadn't informed on him before.'

'Why didn't she?' Farook did not want to know and yet wanted so desperately to understand how the mother had sat silently watching one life after another snuffed from this world.

'She claims she knew nothing. She says if he did something he did it without her knowledge or support,' explained the proprietor, his right eyebrow raised high enough to demonstrate the entire city's lack of belief in her ignorance. He continued his description, not needing Farook's questions about motivations.

'The sight of the two being carted across the city drew a crowd to the Pasha's door and the wails of the old woman could be heard throughout the neighbourhood. By the time they were taken back to the dungeons a mob was waiting for them. I need not explain what this means.'

Farook nodded. It meant mayhem. They would call for blood, a baying horde of people who would not disperse until their demands were met.

'Eventually the cobbler spoke,' continued the proprietor.

'What did he say?'

The proprietor paused for a moment, uncertain about his next piece of news.

'He asked for you,' stated the proprietor, concern crossing his face. 'He said he would not speak to anyone but you.'

49

Market day

On the second day of his confinement, Farook stayed longer in bed and did not allow the proprietor into his room until early afternoon. He listened to the funduq filling and made do with the previous evening's dinner. When the proprietor finally entered, he sniffed the air and wiped his nose. He got straight to the point. His respect for Farook made it difficult to see him this way.

'They were kept in the dungeons for the whole morning. The woman's groans can be heard from outside the prison walls, but they say Mesfewi has not uttered a sound. It's not what you are thinking. They continued to beat them both, but the cobbler refuses to scream or speak for that matter.'

Farook could not fathom the strength it took to tolerate the range of torture techniques used by the makhzan silently. Perhaps the ripping out of the tongue and vocal cords would do the trick he thought. He had met men who were tortured and behind their heavy eyes they carried dark secrets, knowledge about themselves they would prefer to have never discovered.

'A crowd is gathering in Jemaa el-Fnaa. People from all over the region are entering the city. There were even scuffles in the market, fighting over bread. They want justice and are calling for their execution.'

That too was inevitable. What else would become of them but a humiliating and brutal public death?

'Si Yusuf was seen entering the prison in the early morning,' the proprietor stated, inspecting Farook's face for a reaction.

'And the women?' Farook asked. It was a question which had circulated in his mind through the sleepless night. What had happened to the girls?

'Sixteen buried under his shop.' The words were heavy on the proprietor's tongue.

'Have they checked his garden?'

'They are digging it up now. They say they have already found five more. The families have also gathered in Jemaa el-Fnaa and are refusing to leave until something is done.'

The proprietor left his room without another word. His head hung low and his feet dragging him to his chores.

Later that day he returned and entered apprehensively.

'Thirty-six women in total,' he said, almost by way of greeting.

In their conversation Mesfewi had said he was not finished. Farook felt sickened by the thought that the man intended to continue. The cobbler had a specific number in mind. He was seeking revenge and the only way to know how many he intended to kill was to find the history of his tribe or speak directly to him. Did he really want to face Mesfewi again?

'You must leave this room,' the proprietor stated, stopping in front of Farook and staring him directly in the eye. He looked exhausted, his face ashen and dry.

'I have watched you hole yourself up in this room as though this is nothing to do with you, as though you were just a bystander to events. I, for one, have no problem seeing that monster executed in front of the whole city and will take my place in the crowd. He deserves

251

nothing less. But you … you and I both know your work in the city is not finished and that you will not rest until you seek the answers to the questions you have. So, I will bring you some warmed water and food and you will bathe and dress and leave this room.'

The proprietor paused for a moment and retrieved Farook's clothing from the peg on the wall to air. His assertiveness took Farook by surprise. Holding Farook's clothes, the proprietor continued.

'Forgive my imposition, but I think in the time you have been my guest at this funduq I have come to know you. This is not you and you are not a man to hide from the truth.'

'I failed,' said Farook softly. 'My instincts were off and I got there too late.'

'You stopped him,' the proprietor said. 'You stopped him from completing his criminal plan and in doing so you saved others. Assiya was dead before you even knew her name, as is the case with the others. They have announced his punishment. The atmosphere in the city is ripe for rebellion, the makhzan want this to disappear quickly. The woman, they say, will not last the night, but him … they are keeping him alive.'

Farook looked at the proprietor unsure if he wanted the man to continue.

'He is to be crucified in Jemaa el-Fnaa on Thursday, on market day.'

50

A friend from France

It was only once he left the narrow alleyways of his funduq that Farook knew where he was going. He took in a sight that assaulted his vision and every value he held sacred. Jemaa el-Fnaa was the busiest he had ever seen it. The square was thick with crowds who loitered or stood in circles. The sound of the iron castanets and three-string lutes of the gnawa bands entertaining the assembled mass rose above the square, along with the repeated chants of the musicians so that at first appearance one would think it was Eid al-Adha, the Festival of Sacrifice. In fact, that was exactly what it was and it was surrounded with a celebratory atmosphere as though the long month of fasting was over and a feast was about to be served. Among the crowd were sellers of all kinds of produce. Days earlier, the city seemed to have exhausted all of its resources. Now, it burst with provisions. Young boys sat on wooden stalls roasting corn ears still wrapped in their browning husks. Others watched over stalls heaped with walnuts, almonds, dried prunes and apricots. There were stalls selling provision fit for a wedding feast: dough bobbing in cooking oil, inflating into weird and wonderful shapes and rescued from the large pan just as they crisped; sweets drenched in a sugary syrup; stalls serving dollops of thick lentil broth with bread to dip in and devour. And amongst them the gnawa continued to tap their castanets and pluck their lutes rhythmically. Dressed in brightly coloured tunics and harem trousers – blue, red and green – they rotated their heads so that the bobble hanging off their unique knitted hats spun around and around and drew the musicians and their audience into a transcendental state.

Farook walked past the gnawa bands and ignored the men and women standing behind food stalls, calling him to partake in the invigorating taste of blessings to come. He also ignored the guerrab, with their camel bags of fresh water hanging from their hips, their hands stretched out holding brass cups filled with fresh valley water. They satisfied the crowd's need for water and encouraged its thirst for blood.

Farook ignored it all, including the bare-footed children who chased behind him with trinkets and solicitations to his ancestors, the groups of families gathered on tattered rugs, the men who lay back in deep slumber with their faces to the sky, or the women gathered in tight circles whispering to each other under their melhafs. The soft wind carried the sound of laughter and chatter and children at the height of their innocence to accompany the erratic sound of the gnawa. The smells of different foods cooking, unwashed bodies, the sweat of anticipation and adrenalin, all occupied the spaces in the air the sounds did not fill. Farook left the square behind him to turn his back on the festivities. He was continually aware of what the crowd wanted, and the anticipated climax of their celebrations.

Arriving at the Jewish quarter of the city, he observed its surrounding wall and the silence, just as oppressive as the sounds of jubilant celebration only a short distance away. He attempted to push the gate open, but it was locked from the inside. He banged with his fist a repeated thump until he heard the sound of feet shuffling in dust. An old Jewish man opened the door and peered through the gap. Farook explained the reason for his visit and reluctantly the man let him in.

Bolting the gate behind him, the Jewish man stood waiting for Farook to say more. Farook looked the old man up and down. Beyond his kippah, there was very little to indicate that he was Jewish. He wore the same clothes as any Moroccan man might, except that he was stood on the inside of the dividing wall and went bare foot, as Jews in the city were compelled to do.

Disappointed by the visitor's refusal to fill his ears with news of the square, the man ordered Farook to follow him and marched away. He led him through an area of ramshackle houses, where children who were barely dressed and women who stared from their doorways with large curious eyes, babies hanging from their hips as bloated as the camel bags of the water carriers in the square. He entered an alleyway marked by its more refined accommodations and displays of wealth and was left outside a one-story house. The old man knocked on the door and left Farook, not bothering to provide an introduction on his behalf.

The door opened and before him stood Dr Delacroix. A look of surprise crossed over the doctor's face, quickly replaced with a somewhat feigned smile of greeting. Farook followed the doctor into the house and arrived at a reception room. He took no notice of the interior of the house, though it was his first time to visit one in the Jewish quarter. His mind was already focused on the purpose of his visit. Once seated, Farook spoke and wasted no time on formalities or politeness.

'You said once that France is my friend and if I were to ever need her help I need only ask.'

The doctor nodded silently, enjoying the moment more than Farook could imagine.

'What is it you need?' he asked in as soft a tone a possible, not wanting to reveal his pleasure least it cause Farook to silence his plea.

'The murderer … the cobbler,' Farook began. 'I would like to speak with him one final time.'

The doctor stifled a small laugh.

'And how might France, or I for that matter, be able to help you with that?'

'He is to be crucified in the square on Thursday.'

'I am aware. Why do you think the Jewish quarter has closed its gates? And why have I not left it since we last saw each other? It is not safe for anyone, especially someone like me or them.' He indicated the residents of the neighbourhood with a flick of his hand.

'Crucifixion is a horrible death,' Farook ventured.

'The man committed horrible crimes,' the doctor returned.

Farook paused for a moment, wondering how to continue the conversation. He could just come out and say what he wanted or he could coax the doctor to arrive at the same conclusion himself.

'Do you not wonder why the makhzan would choose such a death during these difficult times?'

'I have not thought of it,' admitted the doctor sitting back in his chair.

'Perhaps you should. Was not the son of God crucified?'

The doctor leant forward. His imagination was finally caught in Farook's snare.

'Go on.'

'Perhaps the Pasha is in some way trying to insult the European residents of this city through choosing such a blasphemous form of punishment. Maybe he is even trying to offend you directly. Jesus was not a murderer. He did not kill women,' Farook explained, as he watched the doctor's face flush pink, then red and then drain completely.

'You see, I think it is not so much what you or France can do for me as it is what we can do for each other,' he continued. 'It's simple really. I want to speak to the cobbler and you want to walk about this city with your presence appreciated and your contribution to its development valued.'

'What are you suggesting I do, Monsieur al-Alami? You and I both know the Pasha despises me and would like nothing more than to see me thrown out of the city or perhaps even, like his cobbler, put up on the cross.'

'That is true,' Farook agreed. 'But while the Pasha may be your enemy, he has his own.'

The doctor gave him a blank stare.

'Moulay Hafid,' Farook stated simply. 'The Caliph could be pressed to intervene, to halt the crucifixion because of the offence it might cause the Christian residents of the city. Of course it would have to be explained to him just how offensive it is to European sensibilities. As you know, the Sultan is currently in the midst of negotiating relations with Europe. it would not do for those negotiations to be influenced by the barbarity of the Pasha.'

The doctor looked at Farook with intrigue. He absentmindedly scratched at a small scab on his hand until he exposed the pink skin beneath.

'All this so you can talk to the killer?' he asked, unsure those were Farook's real motivations. 'Why do you wish to speak to him?'

'Professional curiosity, Dr Delacroix. I see it as an opportunity to learn what goes on in the mind of a monster and besides public executions have no place in the modern world. My request is that you assure me time with him.'

'I doubt I am in a position to assure anything,' stated the doctor. 'But while my letters to the makhzan may not always be welcomed, they have in the past proven very effective.'

The doctor stretched his arms above him and arched his back against his chair. He felt strangely enthusiastic. His long days and even longer nights spent in the confines of the Jewish quarter had left his spirit utterly defeated. While he kept up the pretence of strength to his neighbours and the other European residents, in the quiet of his rooms he stared at the bare walls and wondered why he had chosen such a path. Why had he not continued to practice medicine in France, married a good woman and died in his own bed on his own soil? Instead he had taken to this foreign land and insinuated himself in its politics and people. He hoped at least that as a reward France would remember him, include his name in the history of the French empire when it was written. Perhaps she would. Perhaps he would be remembered for civilizing the barbarians after all.

Farook stood up to leave.

'I have a question,' said the doctor.

Farook waited patiently.

'Whose side are you on, Monsieur al-Alami?'

Farook paused for a moment to think through his response.

'I am on the side of the truth, Dr Delacroix.'

51

Thursday comes and goes

Thursday passed with Farook returning to his self-confinement and the city waiting with bated breath. Jemaa el-Fnaa continued to fill with people intent on watching the entertainment: a spectacle which would no doubt ignite their imaginations in a way the storytellers and seers couldn't compete with.

The day progressed with no crucifixion or relief of the crowd's yearning. The victim's families continued to refuse to leave the square displaying their grief in public. They sat huddled together mostly in silence but sometimes breaking out in the ululations of mourning.

By Friday, the peculiar atmosphere of outrage and excitement permeating the city was peppered with annoyance. It seethed out of the square and into the mosques. The calming words of the imams at their pulpits did nothing to sooth emotions or reduce expectations. They were interrupted with calls for God's retribution from the crowd. The worshippers stood from their kneeling positions and marched to the square more determined than ever they would assert their righteousness in this world by sending the damned into the next. Tribal armies passed each other down alleyways, placing their hands on their swords as warning. They jeered at each other, baiting for a confrontation until eventually scuffles broke out over minor infractions: a wrong look or a mumbled insult. Children weaved through the crowds playing chase, not fully comprehending what was about to unfold but certain it would be a spectacle worth remembering. Mothers grabbed them as they passed their homes and tried to confine them, but they would sneak out again and continue their game. Women unable to join the crowd took to their rooftops. They moved their kitchens to the flat roofs and took advantage of the drop in prices in the market by roasting meats on open fires. They looked over the edges towards the square and called out developments, as though passing them from one rooftop to another like clothes down a washing line.

Farook remained in his room and waited to see if his visit to the doctor would amount to anything. Something had obviously caused the postponement of the crucifixion. The proprietor could give him no other news except that the stage had been set and construction of the cross in the middle of Jemaa el-Fnaa had begun early on Thursday before being abruptly aborted. He could give no explanation and Farook did not furnish him with any insight, leaving the possible reasons to the speculation of the proprietor and funduq guests. The fact that the crucifixion had been cancelled encouraged his hopes for a final meeting with the cobbler. The man would die; he had no doubt about that. The demand for a public execution was too high and too far-gone for reason to prevent it. If the horde did not get what they wanted they would turn on each other and the authorities.

As Friday afternoon became Friday evening, the sun setting slowing over the city's unwavering demands and newfound optimism for the future, Farook considered his options. He knew his time in the city was coming to a close and regardless of the outcome of his meeting with the doctor he would soon have to leave.

He began to gather the very last of his belongings. He turned over each item as though it belonged to someone else, hoping perhaps it would reveal something about the owner he did not already know. The few pieces of clothing he brought had not stretched to fit a different man, his scribbled handwriting showed nothing new of his character and his Italian shoes remained as they were, the same shape and size made for only him to walk in. His possessions told him nothing of who he had become and what he had learnt. He spoke to the proprietor to arrange transport and provisions for the road.

As night set in, Farook made ready for sleep, knowing if he did not get his moment with the cobbler soon he would have to leave regardless. As he lay under his covers in the stifling heat of coal fires which burnt in the rooms beneath, he thought back to his life in Tangier and the nights he spent with the windows opened in his bedroom to the sound of the Atlantic and Mediterranean meeting to lull him into a gentle slumber. He was much like that point where the two oceans met, not completely of one or the other, destined to forever swim between the two. He drifted to sleep with these thoughts filling his mind.

The next moment a banging pulled him out of his dreams. He awoke with a start, the dark room giving no hint of time or how long he had slept. It seemed only a moment. He jumped out of bed and flung the door open, instantly raising his hand to shield his eyes from the sunlight. He had slept undisturbed through the night. The day was fully broken and behind the man standing in front of him the funduq was in full swing. For a moment, he did not recognize him, the light casting his face in shadow. As his eyes adjusted, Farook began to recognize him from his shortness and rounded form. Looking at him more closely, Farook noted the changes; he had aged in no time at all.

'You look unwell,' Farook said dismissively as he turned back into the room.

Yusuf looked down at his form and frowned. The last few months had probably resulted in a loss of weight and he certainly no longer had the strength to keep order at home. Postponing thoughts of that problem he drew his attention back to Farook, who stood waiting patiently, a bemused expression painted across his face.

'Come with me,' Yusuf said, hoping his voice would come through as firm as he meant the instruction.

'Please,' he added, getting no response from his old friend.

'I need a moment.' Farook closed the door in Yusuf's face and got dressed without rushing. He splashed his face with the water from the night before and rinsed his mouth. With his jellaba on, he placed his heavy selham over his shoulders and adjusted the hood at the back so it sat symmetrically between his shoulder blades. If he had known he would be in the city for so long he would have packed a summer cloak. Next he sprinkled rose water onto his hands from a silver jar and slapped it on his face and down the front of his clothes and placed his tarboush carefully on his head, adjusting the black tassel. Finally, he bent down and slipped his feet into his shoes, tying the laces into perfect bows.

Reaching the door, he opened it to find Yusuf in his previous position as though frozen by a magical hex. They did not speak. Instead Farook followed Yusuf down the stairwell and into the funduq courtyard. He wondered what time of the morning it was. The courtyard had suddenly emptied leaving only the kitchen boy peering at them as he swept the floor. As they passed him, Farook paused placing his hand on his shoulders.

'Mohammed, do not leave the funduq until I return.'

The boy nodded nervously and continued with his chores.

52

Walled-in

Farook and Yusuf left the funduq and were instantly joined by a small army of men. The men circled the pair as they entered the alleyways of Marrakesh, walled them in from the crowd – shouting their orders with authority – and pushed through those who refused to make a path. Doors opened to their side as others rushed out of their houses to walk towards Jemaa el-Fnaa, the crowd carried them like a wave crashing onto the shore. Yusuf lent towards Farook and shouted into his ear.

'The cobbler seems to have taken a liking to you, Si Farook,' he said

Farook did not respond. If he had had any questions about where he was being taken the growing mass of people had already provided an answer.

'He asked for you repeatedly. That was the only thing he said in fact, until he stopped speaking altogether,' Yusuf continued, regarding Farook's silence with disdain.

'And it seems you also asked for him. The Pasha is well aware of your dealings with the Christians and many in the makhzan consider you a traitor. Despite it working in favour of the Caliph, it is safe to say you are no longer welcome in this city. I suggest you leave at the first opportunity. The only thing shielding you is the Sultan's protection.'

Farook remained silent. In his mind he went back to the day he came face-to-face with the cobbler. He could only imagine what state he would find him in now. Yusuf stopped abruptly at the mouth of the alleyway and turned to face Farook. Looking beyond Yusuf, Farook was struck by the sea of people filling Jemaa el-Fnaa. They occupied every space and continued to pour in from every road leading into it. The crowd jostled to get closer to the centre, nudging ribs and pushing into backs. A gravitational pull drew them in together. Absorbed by the sight, Farook missed what Yusuf was saying. Dragging his eyes away from the square, he looked at Yusuf, trying as best he could to conceal his horror. What were they going to do?

'As I am sure you are aware, the crucifixion was cancelled. The makhzan had a change of heart shall we say. It appears Moulay Hafid intervened, deciding on behalf of the Sultan that crucifixion was an insufficient punishment for such heinous crimes. And as you can see, the people agree.'

Yusuf paused for a moment to further allow Farook to take in the sight and his words. 'You will have five minutes with the cobbler and no more. And then you will leave Marrakesh and not look back,' explained Yusuf. 'That is on the order of the Caliph and to be guaranteed by the Pasha.'

Farook nodded in understanding. He had no desire to stay in the city as it was. The sooner he could set out on his journey to Fez to report to the Sultan and then on to Tangier the better. He looked at Yusuf waiting for him to signal to the guards they were ready to continue towards the square.

Yusuf hesitated for a moment, lowering his eyes in a moment of shame.

'My father raised me with high hopes. He thought his son would one day move up the ranks and write the family name in the history books. Before his illness he asked only that I stay on the right path that I ensure we are remembered for bringing good into the world and not evil. But my time is different to his. If he saw what this city, this entire country, has become he would understand that our choices are no longer that simple. I am only glad he passed before he had to witness it. I am not good; I was not made for good. I am made to follow orders; it is the only thing I understand.' Yusuf stopped talking, unsure where to go from there.

'Nothing has changed, Si Yusuf,' said Farook. 'The world has made unfair demands on Man from the dawn of time. It has tested our beliefs and convictions and will continue to do so long after we leave it. What separates one man from another is not his ability to make the right choice, but his ability to live with the outcomes. You will have to live the outcomes of your choices, whatever they may be, as will I. You are not good or bad, you are just weak.'

Yusuf nodded, understanding this was the most empathy he would get from Farook. He turned to the guards and ordered them to attention.

'Keep close to me, Si Farook. If I lose you in the crowd I may not be able to save you,' Yusuf explained, before turning towards Jamaa el-Fnaa to join the throng of people. They guards kicked into motion once more creating a barrier around them. Farook stayed within the protective circle looking ahead and beyond the bodies pressing in on them.

The crowd was charged with excitement: fists punched the sky; young children were carried on men's shoulders to wave down at their families around them; and women carrying baskets filled with rotting vegetables and meats. The stench was enough to turn anyone's stomach. Farook took in as much as he could of his surroundings. To the right he heard a burst of roars and boos and the guards moved in that direction. They nudged their way through as the crowd thickened and pushed back against them. The path opened before them and was quickly closed again. Time crawled as the roars and screamed insults filled his ears.

Eventually they arrived at a barrier circling a raised makeshift wooden platform. As Yusuf approached a guard opened a section and let them pass. The separation from the crowd gave Farook the opportunity to look into their faces. What he saw would remain with him until his final days. Their eyes were set on the platform behind him. They were delirious with hunger. He saw faces wide with wild smiles and eyes which looked up to the platform braced for a divine miracle. Farook scanned their faces, in search of a different emotion, anything but the rabid hunger for blood. He rested his sight on one woman stood behind the barrier and being held up by her husband. She had been watching him all along, behind her malhaf. She clutched her husband's arm, while refusing to break eye contact with Farook. She showed no rage – no desire for blood – only sorrow and defeat. He walked towards her leaving Yusuf behind him. As he approached her eyes widened with rage. Her husband gripped at his wife holding her upright. Farook looked at Assiya's parents. 'I promised to restore your honour,' he said. 'This is the best I can do.' He withdrew Assiya's last letter from beneath his selham and handed it to her mother. She hesitated for a moment, unsure of what to do. Eventually she took it and placed it beneath her malhaf. She glanced behind him and the rage that filled her eyes only moments ago was suddenly replaced with terror.

Turning around, Farook saw Mesfewi being dragged up the wooden steps of the platform. His feet were chained together as were his hands and he hung between the two guards carrying him as though his spirit had already left his body. His clothes were caked in blood and dirt and his head hung low. His eyes were so swollen they were completely closed and around his ears blood had crusted. He looked unrecognizable. His face was covered in black and purple bruises and the sharp bend in his newly cracked nose changed his profile. Around the edge of the platform men began to build makeshift walls from mud and rocks. Farook watched the walls take shape. They rose up around the cobbler, who was now tied to a beam in the middle of the platform. He tried to process what was happening before him, but the eruption of screams and shouts from the mass of people crowded his thoughts. They roared insults and curses at Mesfewi, his ancestors, and every unfortunate person to have ever held affection for him. They condemned him and his forefathers to the eternal fire, spat out his name, and stamped it into the dirt. Rotting fruit and vegetables sailed through the air, some missing the cobbler entirely and others smacking into his face and chest: apples, melons, cabbage and anything else that might travel the distance. Farook swirled in the chaos around him, lost in the roar of the crowd and the sight of Mesfewi's battered body, which shook back against the beam every time an object crashed into him. A rock smashed into the cobbler's temple and blood burst out, covering his eyes. The crowd cheered and roared with pleasure.

'Si Farook,' he heard Yusuf call to him from afar. Farook turned to look for him. He found him to his left. He focused his vision on a man he once thought he could trust.

'When the wall is high enough, I will take you to him. But remember, you have only five minutes and then you must leave,' he shouted above the sound of the crowd.

Farook leaned forward and shouted into Yusuf's ear, 'What is his punishment?'

'Time, Si Farook,' shouted Yusuf. 'And public entombment right here in Jemaa el-Fnaa. It is a fitting death.' Farook stepped away from Yusuf. He looked at Mesfewi and wondered how long he would last: what would kill him in the end? Thirst, insanity or the barrage of rotting fruit.

He returned his gaze to Yusuf.

'What does his death make us, Si Yusuf?' Farook was shouting, no longer able to keep his voice or face neutral. 'What kind of people do we become by being witness to it, contributing to it bit by bit?'

Yusuf ignored his question and shook his head in disappointment.

'The Pasha would like you to know we do not answer to Europe,' Yusuf continued. 'Nor to her people, who are here as guests of this country. They may be able to tell us how not to kill, but they will never dictate to us who is worthy of death. They may point a finger at an act and call it savagery, but we will show them that is merely the limits of their imagination. It is Morocco who draws the line between savage and civilized in her soil, not them. Tell me Si Farook, which is worse, physical torture or mental suffering?'

'I don't know,' answered Farook, unwilling to think of either.

'The suffering, Si Farook. The body can only take so much pain until it surrenders to the sensation, at best it stops feeling it and at worst gets used to it. The mind ... Well, the mind can torture the spirit until its last breath.'

Yusuf nudged his head in the direction of the platform. Farook turned towards it and made his way up the steps. As he approached, the cobbler raised his head and looked in his direction. Through the blood and bruises blinding his vision, he managed a wry smile. 'I am not a bad man,' he said. 'I have done some bad things, but I am not a bad man ...'

Epilogue

Farook stood in the courtyard of his funduq. He looked at the rooms on the upper floor and inspected the interior. It really was a beautiful city. Its beauty was layered, hidden beneath the dust that coated every surface. To see it, you had to open more than your eyes. It had to be looked for in the daily assault of the nostrils. Mules, sweat, spices, roasting meat and sewage all mixed together so that your eyes stung. And while you continued to search for the beauty the city screamed into your ear: traders passed through quiet alleyways shouting their wares; children played, worked, or were disciplined; women chattered on rooftops; mules brayed; musicians tapped tambourines and clicked castanets for a coin or loaf of bread.

There was beauty in the city, the whole country; Morocco was like its food, sweet yet savoury.

Farook watched as two men lifted his trunk from the floor. They carried it to the room behind him. It was his only luggage; he preferred to travel light. The proprietor acquired the appropriate transportation for him, despite his reservations. They had been kept in a stable beneath his room, with the kitchen boy ensuring they were fattened up for the long journey, one horse and one mule. Farook handpicked his guide. The man knew the landscape and was trustworthy. That was all that mattered.

Now the only thing keeping him was the last preparations: the packing of provisions and checking of his pistol. The kitchen boy ran between the stable and the courtyard assisting the lifters. The proprietor stood nearby biting his nails and barking orders. He watched Farook from the corner of his eye. Eventually he shuffled over. 'Si Farook, are you sure about this? I must stress your friend assigned me responsibility over you and I cannot let you travel out of this city with one guide. If anything were to happen I would feel eternally responsible. Please let me acquire you some security at least.'

'Do not worry,' replied Farook, slapping the proprietor on the back and smiling. 'This is how I travel.'

'But Si–'

'My friend, he is well aware of how I travel and is under no delusion that you can prevent it,' interrupted Farook. 'You get me to the city gate and you will have fulfilled your oath to him.'

The proprietor nodded, accepting his responsibility towards Farook would end soon. 'I must thank you for your hospitality,' Farook said, placing his hand on the proprietor's shoulder. 'I could not have completed my work without you.'

The proprietor lowered his eyes blinking rapidly. He nodded away the beginning of tears.

'I only wish your visit was under less awful circumstances, Si Farook. It's unfathomable that a man can feel justified inflicting such violence on innocent women, who God has ordered us to protect. They had no part in the death of his tribesmen. I was in the city when they rebelled; the Mesfewi were always a troublesome people.'

Farook paused for a moment, the memory of his final conversation with the cobbler still vivid. Despite the torture and his closeness to death, the cobbler had managed to maintain his composure. With an unsettling calmness, he explained:

"Revenge is an awful thing. If it remains unresolved it eats away at a person. The people of this city, I have made them share the pain my mother and I felt. I have shown the Sultan he isn't untouchable. Look at this mob, see them braying. It cannot last. You understand, surely? You too are an outsider."

Mesfewi had closed his eyes, his battered face barely recognizable as the man Farook had first encountered in his shop. The walls of his tomb were almost complete.

"Now I can join my assembly. We must learn to let go our anger and prejudices."

The proprietor looked up at Farook as he repeated Mesfewi's last words under his breath.

'If I am honest, I will miss you in the funduq. Perhaps you can stay on for a few more days, the weather uncertain as it is.'

'I will travel today,' replied Farook, shaking his head.

'Si Farook, you are by far the strangest man to have ever lodged at my establishment. You are an adviser to the Sultan, you have his ear, and yet you travel like you have nothing but a donkey and cart. You show no interest in money, liquor or women, and yet you never attend the mosque. You are a man of so few words and yet there is little doubt about what you mean. You abstain from mint tea as though it is an intoxicant. You carry your jellaba and selham like a man proud and yet wear foreign shoes. I cannot make sense of you, Si Farook.'

Farook looked down at his feet.

'I am not wearing them now.'

'No, they would be ruined by the journey. They are beautiful shoes and it would be a tragedy.'

'So, you like my shoes,' replied Farook, more a statement than a question.

The proprietor looked aghast. He did have a way of exaggerating.

'Of course, they are the most beautiful things I have ever seen. Who would not like them, Si Farook?'

The kitchen boy ran and stood in front of Farook and the proprietor. He breathed heavily, struggling to speak.

Catching his breath, he said, 'It's all ready master and the guide is waiting at the gate.' The proprietor clicked his tongue in irritation. Farook looked down at the boy. He looked back at the proprietor.

'Tell me,' he asked, 'what would you give for my shoes?'

The proprietor looked shocked by the question. The kitchen boy watched on silently.

'I … I don't have anything of any value, Si Farook. If I did I would give it gladly. I have my grandmother's gold wrist band. It is not worth much but I think that would be a fair exchange. Si Farook, if I had known I would have sold some things.'

Farook paused for a moment.

'Let's walk to the gate shall we? It is time I start on my journey,' he said.

They walked towards the door, passing the kitchen boy, who spun around to watch them go. Farook stopped to look at him.

'Mohammed, you come too.'

The boy smiled and followed after them. The lifters pulled the horse and mule out of the stables and followed from a distance.

Outside the city seemed to have returned to normal. It had taken the cobbler three days to die. On the first night his screams kept the city awake, but by the second he had quietened down until it fell completely silent on the third morning and the crowd grew restless. On the third night people began to disperse. Some complained the punishment was insufficient. He had died too quickly. Farook stayed away. He took the time to write in his journal and prepare for his travel. Walking through the alleyways it was as though nothing at all had happened. The city had an airiness Farook had not felt before. Summer was coming and though the sun would scorch the backs of its residents, optimism had returned. The seasons came and went and as each one ended and each one began the inhabitants shed their memories and looked forward with new hope.

They walked in silence. The proprietor resisted indulging in nostalgia and Farook looked to the path ahead. They arrived at the gate and stopped under its archway. The door was old: perhaps one of the first to be built and ahead lay the long road to Fez. It would not be long before he was home in Tangier. The kitchen boy stopped just within earshot as they waited for the horse and mule to arrive.

The proprietor lowered his head. 'I am very sad to see you leave, Si Farook. You are always welcome in my—'

'About my shoes,' Farook interrupted, with a slightly raised voice. The proprietor creased his eyebrows not sure what to make of Farook's refusal to drop the topic. 'I am in need of a personal assistant,' he explained. 'Someone whom I can trust and train to look after my affairs. Someone smart, who learns fast and can assist with writing and help me with my professional work – that sort of thing. I will pay him a salary of which I will store in safe keeping until he decides what to do with it if he so wishes, or he can have it at the end of every month. It is his choice, but during his time with me he will have no fear of hunger.'

'Why, Si Farook, whoever acquired such a role would be honoured,' said the proprietor in surprise. 'If my only son was not already married and in trade I would suggest him. There are hundreds of young men ready to jump at the opportunity, but I need time to find the right one.'

'What about the boy?'

The proprietor looked at Mohammed, confused. A laugh escaped his throat, which he quickly stifled on seeing the seriousness in Farook's face.

'But Si Farook, he cannot even hold a quill, let alone read and write.'

'I will teach him. He will have a tutor,' said Farook.

'Si Farook, he is not the brightest. He can hardly follow the most

273

basic of instructions, let alone learn to read or appear at the palace with you. Really you would curse me if I allowed it.'

'I accept the offer,' called Mohammed, having listened to the entire conversation

'It is not a question of your acceptance, boy, it is a question of property,' snapped the proprietor.

'Which is why I offer my shoes in exchange,' said Farook. 'I feel perhaps they are not enough for you.'

'No ... no ... no,' rushed the proprietor. He looked at Mohammed with supressed scorn. The situation allowed for no other choice and, really, what was a kitchen boy compared to ownership of an item so rare?

'I think it is a fair exchange,' said the proprietor reaching out his hand to Farook. They shook. Before more could be said, Mohammed rushed to the mule and pulled the shoes from the trunk. He handed them to the proprietor and turned to Farook.

'I will travel on the mule, master. I have no possessions to take with me.'

Farook turned, climbed onto his horse, and waited for Mohammed to jump onto the mule.

'As you wish,' called Farook as his kicked his horse into life. 'But stay close and if you spot danger then bring the mule beside me. And please do not call me master. "Si Farook" will do.'

Mohammed nodded, 'As you wish, master.'

They set off on the road ahead.

Historical note

Hadj Mohammed Mesfewi was immured in Jemaa el-Fnaa, the place of public execution in Marrakesh on 11 June 1906 for the murder of thirty-six women. Few records exist of his crimes, except some reports in European newspapers where he was referred to as 'a Moorish Jack the Ripper.'

He lived in the Riyad Zeytoun district of Marrakesh where he owned a shop and worked as a cobbler and letter writer. The date he began his murder spree is unknown, but he was arrested in May 1906 after the parents of one of the victims traced their daughter to his accomplice Rahalia, a 70-year-old woman, who also went by the name Annah.

The Marrakesh authorities dug up his shop and found the remains of 26 women. The remains of a further ten women were found buried in his private garden. Mesfewi and Rahalia confessed to the crimes under torture. Initially, Mesfewi claimed to have committed the murders under the instruction of three men. There is little indication this assertion was investigated by city authorities. Rahalia died under torture. Before her death she claimed she knew nothing of the crimes, placing the blame entirely on Mesfewi.

The women were lured to the cobbler's shop with a dinner invitation, or they visited the shop to dictate letters. They were fed a narcotic causing them to fall asleep. Mesfewi then murdered the women before mutilating their bodies with a dagger. European newspaper reports suggest robbery as a cause with no indication of a sexual motive. No details about the women or their lives were reported. They have simply been recorded in history as 36 murder victims, faceless and nameless.

The discovery of the bodies caused public outrage in Marrakesh with the city residents demanding a harsh punishment for Mesfewi. In response, the authorities sentenced the cobbler to public crucifixion in Jemaa el-Fnaa, which means 'the assembly of the dead.' However, the European residents of the city protested against this form of punishment and the construction of the crucifix within the square was halted. Under increasing pressure from the public to inflict a severe punishment, the city authorities ordered Mesfewi to be publically immured. After undergoing daily whippings and torture, Mesfewi was paraded on a donkey through Jemaa el-Fnaa in front of a baying crowd and entombed. He died on 13 June 1906, three days after his immurement. European newspapers reported that his screams filled Jemaa el-Fnaa on the first two days before he fell silent, eventually dying of exhaustion. The crowd who had camped in the square, along with the victims' families, dispersed, while making complaints that Mesfewi had not suffered enough. After his death, European newspapers suggested the makzan had 'blinded the eyes of foreign residents' by dealing out a harsher punishment than crucifixion and claimed it would have been better for Mesfewi if they had remained silent.

A police force did not exist in Morocco in 1906. In Morocco, citizens wishing to report a crime or injustice logged a case at the Ministry of Complaints, which then assigned a civilian or court judge to investigate. There is no suggestion in the historical records used in the telling of this story that a complaint was made to the Minister of Complaints regarding the missing women.

1906 was also the year of the Algeciras Conference in Spain, organized in response to the First Morocco Crisis and where European superpowers agreed on their territorial claims over much of Africa. During the conference France was given influence over most of Morocco, with Spain claiming parts of the country's northern territory. Sultan Abd al-Aziz was young and brought into power on the sudden death of his father by his Chamberlain Ba Ahmad who ruled vicariously until his death in 1900. Aged only 16, the young Sultan was known for his extravagance and love of European consumer goods. By 1906 he was politically weak, due to heavy foreign debts, growing domestic resentment towards European influence over Morocco, and tribal rebellion. His reign has been characterized as the end of the old empire.

Abd al-Aziz abdicated in 1908, handing authority over to his brother Moulay Abd al-Hafid. Morocco became a French protectorate in 1912.

Farook al-Alami is fictional. He is based loosely on a growing class of men assigned as emissaries to Europe by the Moroccan Sultan to negotiate loans, trade and engage in cultural exchange during this period. Tangier was an important place of Moroccan and European cultural exchange in the build up to the French protectorate. It had a significant number of European residents.

Dr Delacroix is also fictional. He is based loosely on the character Dr Emile Mauchamp, a French resident in Marrakesh, who was murdered by a mob in the city alleyways under accusations of spying in 1907. Medicine was used as a force for colonialism and modernization by the French in Morocco and Dr Mauchamp's death became the pretext for France's occupation of Morocco.

The Assembly of the Dead is a fictional telling of Mesfewi's murders based loosely on the newspaper clippings and records of his crimes that have survived.

Glossary of terms

adhan	Muslim call to prayer
baboush	Moroccan slipper traditionally dyed yellow
balek	A word used by traders in markets to make room for their carts. Means 'mind your back'
Blue Men/ Tuareg	A tribe from the Saharan desert often called the Blue Men because of their indigo-dye coloured clothes, which stains their skin
Caliph	The Sultan's official representative in a city
Caliphate	Islamic stewardship over Muslim land
djinn	Intelligent spirits who can be good, evil or neutral and are made of fire
funduq	A traditional hotel built to store goods and house pack animals on the lower floor and accommodate merchants and travellers on the upper floor
Glaoui	A Berber tribe of southern Morocco whose chief rose in prominence during the French protectorate
gnawa	Ancient African Islamic spiritual music based on chants

	and repetition to induce a trance straight, with iron castanets and three-string lute instruments
guerrab	Water-carriers who traditional roam a city selling fresh water from a camel sack
Hajj	A title given to a person who has performed the Muslim pilgrimage to Mecca
hammam	A communal bathhouse with separate facilities or times for men and women. Traditionally contains three rooms with varying temperatures and steam
henna	A natural red or orange dye used to decorate hands or to colour hair
jabador	A traditional garment composed of tunic and pants in the same colour
jellaba	A loose-fitting outer robe with full sleeves and a hood that hangs from the back
jihad	A struggle as part of religious duty
jihad al-nafs	A struggle against one's ego
kippah	A brimless cap worn by Jews, usually made of cloth
makhzan	The governing institution, state or government
malhaf	A long rectangular piece of cloth, traditionally black or white and wrapped around the body to form a dress and then placed over the head and shoulders
marabout	A wandering saint or holy man
mellah	The Jewish quarter of a Moroccan city, literal meaning is salt, as Jews were assigned the responsibility of salting the heads of enemies to be displayed on the city gates
muaddin	The crier who calls Muslims to prayer from the mosque minaret
mushaf	The Qu'ran as a book or in its written form
Pasha	A high ranking city official
Qadi	A judge or magistrate of court

Sayyid	A title used to denote respect and claiming descent from Mohammed, the Prophet of Islam
selham	A longer outer cloak worn over the jellaba
Shamaliyin	People from the North of Morocco/Northerners
souk	An open-air market place
tarboush	A man's cap similar to a fez, typically of red felt with a tassel at the top
thobe	A robe or outer garment similar to a jellaba, but without the hood
Tuareg	*see* Blue Men
zataar	A herb used in food and tea typically including oregano and thyme

Acknowledgements

This book would not have been possible without the support and encouragement of many people. Firstly, I would like to thank my parents and siblings who have spurred me on in ways only they can.

I must also thank Karima Sbitri and James Brown for believing in the story before the first word was written and Sally Ann Scott for believing in my ability to write it when it appeared an impossible task. Your conviction has seen me through long nights of doubt.

Thank you to friends who created a much-needed space in their homes allowing me retreat into the story. Annette Weppelmann in Germany, Cory Don Merritt and Phillippe Caron-Audet in Tunisia and Andy Whall in France, I am very grateful. A special thank you to Birgit Bihler for giving me a home from home in Marrakesh and embracing my presence in the city. Thank you also to Bouchra and Jerome Bourdel for looking after me during my stay in the old medina of Marrakesh. You offered me a sanctuary amidst the chaos in Riad Ineslisa.

I must also extend my thanks to the staff at Maison de la Photographie in Marrakesh for allowing me to browse through the postcard archive; those images have left their mark on these pages. Thanks also to the American Legation in Tangier and Latifa Samadi for help in accessing the newspaper archives and the reading room staff at the British Library in London for help in sourcing information.

During the research for this book I contacted many writers, academics and historians with a specialism or interest in Morocco. I would like to thank them for their words of encouragement and invaluable advice. A special thank you to Tahir Shah, Richard Hamilton and Jonathan Katz for reading the manuscript and offering their thoughts and reviews.

Finally, I must thank the staff at Impress Books, including Richard Willis, Rachel Singleton and Sarah Sleath. I am especially grateful to Adam Bell and David Lancett for their editing of this book and helping to make it a better story.